THE WITCHER®

THE WITCHER: FADING MEMORIES #1 VARIANT COVER ART BY
JEREMY WILSON

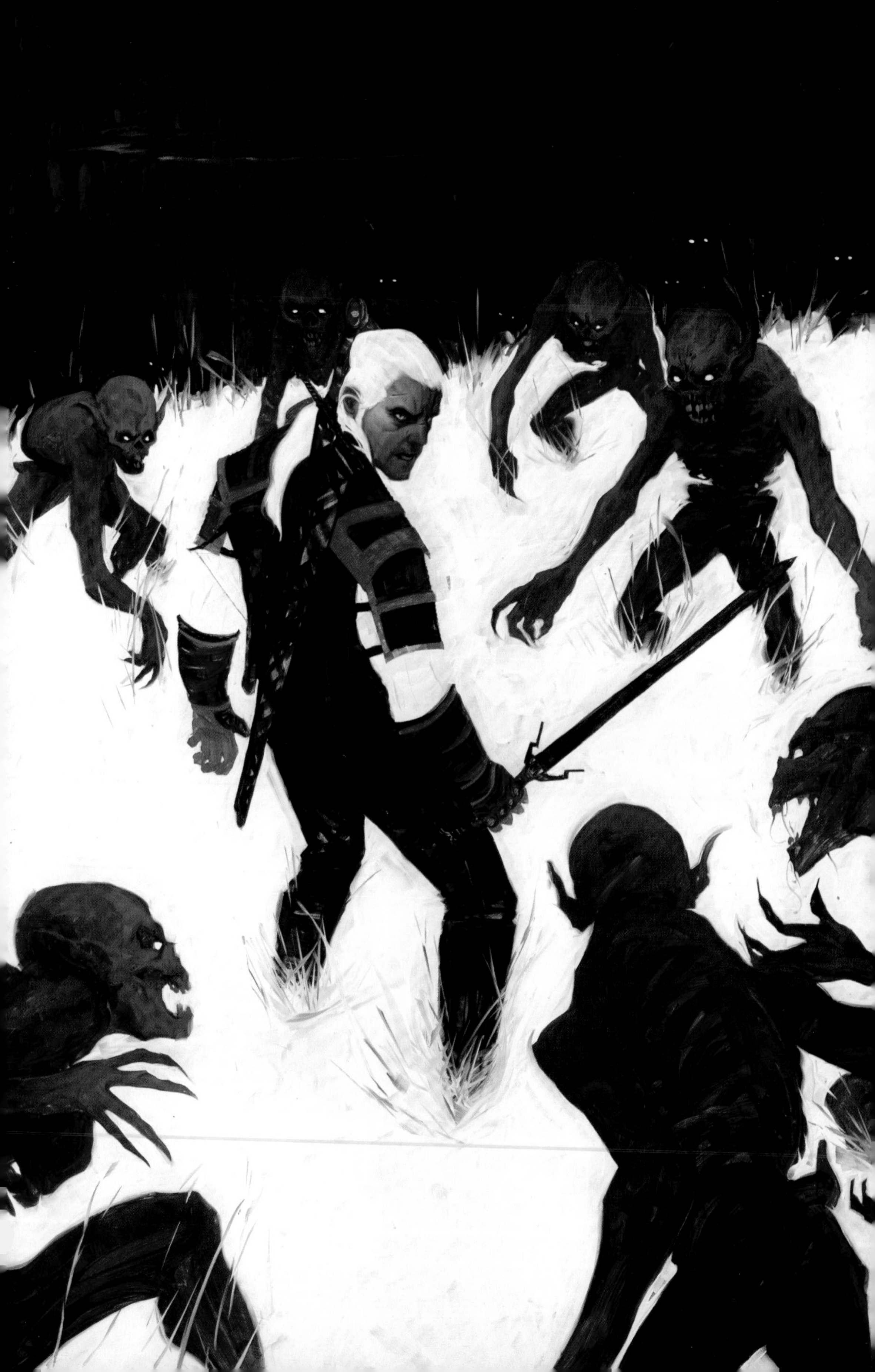

THE WITCHER®

FADING MEMORIES

STORY
Bartosz Sztybor

ART
Amad Mir

COLORS
Hamidreza Sheykh

LETTERS
Steve Dutro

COVER AND CHAPTER BREAK ART
Evan Cagle

DARK HORSE BOOKS

PUBLISHER...Mike Richardson
EDITOR..Megan Walker
ASSISTANT EDITOR...Judy Khuu
DESIGNER...Brennan Thome
DIGITAL ART TECHNICIAN.....................................Allyson Haller
CD PROJEKT RED EDITORIAL................................Rafał Jaki and Bartosz Sztybor
CD PROJEKT RED ENGLISH DIALOGUE ADAPTATION.............Travis Currit

Special thanks to **CD Projekt Red**, including: *Michał Nowakowski, SVP of Business Development* • *Adam Badowski, Head of Studio* • *Marcin Blacha, Story Director*

The Witcher *game is based on a novel of Andrzej Sapkowski.*

THE WITCHER VOLUME 5: FADING MEMORIES

This volume collects issues #1 through #4 of the Dark Horse Comics series *The Witcher: Fading Memories*.

Published by
Dark Horse Books
A division of
Dark Horse Comics LLC
10956 SE Main Street
Milwaukie, OR 97222

DarkHorse.com
TheWitcher.com
Facebook.com/DarkHorseComics
Twitter.com/DarkHorseComics

First edition: July 2021
Ebook ISBN 978-1-50671-658-9
Trade Paperback ISBN 978-1-50671-657-2

10 9 8 7 6 5 4 3 2 1
Printed in China

Neil Hankerson *Executive Vice President* • Tom Weddle *Chief Financial Officer* • Randy Stradley *Vice President of Publishing* • Nick McWhorter *Chief Business Development Officer* • Dale LaFountain *Chief Information Officer* • Matt Parkinson *Vice President of Marketing* • Vanessa Todd-Holmes *Vice President of Production and Scheduling* • Mark Bernardi *Vice President of Book Trade and Digital Sales* • Ken Lizzi *General Counsel* • Dave Marshall *Editor in Chief* • Davey Estrada *Editorial Director* • Chris Warner *Senior Books Editor* • Cary Grazzini *Director of Specialty Projects* • Lia Ribacchi *Art Director* • Matt Dryer *Director of Digital Art and Prepress* • Michael Gombos *Senior Director of Licensed Publications* • Kari Yadro *Director of Custom Programs* • Kari Torson *Director of International Licensing* • Sean Brice *Director of Trade Sales*

Library of Congress Cataloging-in-Publication Data

Names: Sztybor, Bartosz, writer. | Mir, Amad, artist. | Sheykh, Hamid, colourist. | Dutro, Steve, letterer. | Sapkowski, Andrzej. Wiedźmin.
Title: Fading memories / story, Bartosz Sztybor ; art, Amad Mir ; colors, Hamid Sheykh ; letters, Steve Dutro.
Description: Milwaukie, OR : Dark Horse Books, 2021. | Series: The Witcher; volume 5 | The Witcher game is based on a novel of Andrzej Sapkowski"
Identifiers: LCCN 2020031940 | ISBN 9781506716572 (paperback) | ISBN 9781506716589 (ebook)
Subjects: LCSH: Comic books, strips, etc.
Classification: LCC PN6728.W5887 S97 2021 | DDC 741.5/973--dc23
LC record available at https://lccn.loc.gov/2020031940

CD PROJEKT RED®

CHAPTER ONE

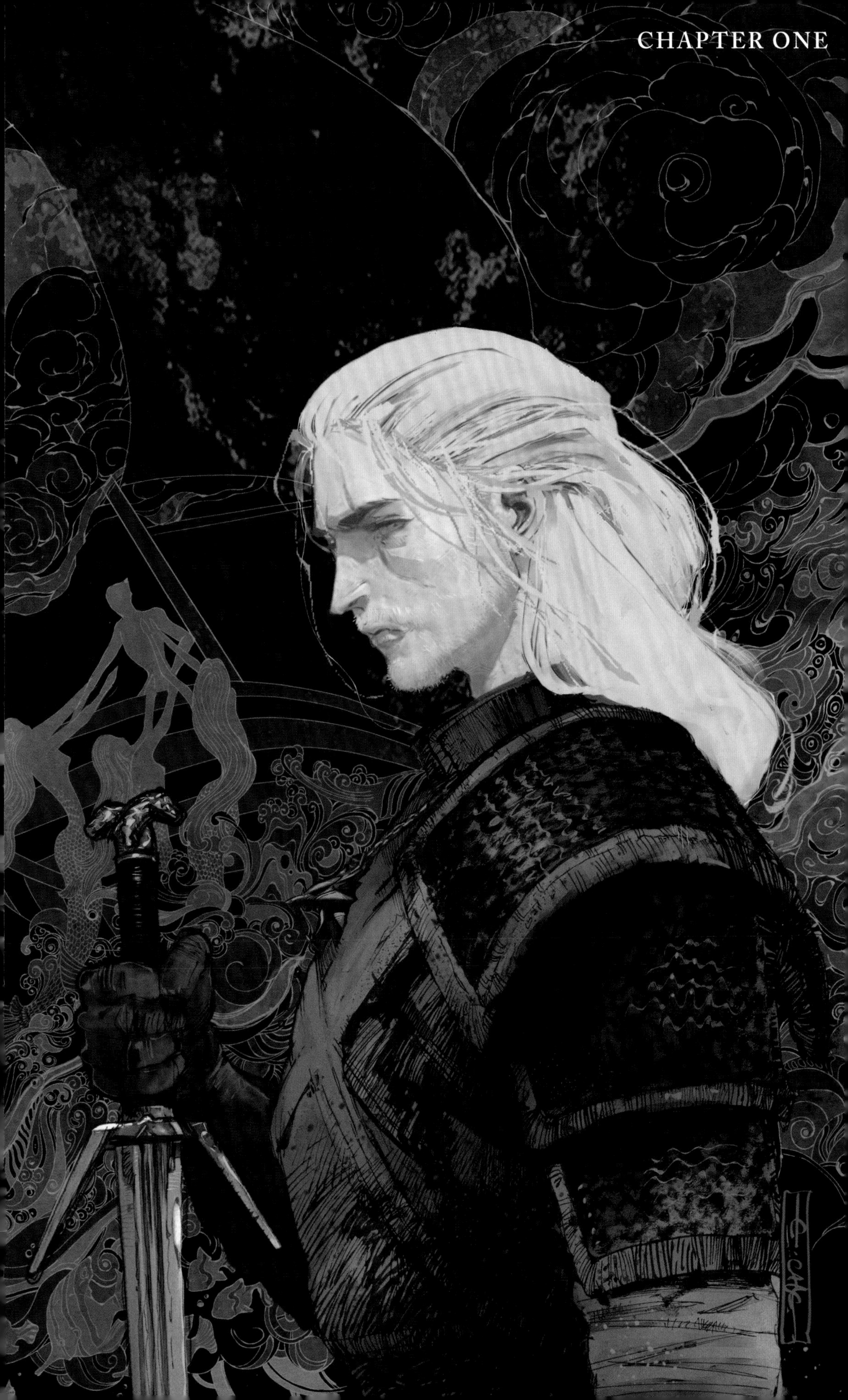

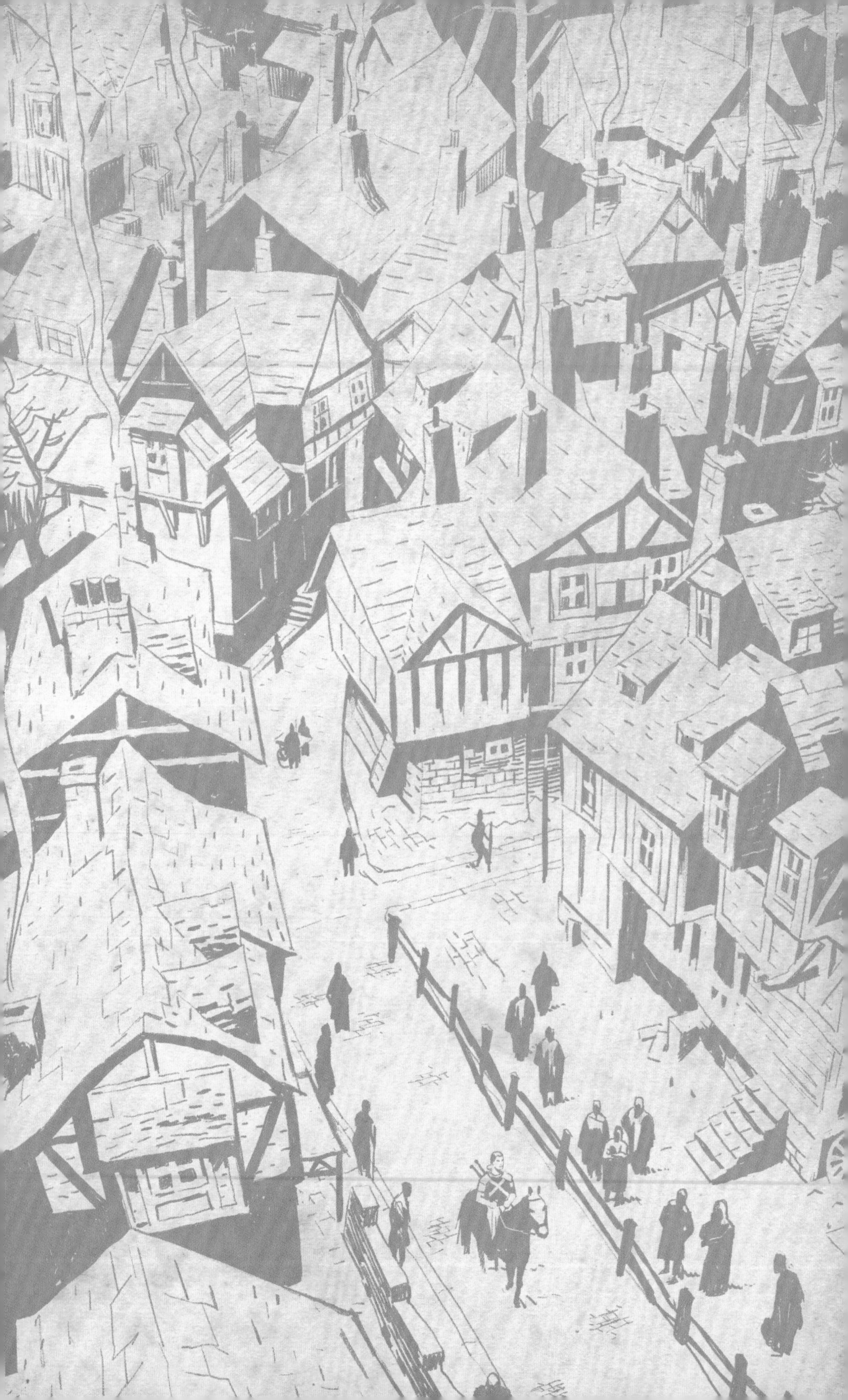

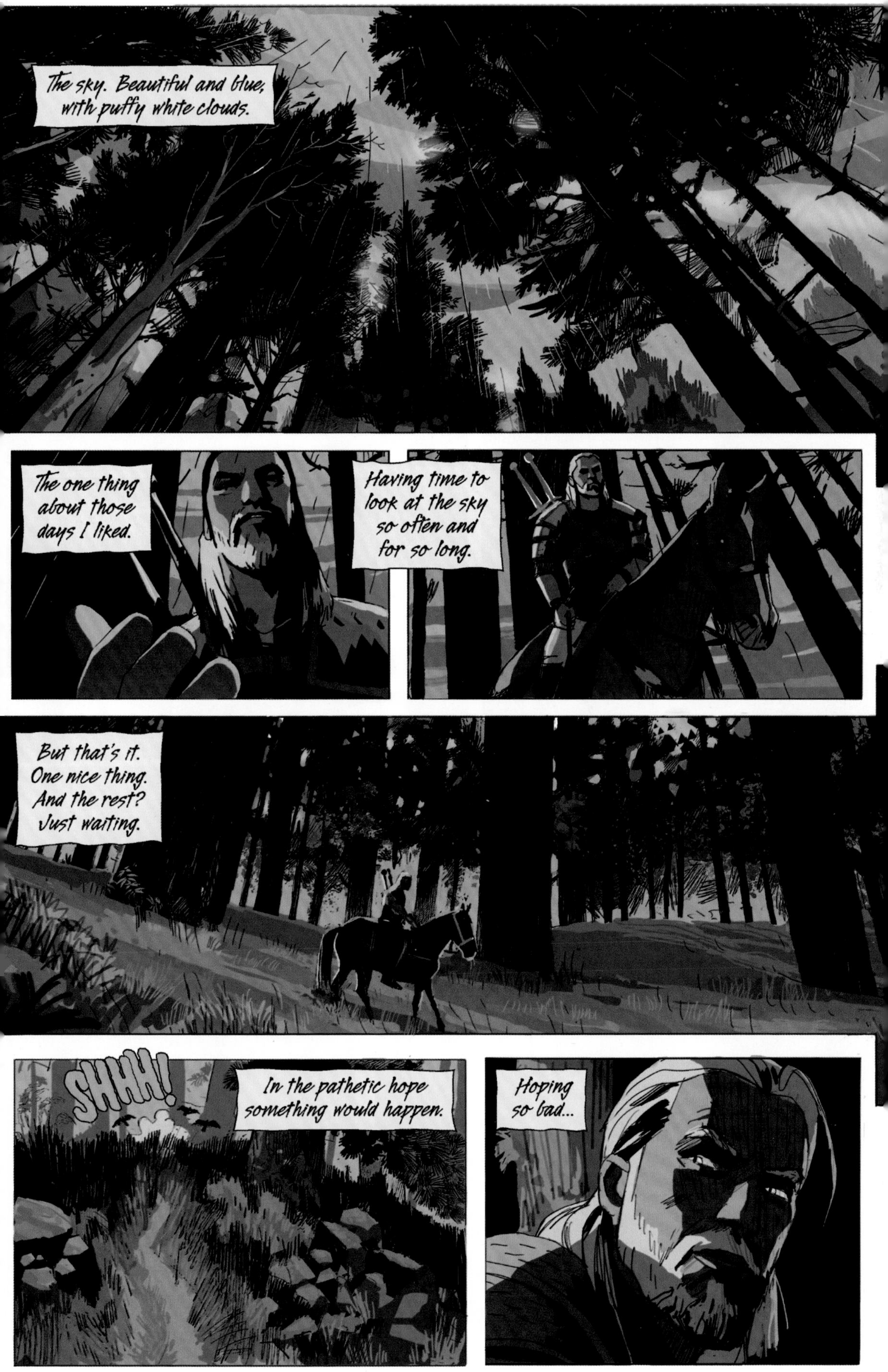
The sky. Beautiful and blue, with puffy white clouds.
The one thing about those days I liked.
Having time to look at the sky so often and for so long.
But that's it. One nice thing. And the rest? Just waiting.
SHHH!
In the pathetic hope something would happen.
Hoping so bad...

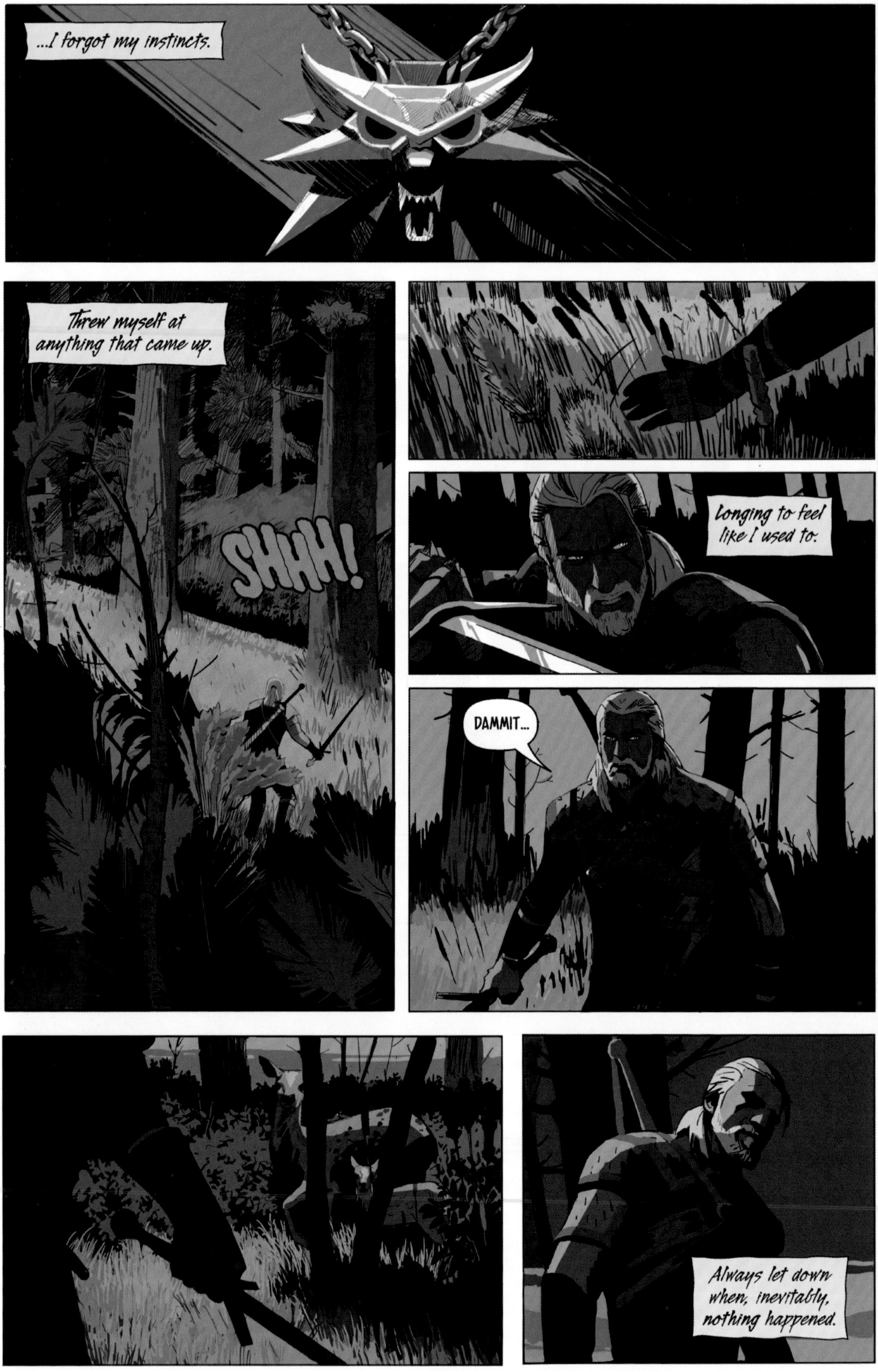

...I forgot my instincts.
Threw myself at anything that came up.
SHHH!
Longing to feel like I used to.
DAMMIT...
Always let down when, inevitably, nothing happened.

And maybe never would.

SOMEWHERE IN POVISS.

A *WITCHER*, WHY, AIN'T SEEN ONE O' YOUSE 'ROUND HERE FOR AGES...

WE'VE NOT GOT ANY MONSTERS.

ONLY A FEW GOOD FOLK AND...

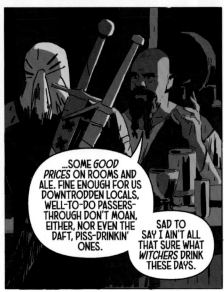

...SOME *GOOD PRICES* ON ROOMS AND ALE. FINE ENOUGH FOR US DOWNTRODDEN LOCALS, WELL-TO-DO PASSERS-THROUGH DON'T MOAN, EITHER, NOR EVEN THE DAFT, PISS-DRINKIN' ONES.

SAD TO SAY I AIN'T ALL THAT SURE WHAT *WITCHERS* DRINK THESE DAYS.

HERE TO *EARN COIN,* NOT *SPEND* IT.

THEN STOP NATTERING WITH THE INNKEEP. IF YOU WISH TO EARN COIN...

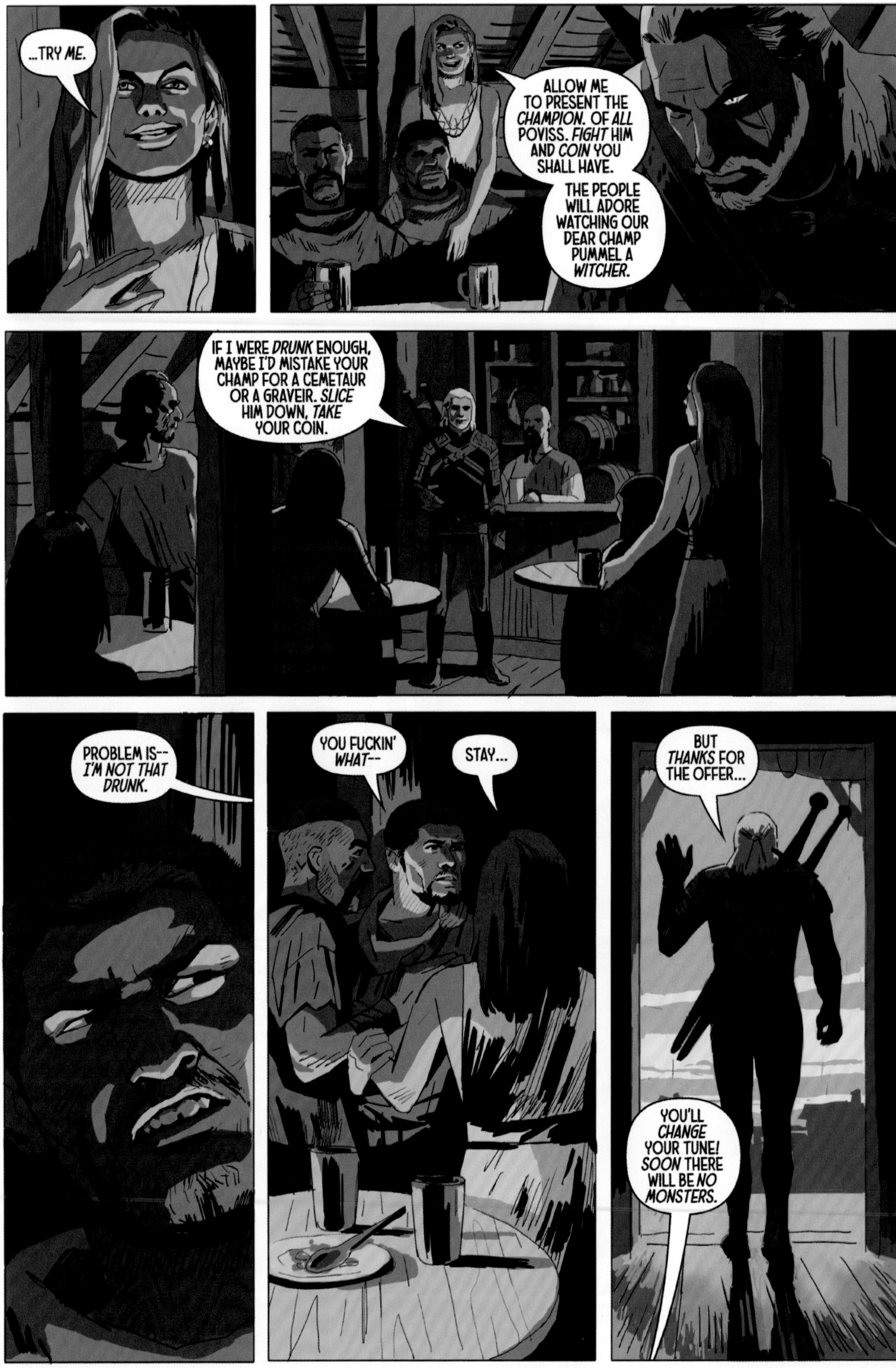
...TRY ME.
ALLOW ME TO PRESENT THE CHAMPION. OF ALL POVISS. FIGHT HIM AND COIN YOU SHALL HAVE.
THE PEOPLE WILL ADORE WATCHING OUR DEAR CHAMP PUMMEL A WITCHER.
IF I WERE DRUNK ENOUGH, MAYBE I'D MISTAKE YOUR CHAMP FOR A CEMETAUR OR A GRAVEIR. SLICE HIM DOWN, TAKE YOUR COIN.
PROBLEM IS-- I'M NOT THAT DRUNK.
YOU FUCKIN' WHAT--
STAY...
BUT THANKS FOR THE OFFER...
YOU'LL CHANGE YOUR TUNE! SOON THERE WILL BE NO MONSTERS.

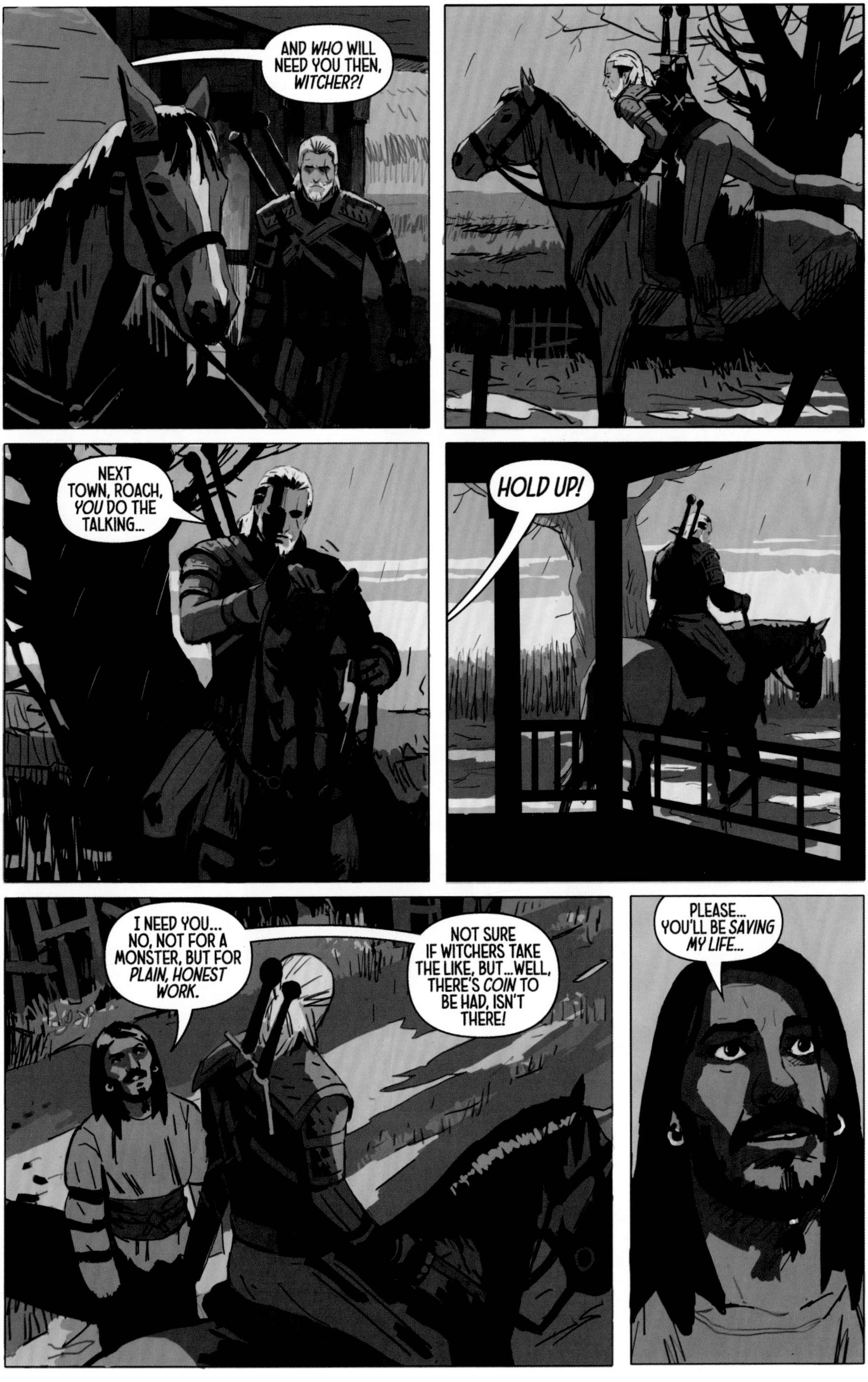

AND *WHO* WILL NEED YOU THEN, *WITCHER?!*
NEXT TOWN, ROACH, *YOU* DO THE TALKING...
HOLD UP!
I NEED YOU... NO, NOT FOR A MONSTER, BUT FOR *PLAIN, HONEST* WORK.
NOT SURE IF WITCHERS TAKE THE LIKE, BUT...WELL, THERE'S *COIN* TO BE HAD, ISN'T THERE!
PLEASE... YOU'LL BE *SAVING MY LIFE...*

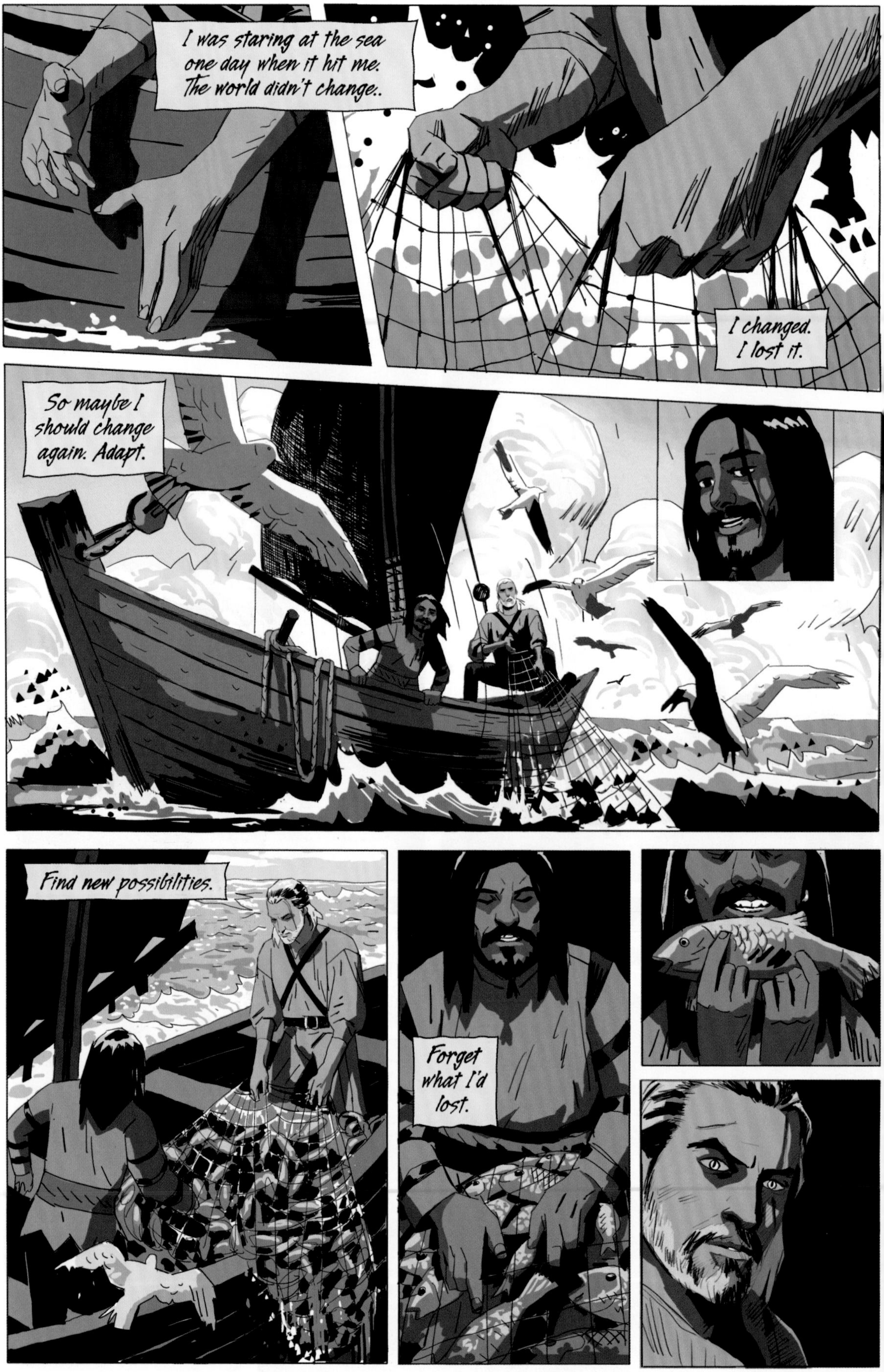
I was staring at the sea one day when it hit me. The world didn't change..
I changed. I lost it.
So maybe I should change again. Adapt.
Find new possibilities.
Forget what I'd lost.

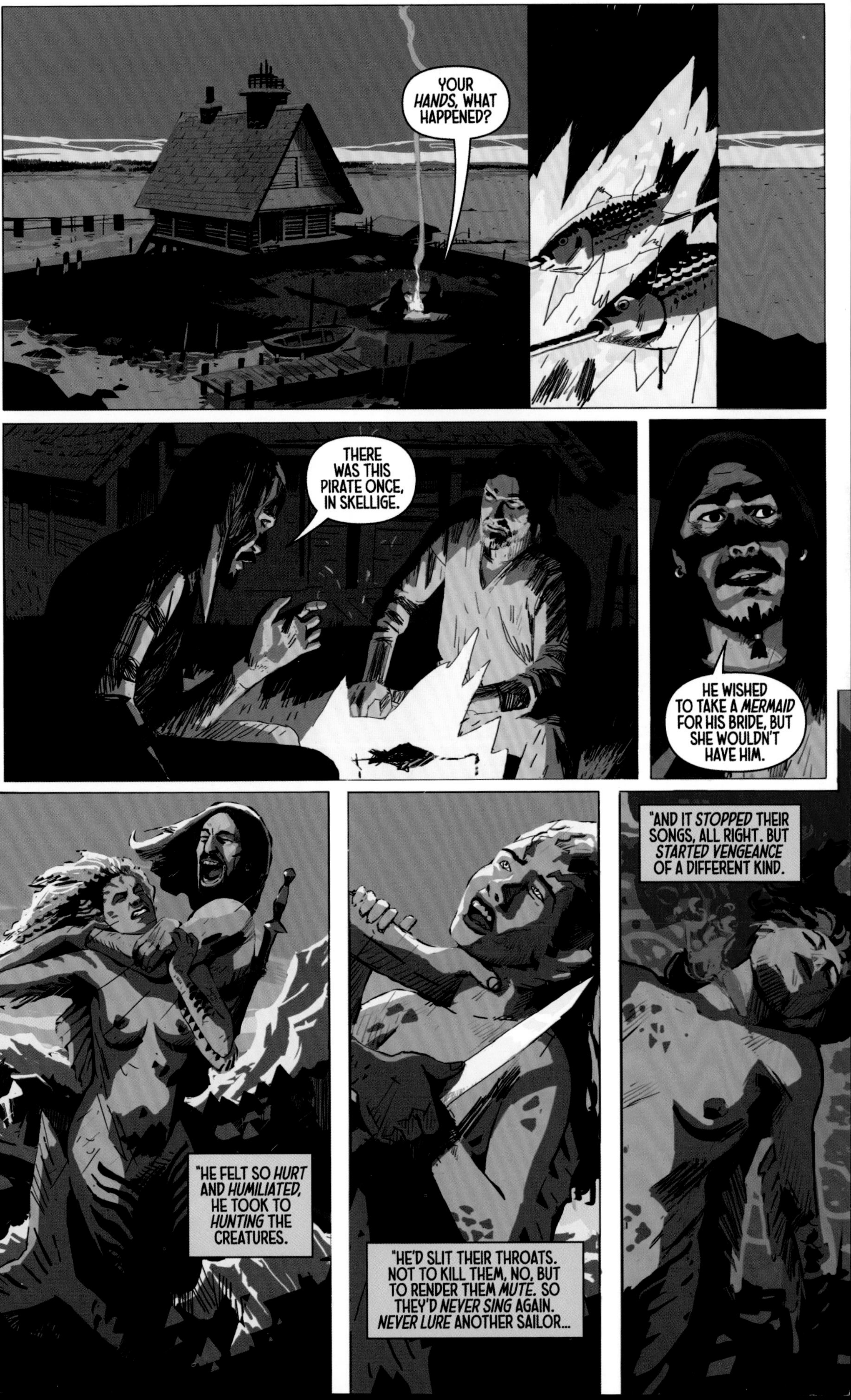
YOUR *HANDS*, WHAT HAPPENED?
THERE WAS THIS PIRATE ONCE, IN SKELLIGE.
HE WISHED TO TAKE A *MERMAID* FOR HIS BRIDE, BUT SHE WOULDN'T HAVE HIM.
"HE FELT SO *HURT* AND *HUMILIATED*, HE TOOK TO *HUNTING* THE CREATURES.
"HE'D SLIT THEIR THROATS. NOT TO KILL THEM, NO, BUT TO RENDER THEM *MUTE*. SO THEY'D *NEVER SING* AGAIN. *NEVER LURE* ANOTHER SAILOR...
"AND IT *STOPPED* THEIR SONGS, ALL RIGHT. BUT *STARTED VENGEANCE* OF A DIFFERENT KIND.

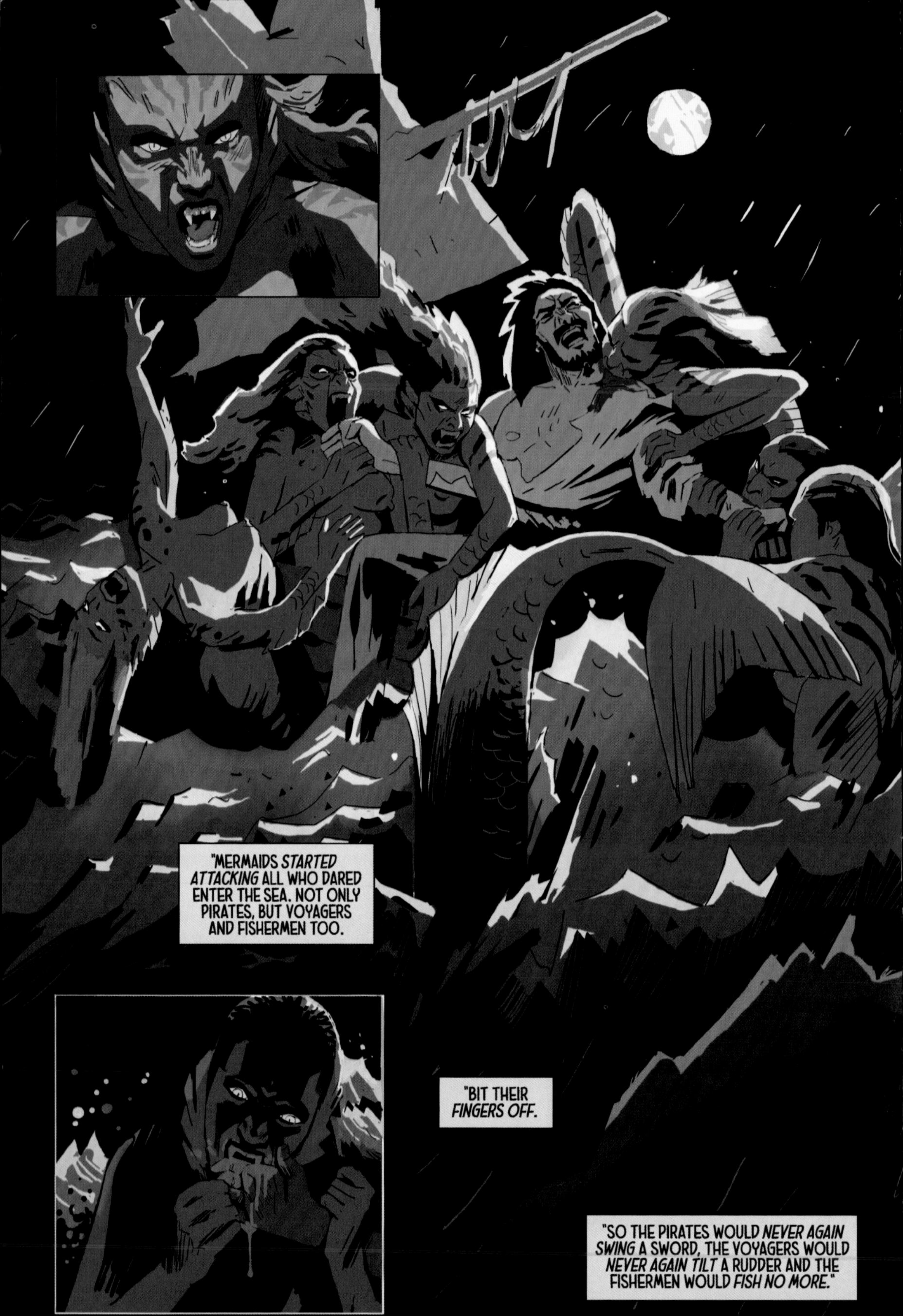
"MERMAIDS *STARTED ATTACKING* ALL WHO DARED ENTER THE SEA. NOT ONLY PIRATES, BUT VOYAGERS AND FISHERMEN TOO.
"BIT THEIR *FINGERS OFF*.
"SO THE PIRATES WOULD *NEVER AGAIN SWING* A SWORD, THE VOYAGERS WOULD *NEVER AGAIN TILT* A RUDDER AND THE FISHERMEN WOULD *FISH NO MORE*."

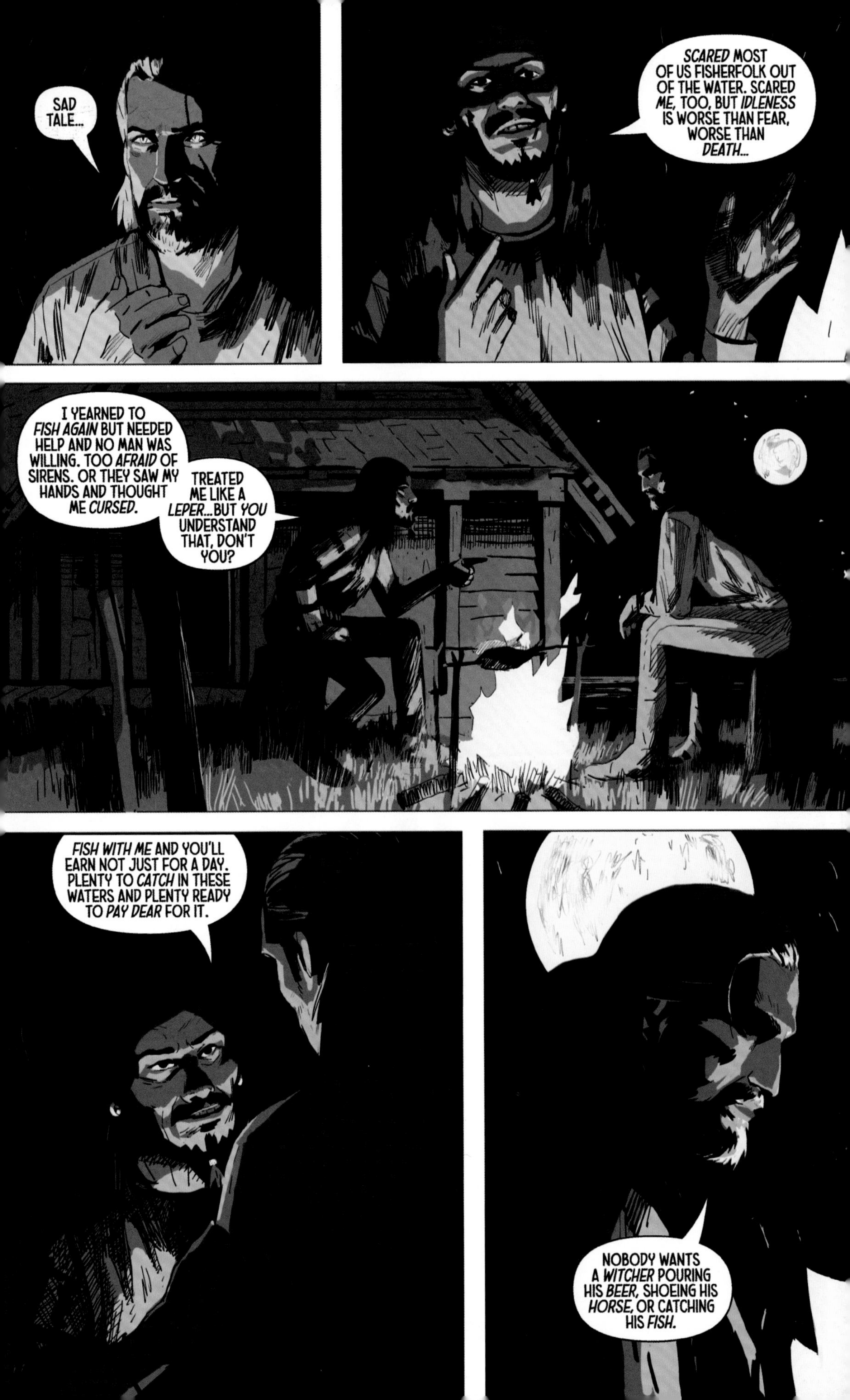
SAD TALE...
SCARED MOST OF US FISHERFOLK OUT OF THE WATER. SCARED ME, TOO, BUT IDLENESS IS WORSE THAN FEAR, WORSE THAN DEATH...
I YEARNED TO FISH AGAIN BUT NEEDED HELP AND NO MAN WAS WILLING. TOO AFRAID OF SIRENS. OR THEY SAW MY HANDS AND THOUGHT ME CURSED.
TREATED ME LIKE A LEPER...BUT YOU UNDERSTAND THAT, DON'T YOU?
FISH WITH ME AND YOU'LL EARN NOT JUST FOR A DAY. PLENTY TO CATCH IN THESE WATERS AND PLENTY READY TO PAY DEAR FOR IT.
NOBODY WANTS A WITCHER POURING HIS BEER, SHOEING HIS HORSE, OR CATCHING HIS FISH.

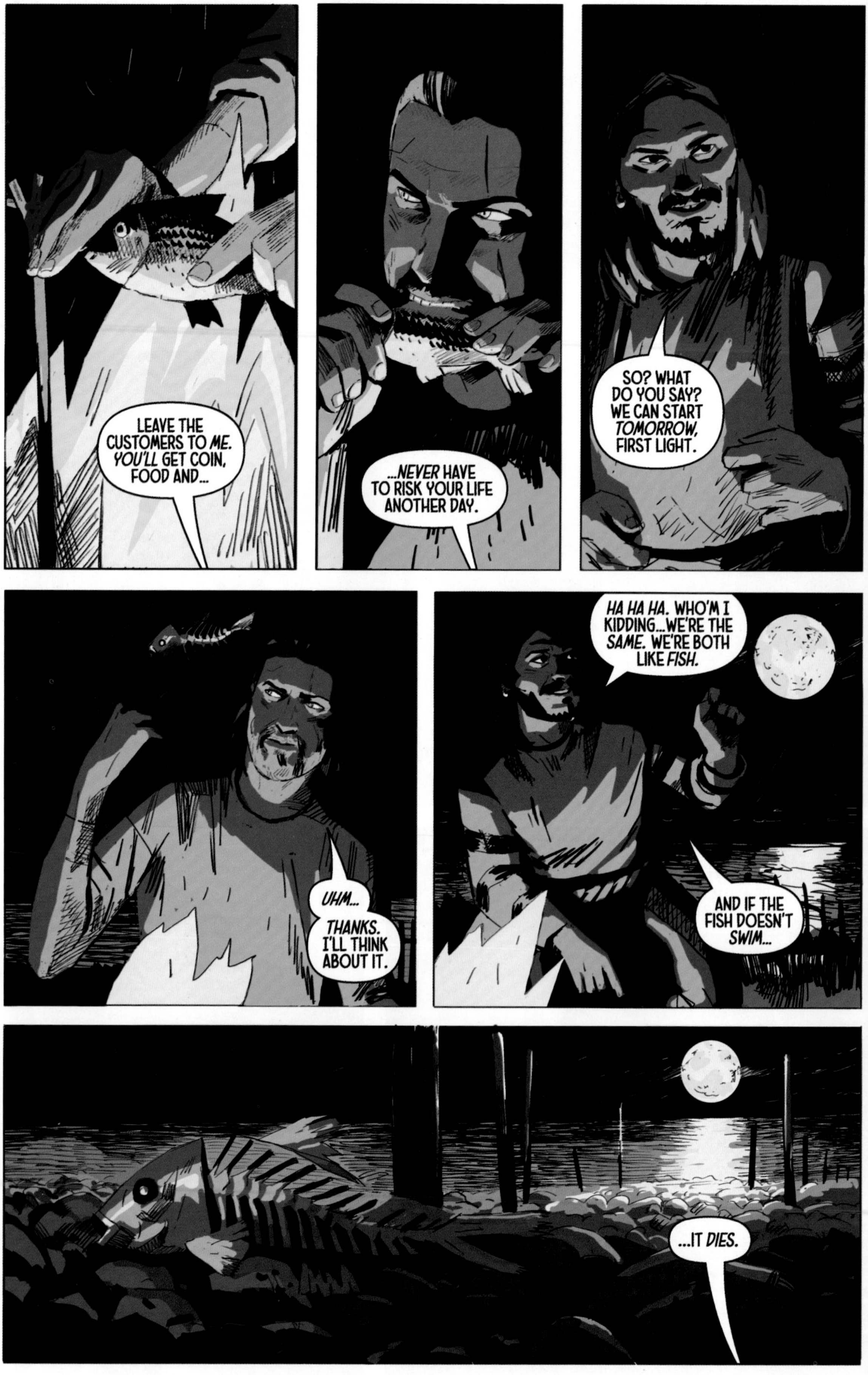
LEAVE THE CUSTOMERS TO *ME*. *YOU'LL* GET COIN, FOOD AND...
...*NEVER* HAVE TO RISK YOUR LIFE ANOTHER DAY.
SO? WHAT DO YOU SAY? WE CAN START *TOMORROW*, FIRST LIGHT.
UHM...
THANKS. I'LL THINK ABOUT IT.
HA HA HA. WHO'M I KIDDING...WE'RE THE *SAME.* WE'RE BOTH LIKE *FISH.*
AND IF THE FISH DOESN'T *SWIM*...
...IT *DIES.*

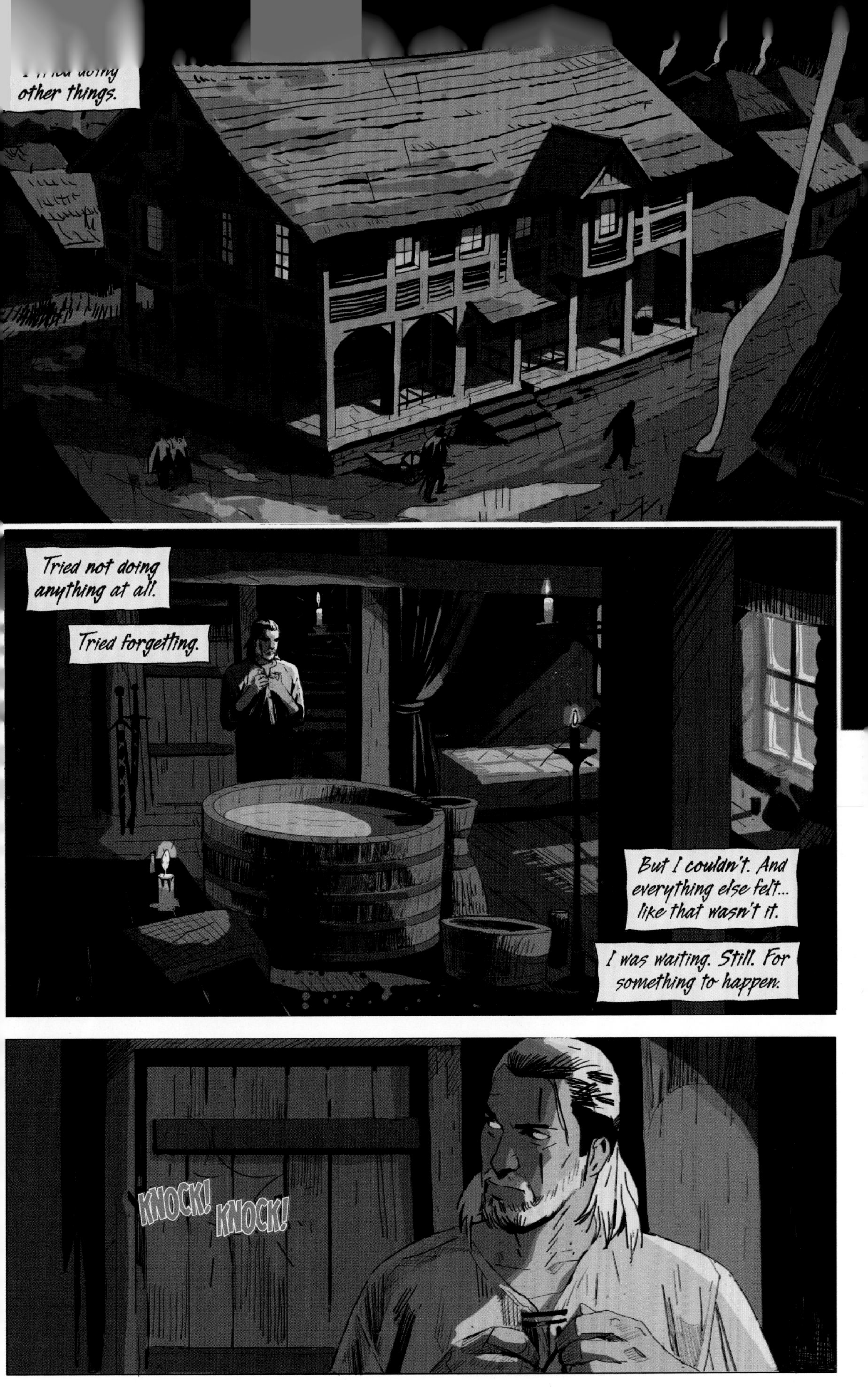

other things.
Tried not doing anything at all.
Tried forgetting.
But I couldn't. And everything else felt... like that wasn't it.
I was waiting. Still. For something to happen.
KNOCK! KNOCK!

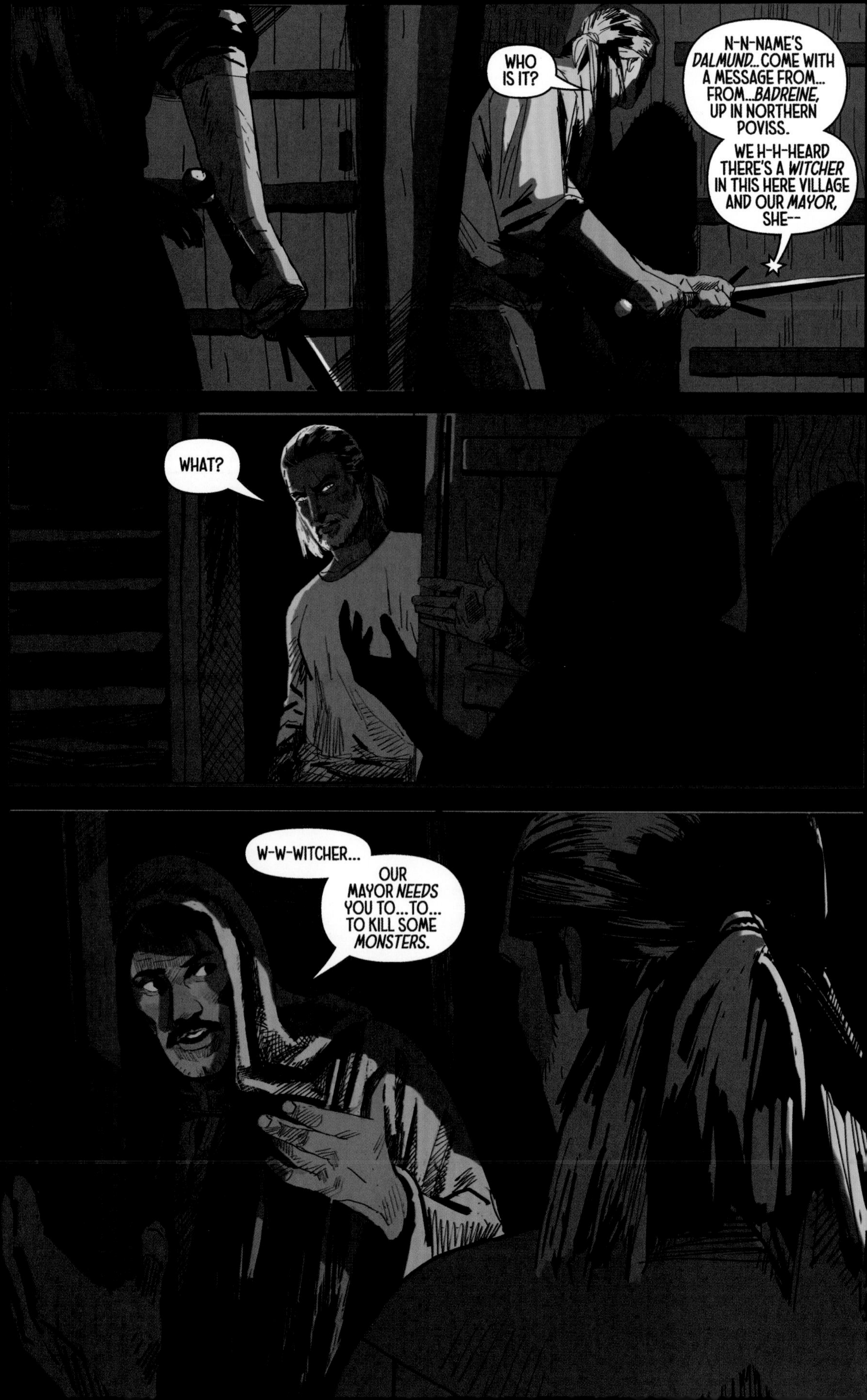
WHO IS IT?
N-N-NAME'S *DALMUND*...COME WITH A MESSAGE FROM... FROM...*BADREINE,* UP IN NORTHERN POVISS.
WE H-H-HEARD THERE'S A *WITCHER* IN THIS HERE VILLAGE AND OUR *MAYOR,* SHE--
WHAT?
W-W-WITCHER...
OUR MAYOR *NEEDS* YOU TO...TO... TO KILL SOME *MONSTERS.*

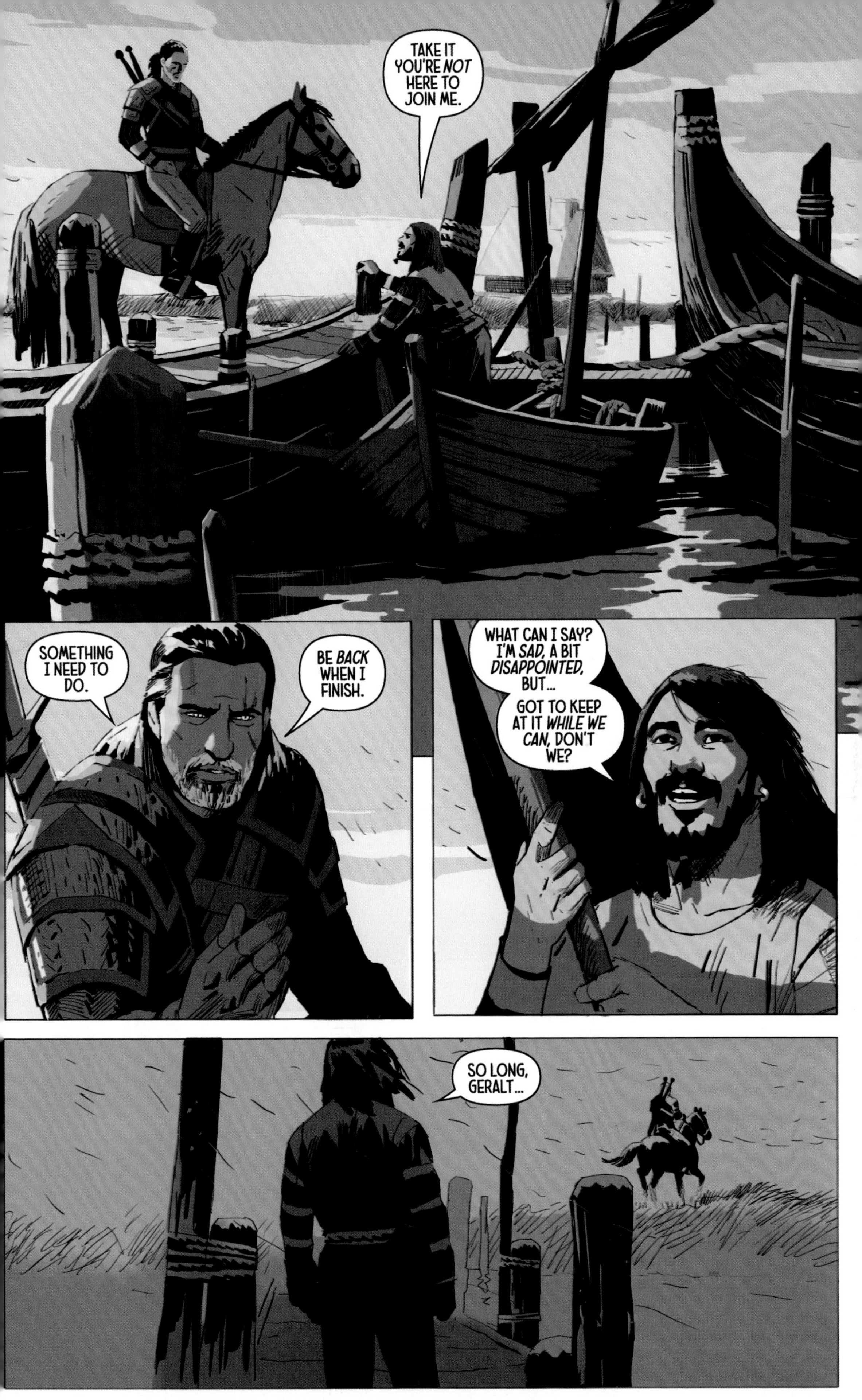
TAKE IT YOU'RE NOT HERE TO JOIN ME.
SOMETHING I NEED TO DO.
BE BACK WHEN I FINISH.
WHAT CAN I SAY? I'M SAD, A BIT DISAPPOINTED, BUT...
GOT TO KEEP AT IT WHILE WE CAN, DON'T WE?
SO LONG, GERALT...

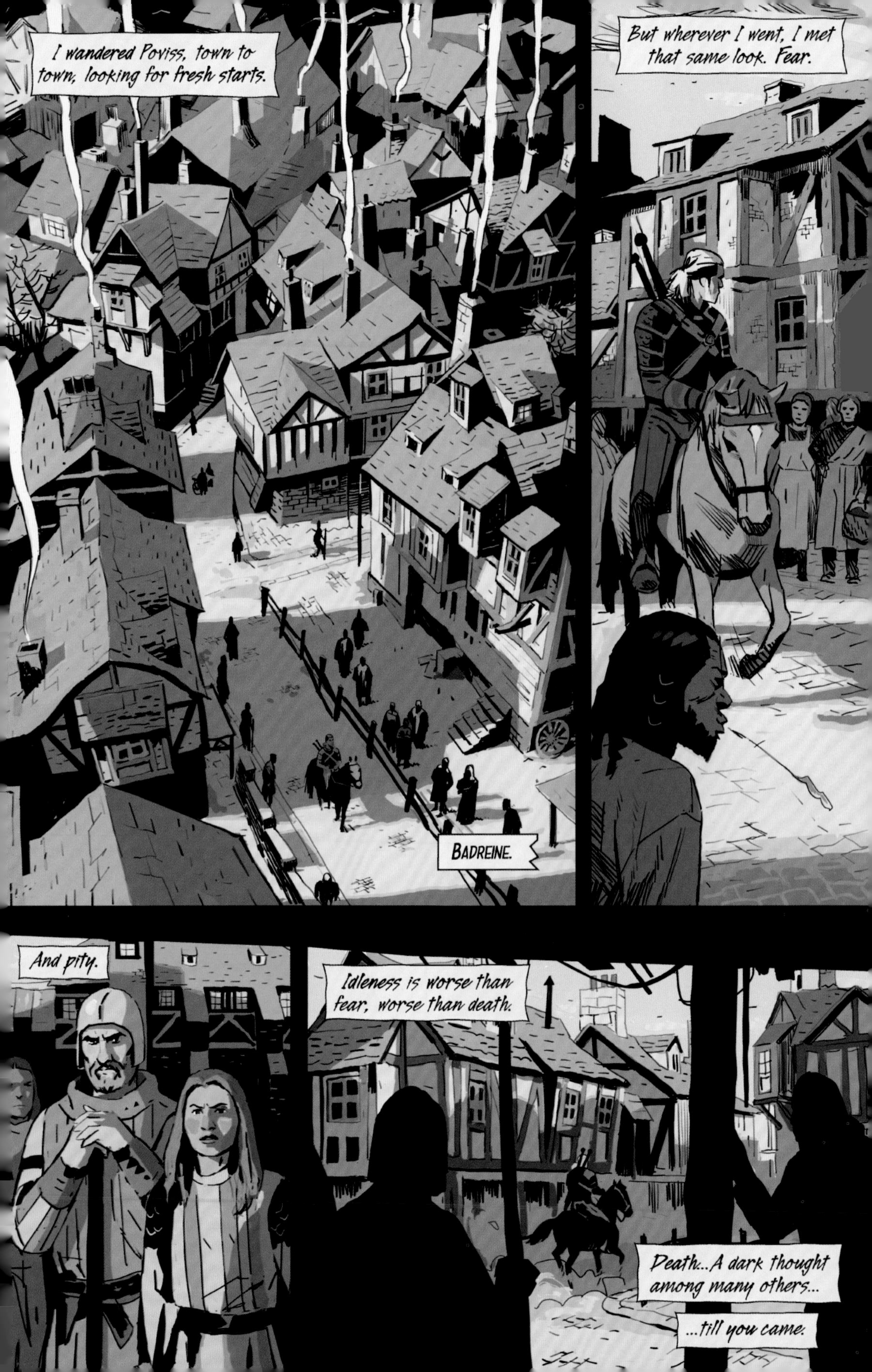

I wandered Poviss, town to town, looking for fresh starts.
BADREINE.
But wherever I went, I met that same look. Fear.
And pity.
Idleness is worse than fear, worse than death.
Death... A dark thought among many others...
...till you came.

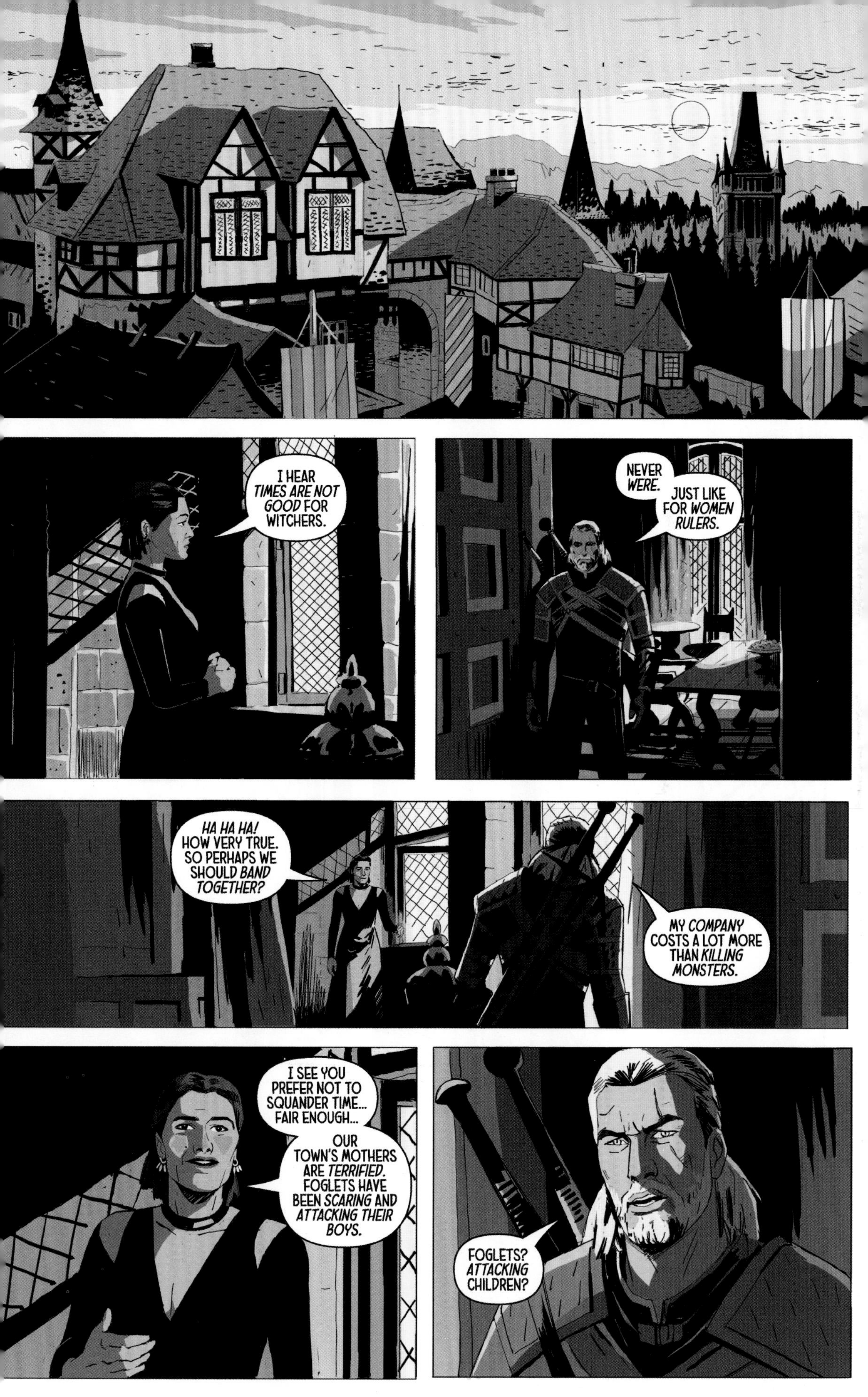
I HEAR *TIMES ARE NOT GOOD* FOR WITCHERS.
NEVER *WERE*.
JUST LIKE FOR *WOMEN RULERS*.
HA HA HA! HOW VERY TRUE. SO PERHAPS WE SHOULD *BAND TOGETHER?*
MY *COMPANY* COSTS A LOT MORE THAN *KILLING MONSTERS*.
I SEE YOU PREFER NOT TO SQUANDER TIME... FAIR ENOUGH...
OUR TOWN'S MOTHERS ARE *TERRIFIED*. FOGLETS HAVE BEEN *SCARING* AND *ATTACKING THEIR* BOYS.
FOGLETS? *ATTACKING* CHILDREN?

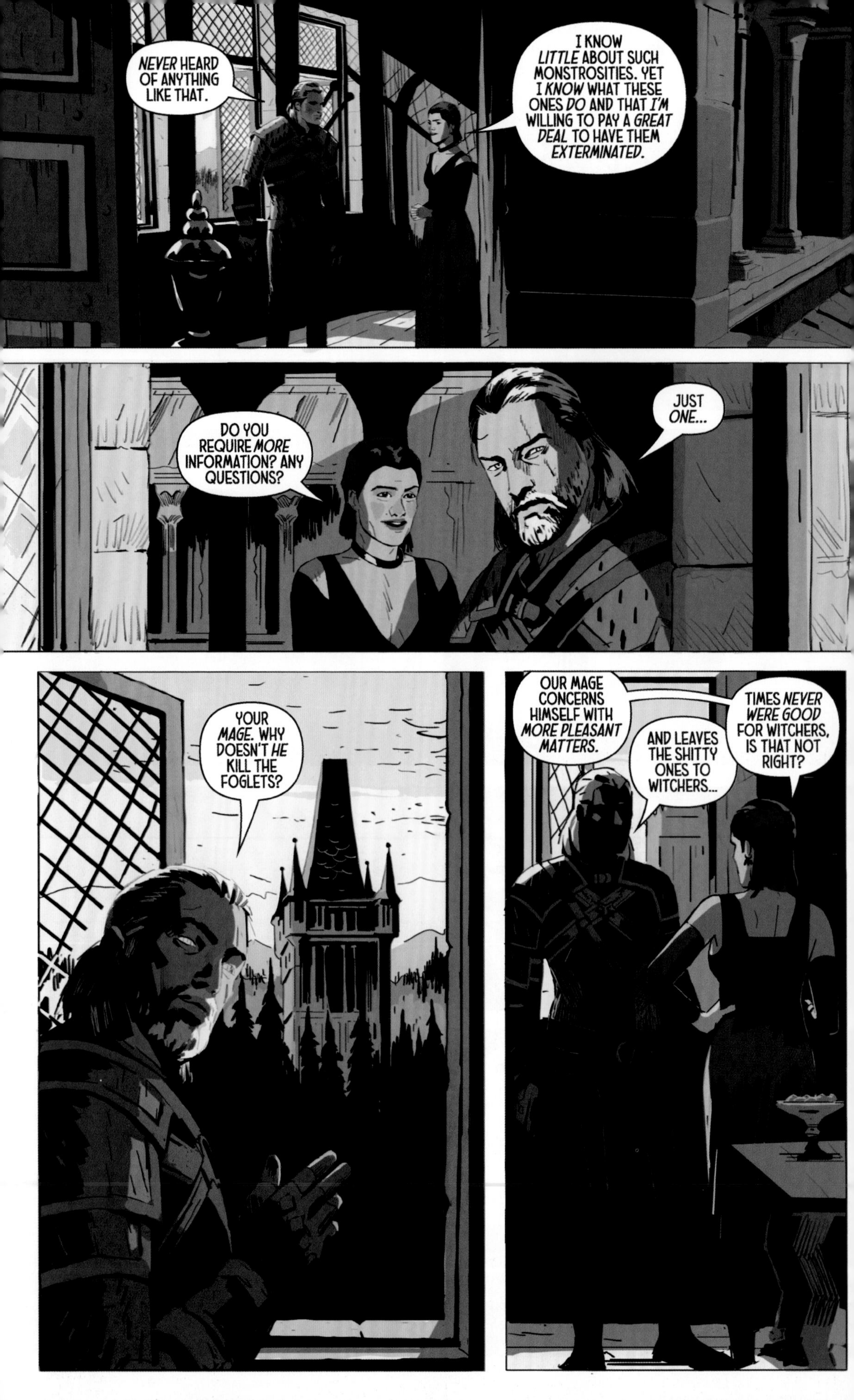
NEVER HEARD OF ANYTHING LIKE THAT.
I KNOW LITTLE ABOUT SUCH MONSTROSITIES. YET I KNOW WHAT THESE ONES DO AND THAT I'M WILLING TO PAY A GREAT DEAL TO HAVE THEM EXTERMINATED.
DO YOU REQUIRE MORE INFORMATION? ANY QUESTIONS?
JUST ONE...
YOUR MAGE. WHY DOESN'T HE KILL THE FOGLETS?
OUR MAGE CONCERNS HIMSELF WITH MORE PLEASANT MATTERS.
AND LEAVES THE SHITTY ONES TO WITCHERS...
TIMES NEVER WERE GOOD FOR WITCHERS, IS THAT NOT RIGHT?

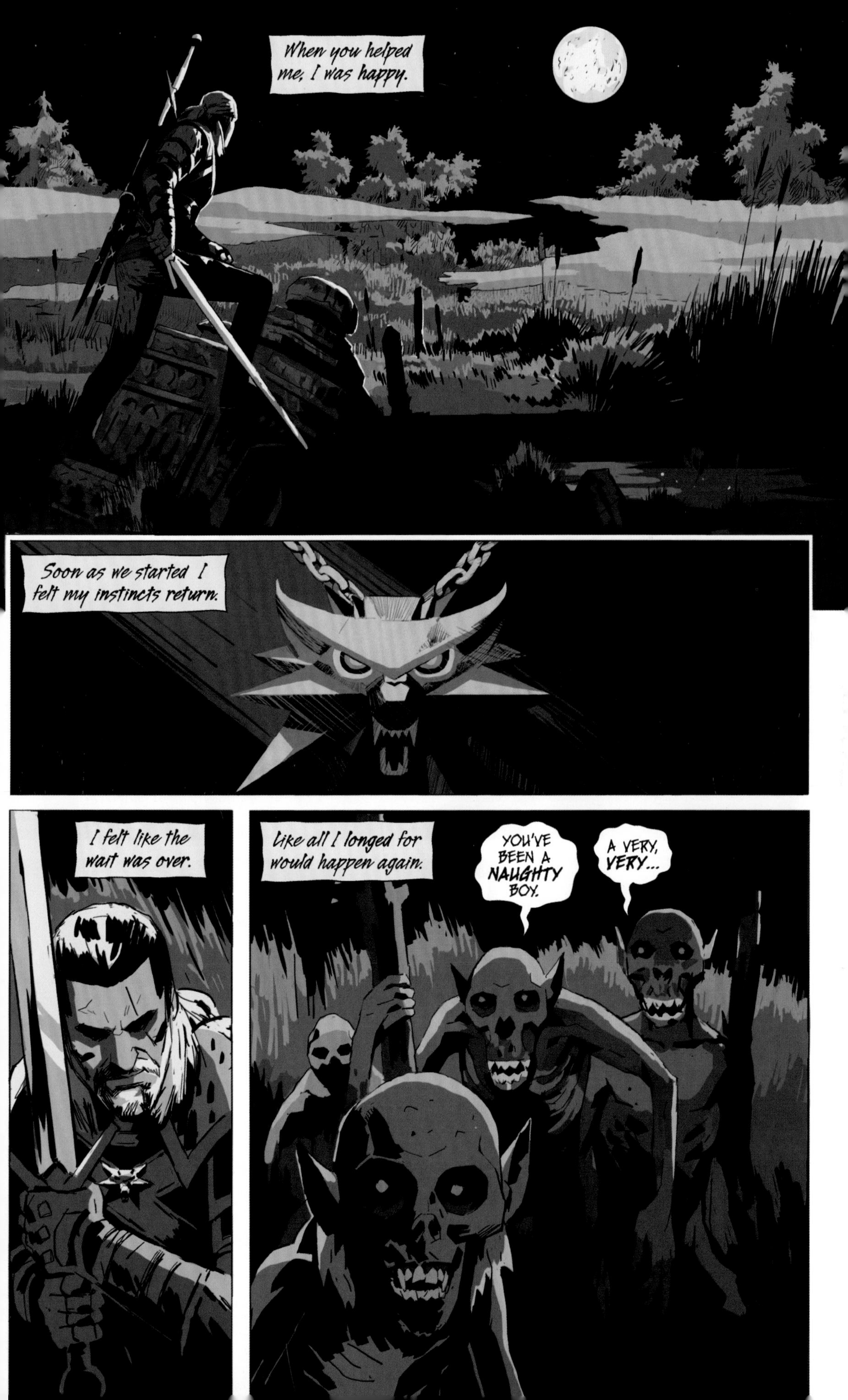
When you helped me, I was happy.
Soon as we started I felt my instincts return.
I felt like the wait was over.
Like all I longed for would happen again.
YOU'VE BEEN A NAUGHTY BOY.
A VERY, VERY...

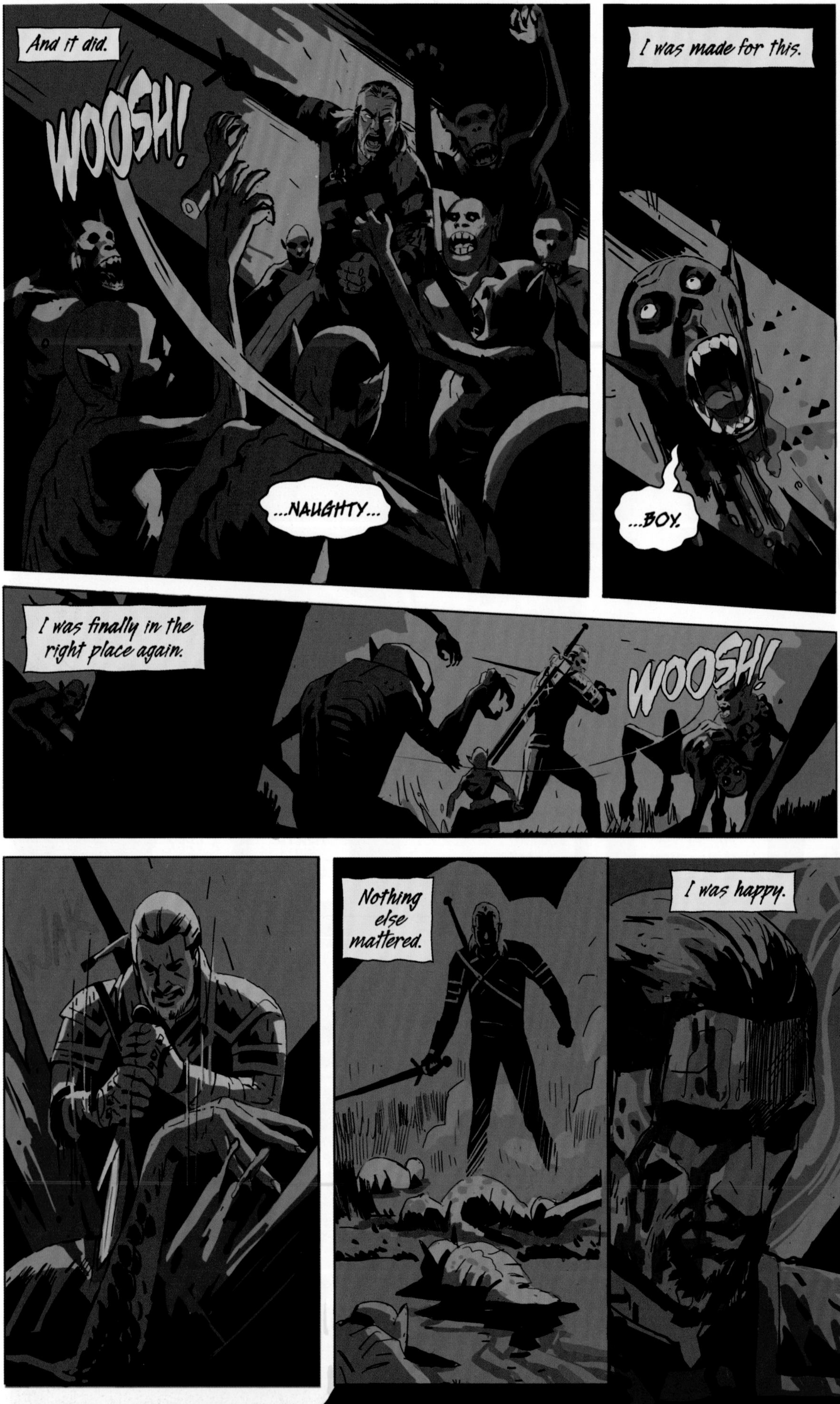
And it did.
WOOSH!
...NAUGHTY...
I was made for this.
...BOY.
I was finally in the right place again.
WOOSH!
Nothing else mattered.
I was happy.

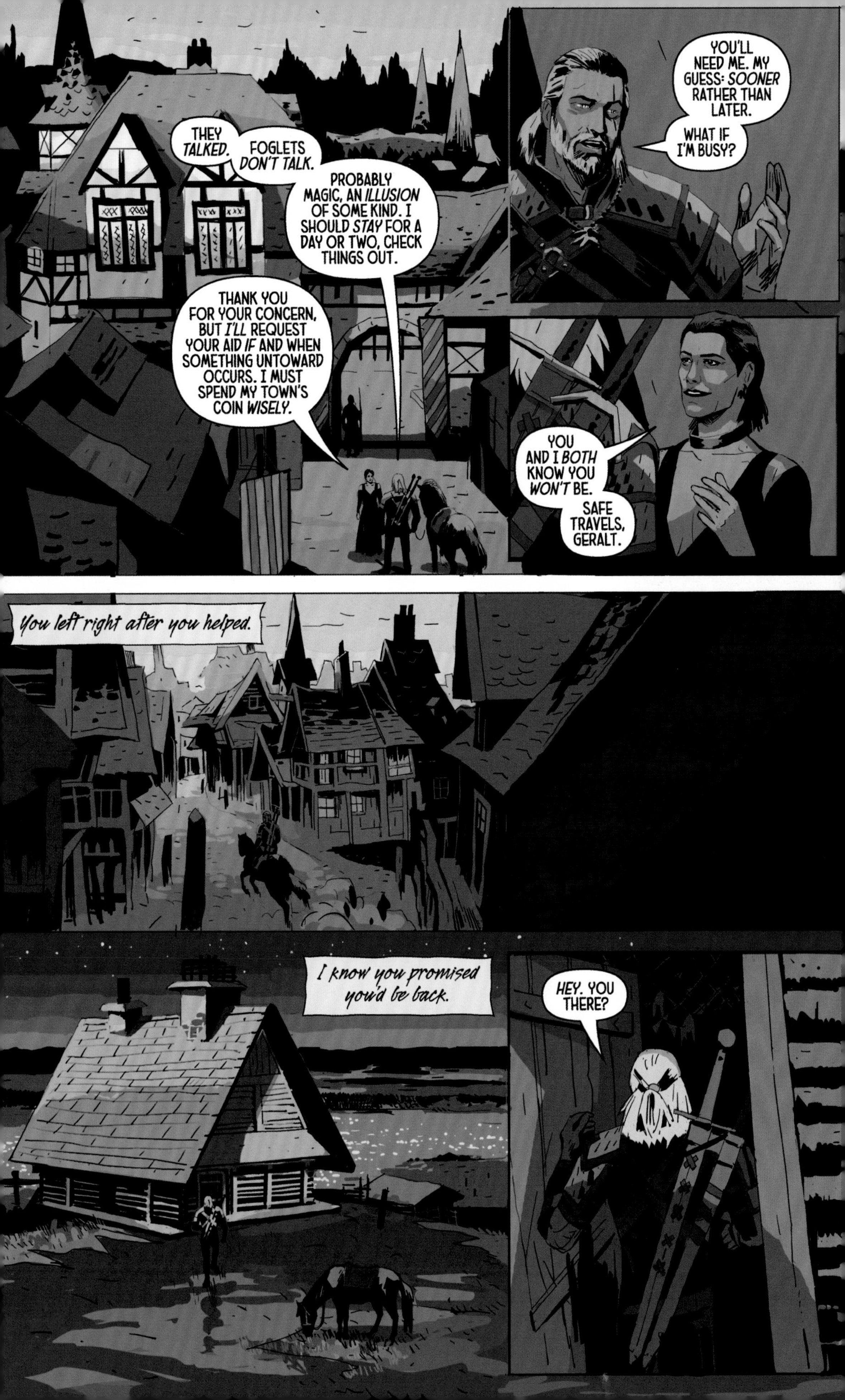
THEY TALKED.
FOGLETS DON'T TALK.
PROBABLY MAGIC, AN ILLUSION OF SOME KIND. I SHOULD STAY FOR A DAY OR TWO, CHECK THINGS OUT.
THANK YOU FOR YOUR CONCERN, BUT I'LL REQUEST YOUR AID IF AND WHEN SOMETHING UNTOWARD OCCURS. I MUST SPEND MY TOWN'S COIN WISELY.
YOU'LL NEED ME. MY GUESS: SOONER RATHER THAN LATER.
WHAT IF I'M BUSY?
YOU AND I BOTH KNOW YOU WON'T BE.
SAFE TRAVELS, GERALT.
You left right after you helped.
I know you promised you'd be back.
HEY. YOU THERE?

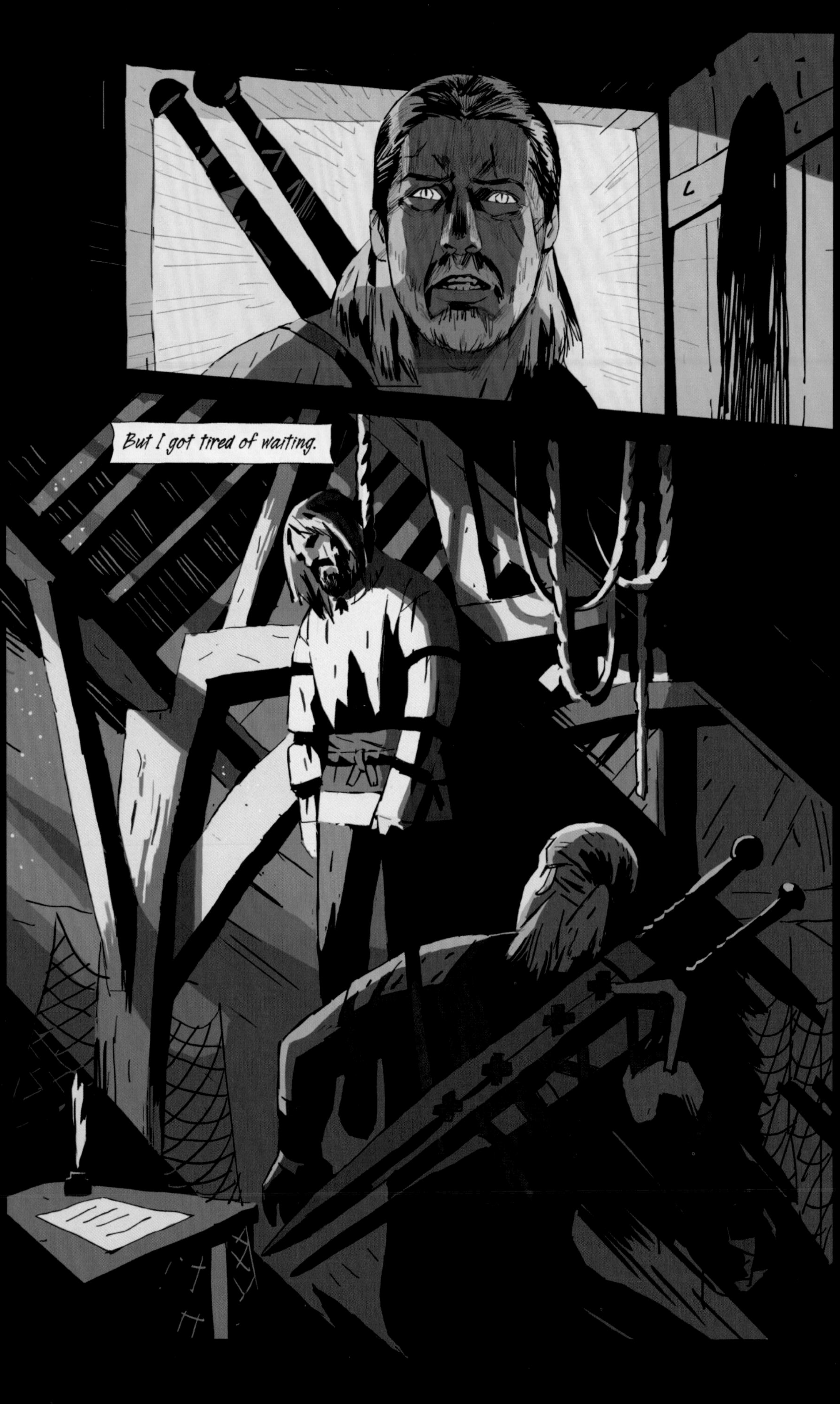
But I got tired of waiting.

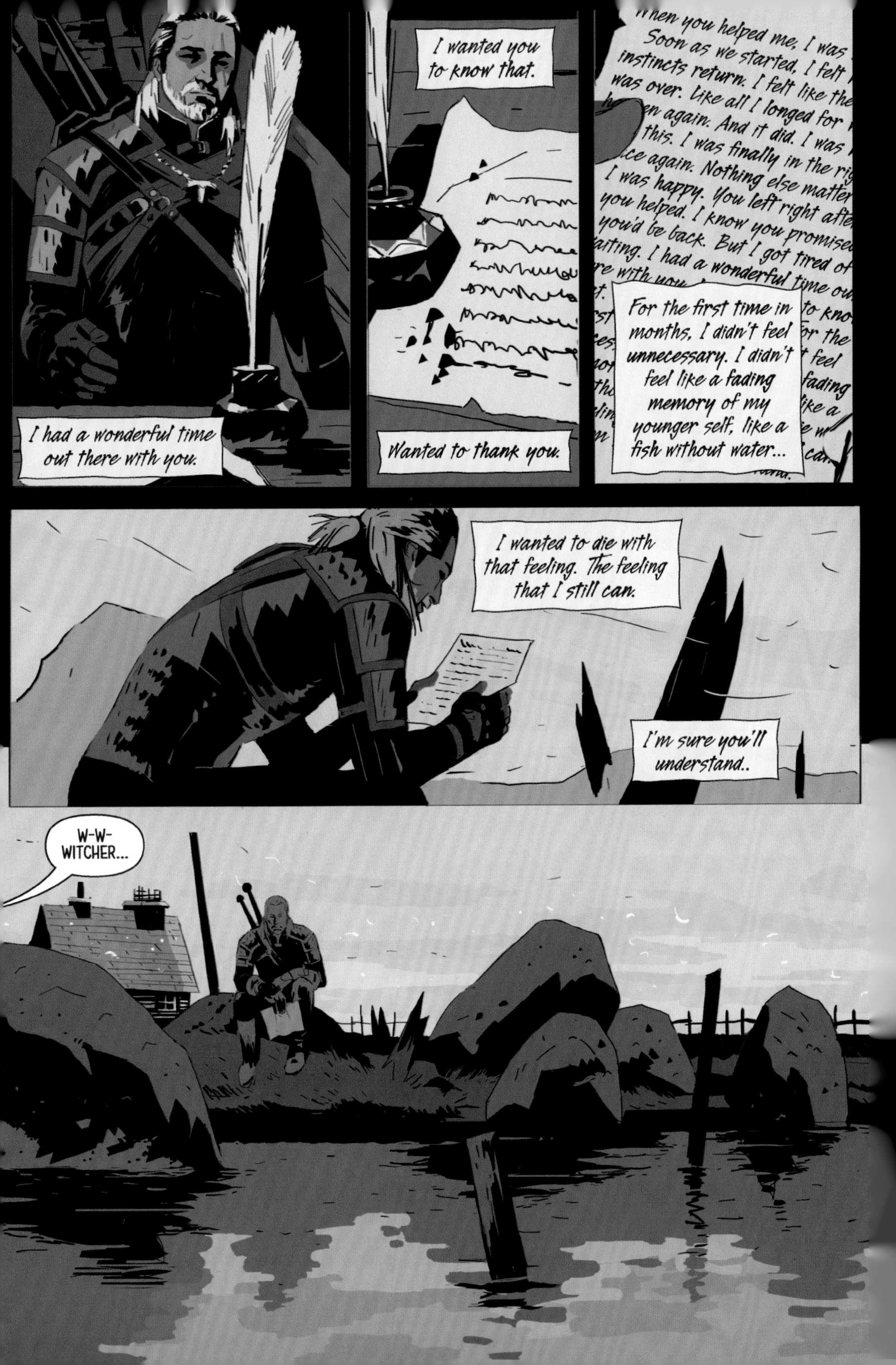
I had a wonderful time out there with you.
I wanted you to know that.
Wanted to thank you.
For the first time in months, I didn't feel unnecessary. I didn't feel like a fading memory of my younger self, like a fish without water...
I wanted to die with that feeling. The feeling that I still can.
I'm sure you'll understand..
W-W-WITCHER...

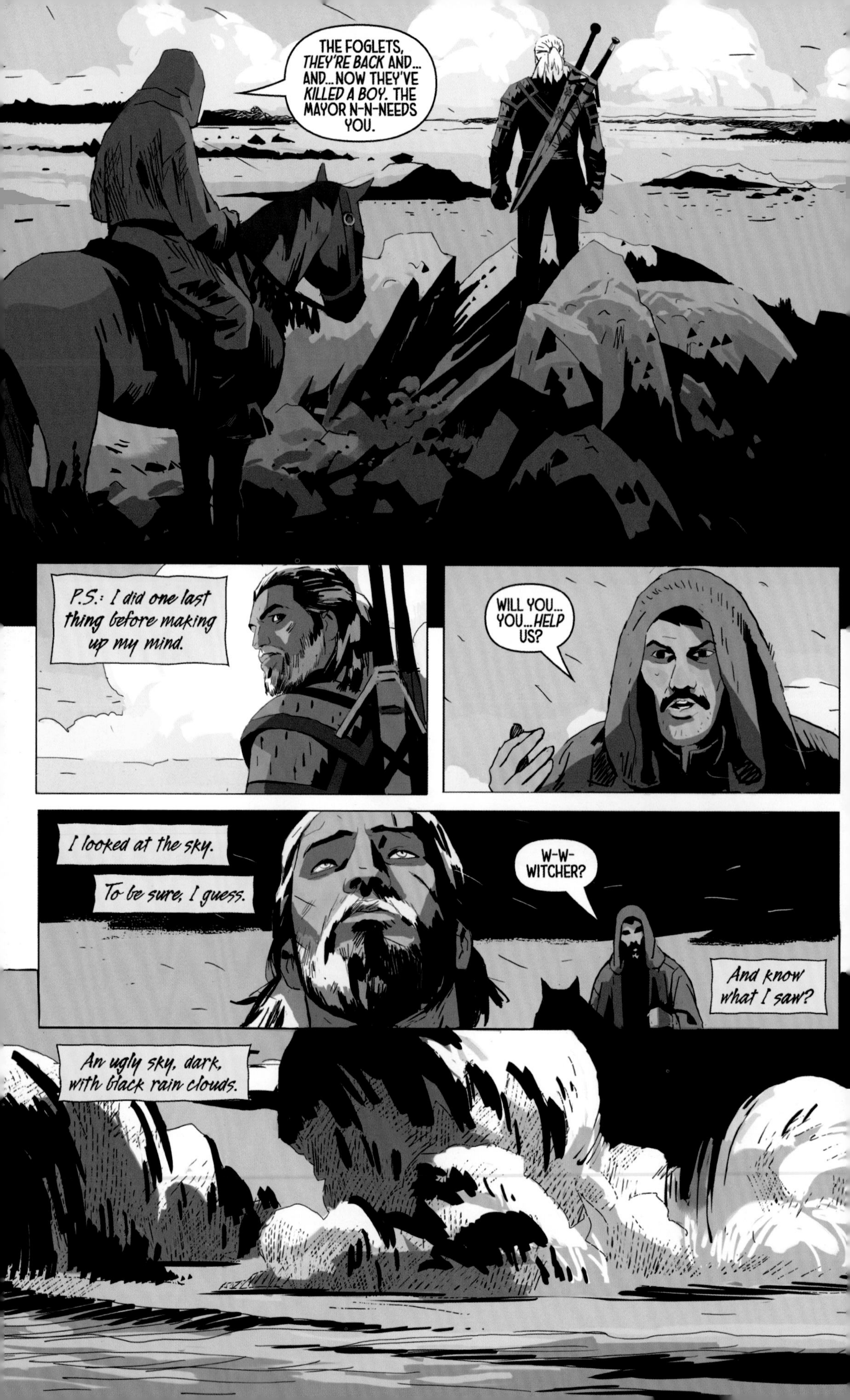
THE FOGLETS, *THEY'RE BACK* AND... AND...NOW THEY'VE *KILLED A BOY*. THE MAYOR N-N-NEEDS YOU.
P.S.: I did one last thing before making up my mind.
WILL YOU... YOU...*HELP* US?
I looked at the sky.
To be sure, I guess.
W-W-WITCHER?
And know what I saw?
An ugly sky, dark, with black rain clouds.

CHAPTER TWO

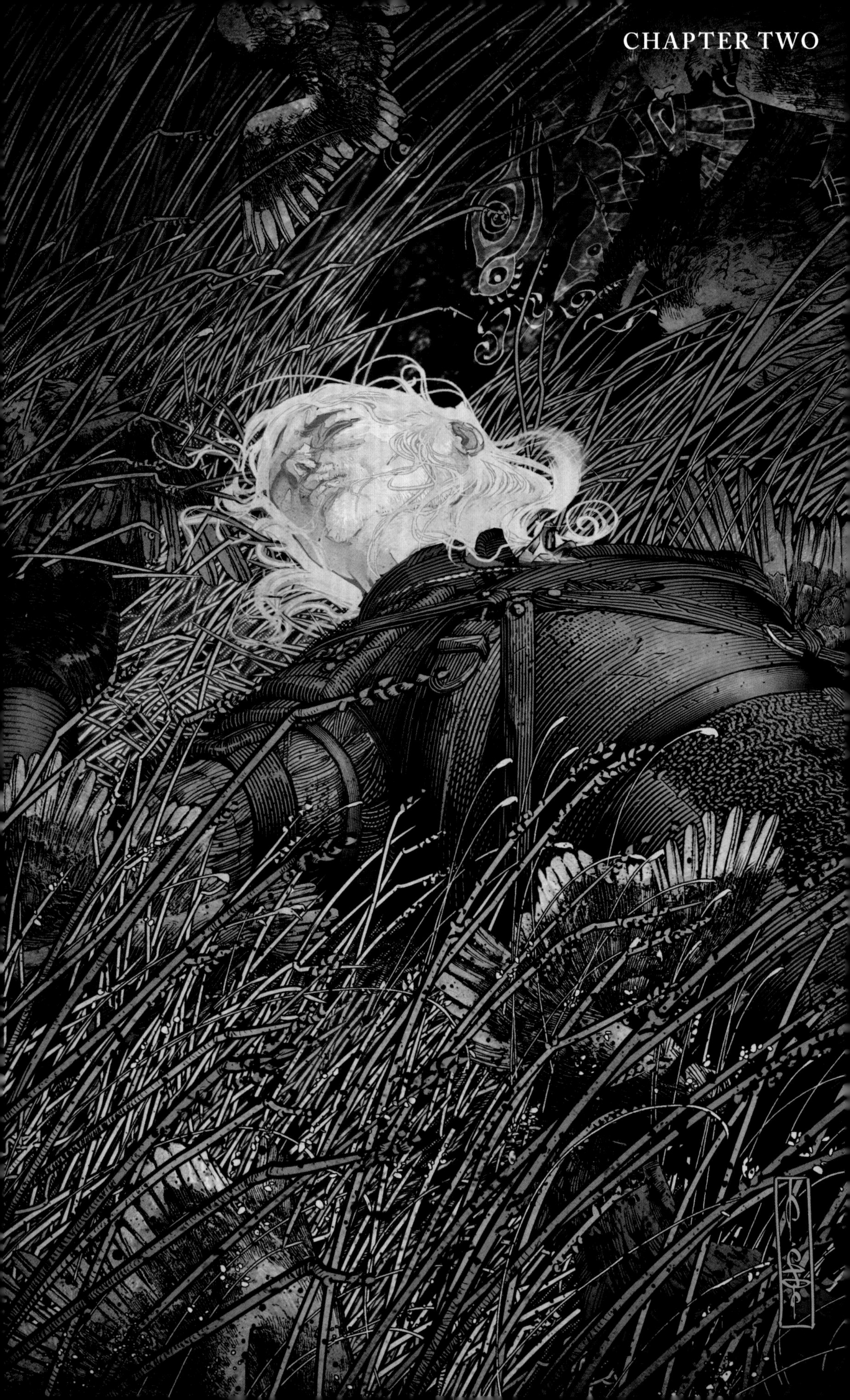

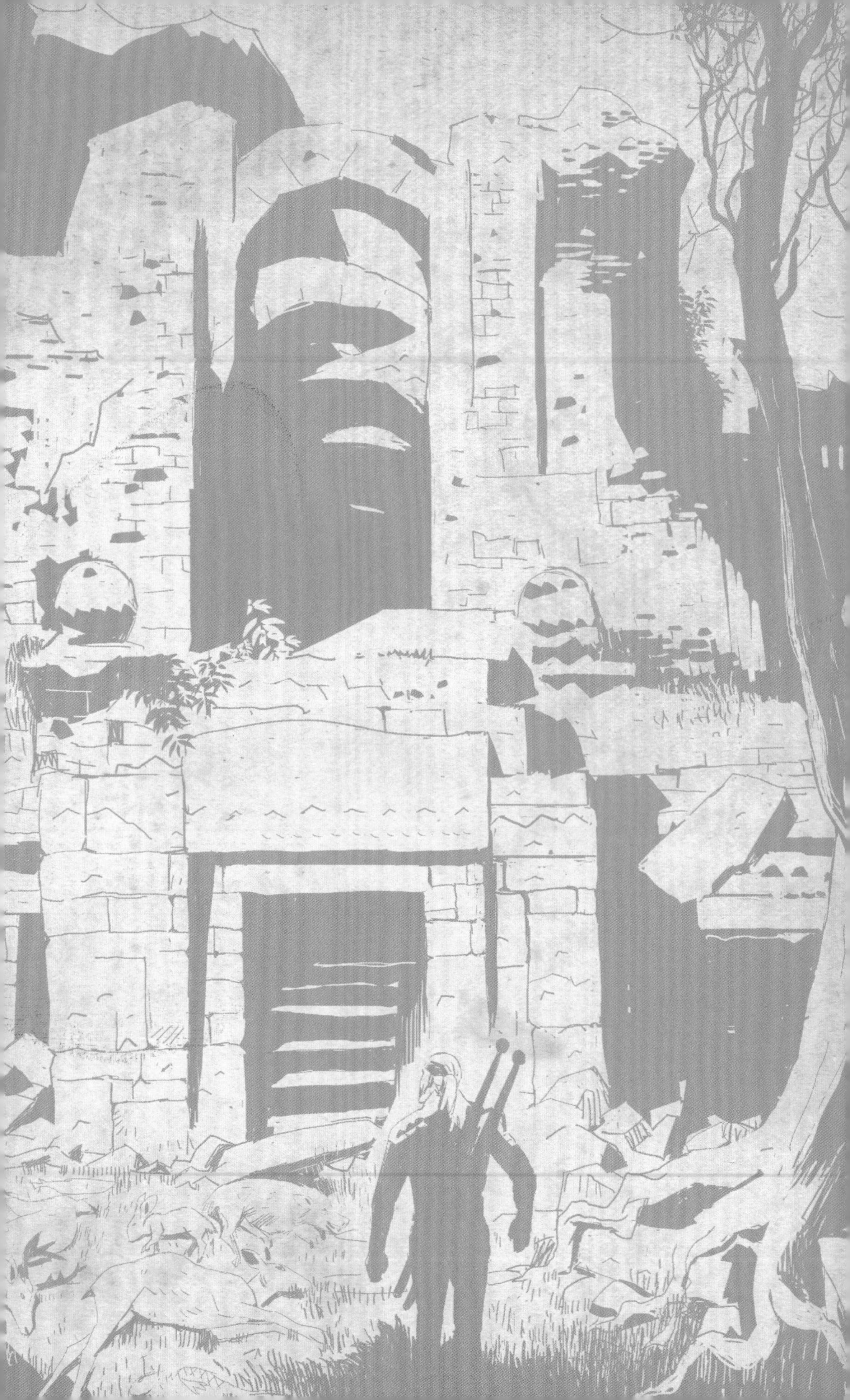

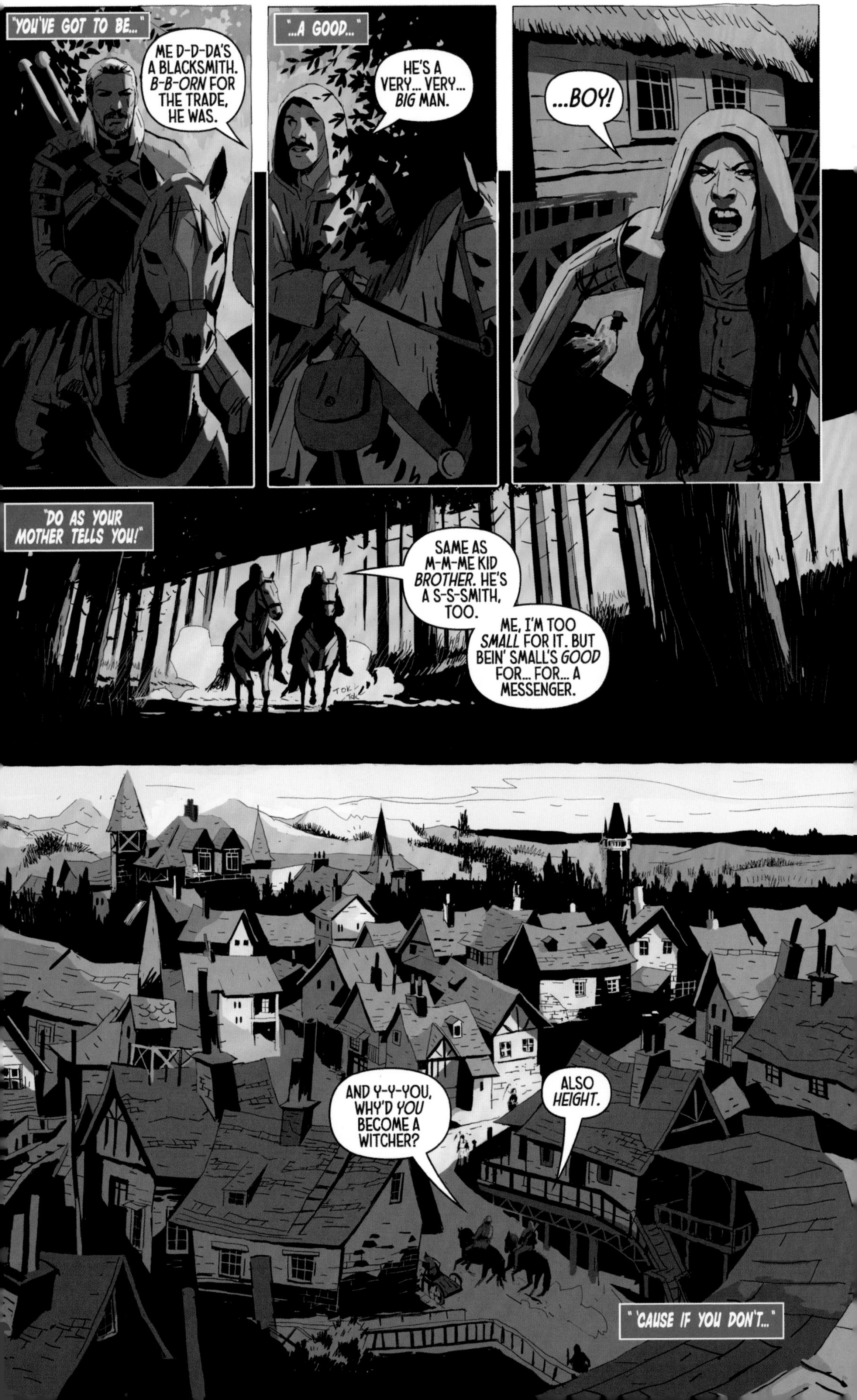
"YOU'VE GOT TO BE..."
ME D-D-DA'S A BLACKSMITH. B-B-ORN FOR THE TRADE, HE WAS.
"...A GOOD..."
HE'S A VERY... VERY... BIG MAN.
...BOY!
"DO AS YOUR MOTHER TELLS YOU!"
SAME AS M-M-ME KID BROTHER. HE'S A S-S-SMITH, TOO.
ME, I'M TOO SMALL FOR IT. BUT BEIN' SMALL'S GOOD FOR... FOR... A MESSENGER.
TOK TOK
AND Y-Y-YOU, WHY'D YOU BECOME A WITCHER?
ALSO HEIGHT.
"'CAUSE IF YOU DON'T..."

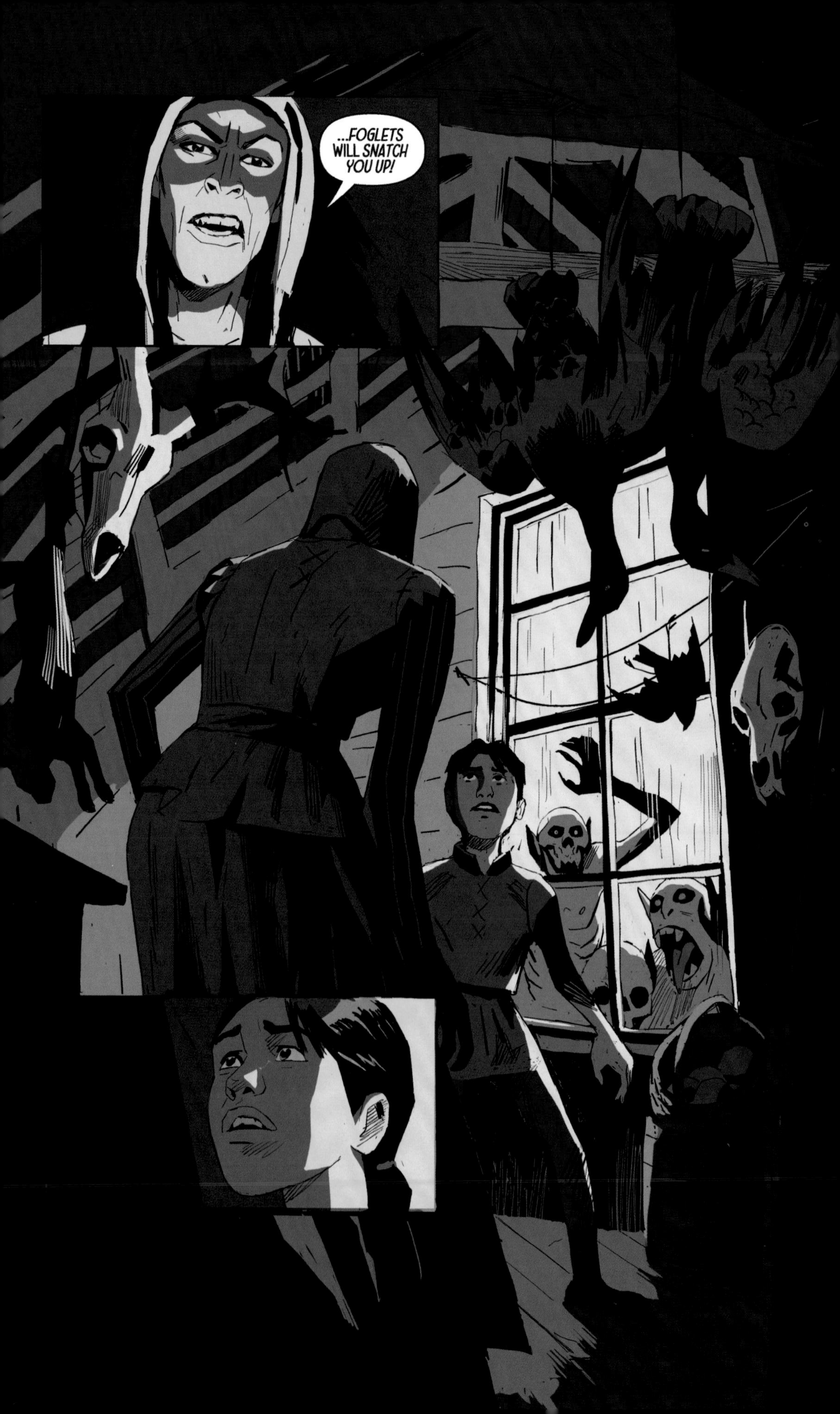
...FOGLETS WILL SNATCH YOU UP!

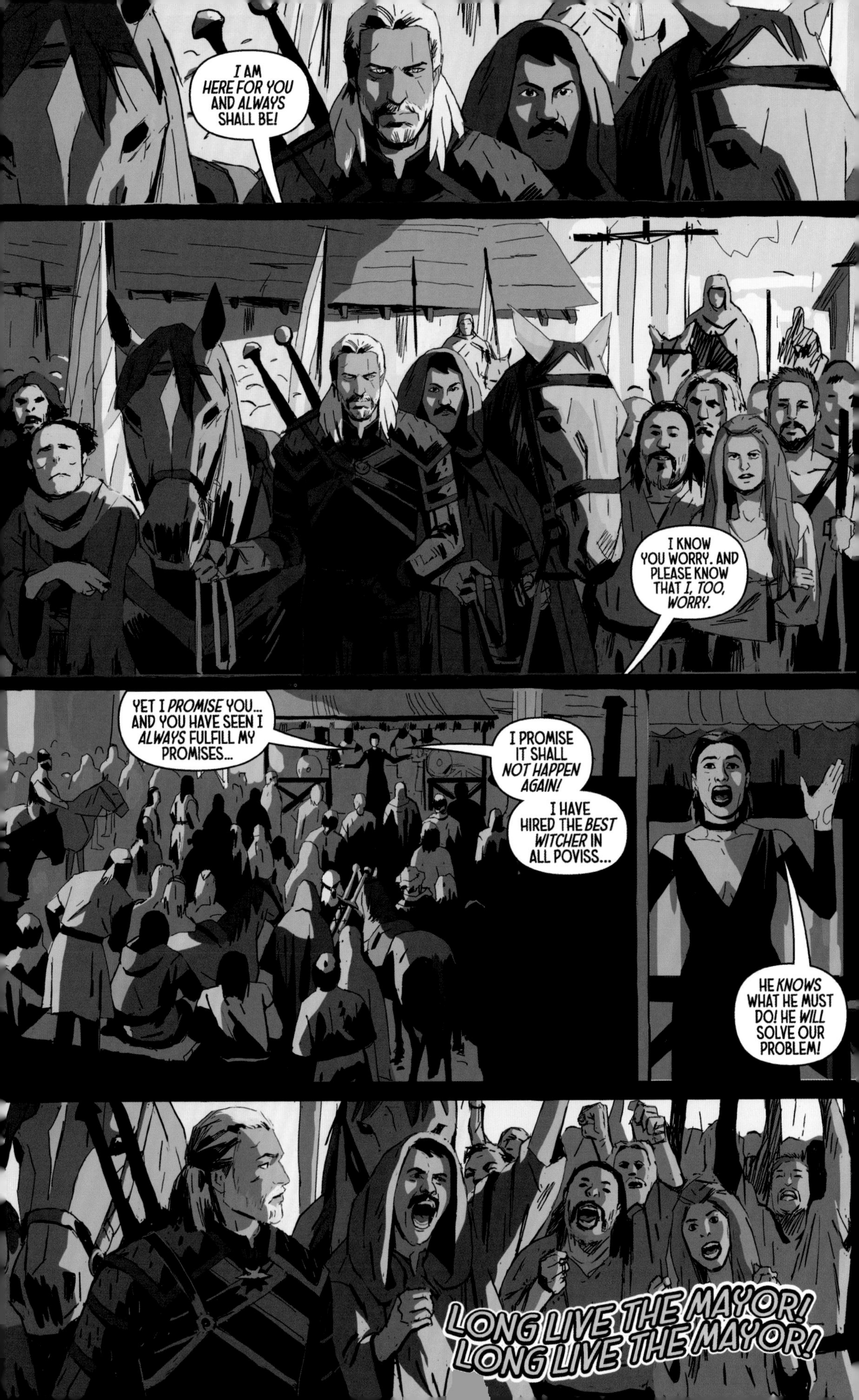
I AM HERE FOR YOU AND ALWAYS SHALL BE!
I KNOW YOU WORRY. AND PLEASE KNOW THAT I, TOO, WORRY.
YET I PROMISE YOU... AND YOU HAVE SEEN I ALWAYS FULFILL MY PROMISES...
I PROMISE IT SHALL NOT HAPPEN AGAIN!
I HAVE HIRED THE BEST WITCHER IN ALL POVISS...
HE KNOWS WHAT HE MUST DO! HE WILL SOLVE OUR PROBLEM!
LONG LIVE THE MAYOR! LONG LIVE THE MAYOR!

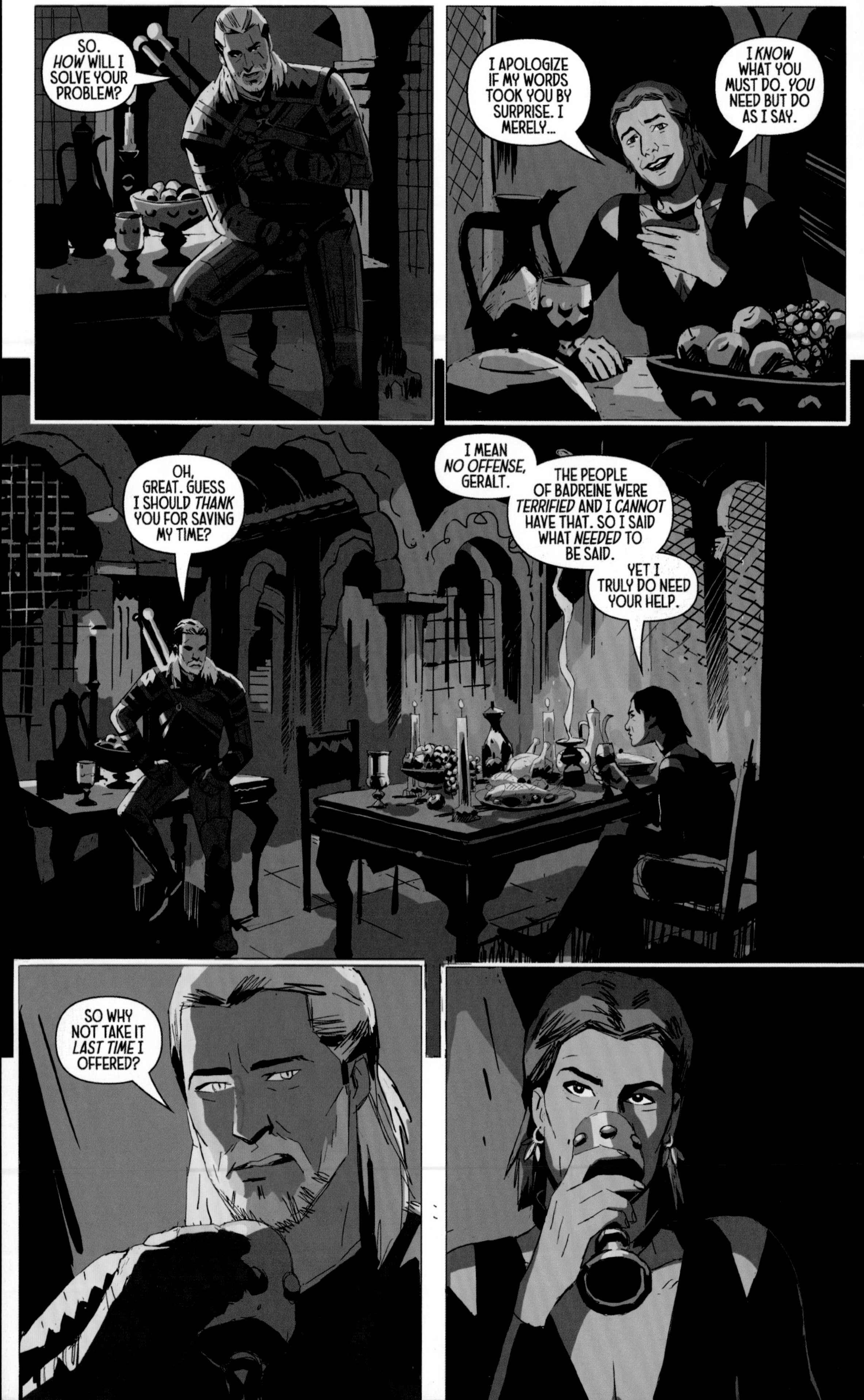
SO. *HOW* WILL I SOLVE YOUR PROBLEM?
I APOLOGIZE IF MY WORDS TOOK YOU BY SURPRISE. I MERELY...
I *KNOW* WHAT YOU MUST DO. *YOU* NEED BUT DO AS I SAY.
OH, GREAT. GUESS I SHOULD *THANK* YOU FOR SAVING MY TIME?
I MEAN *NO OFFENSE,* GERALT.
THE PEOPLE OF BADREINE WERE *TERRIFIED* AND I *CANNOT* HAVE THAT. SO I SAID WHAT *NEEDED* TO BE SAID.
YET I TRULY DO NEED YOUR HELP.
SO WHY NOT TAKE IT *LAST TIME* I OFFERED?

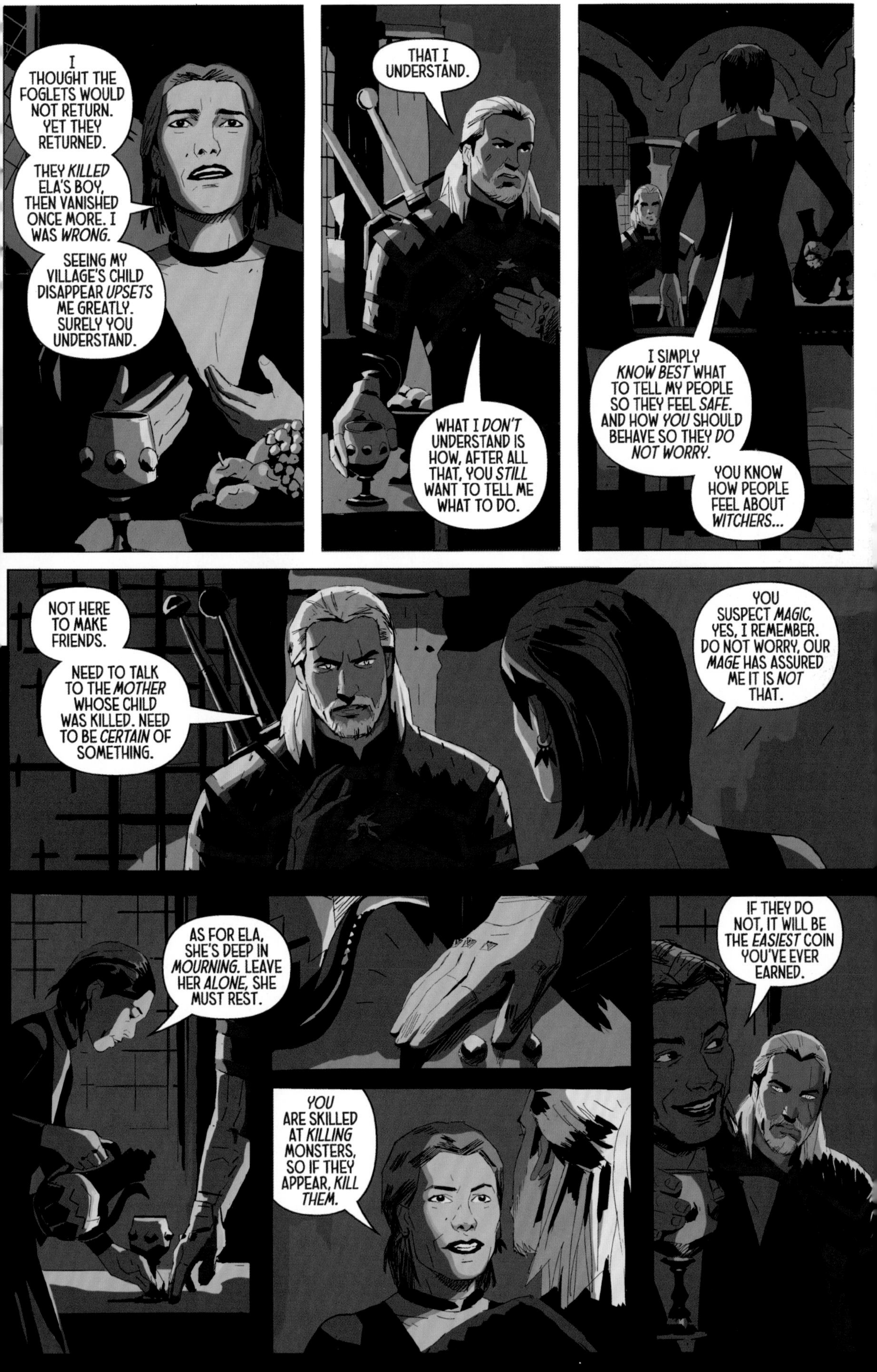
I THOUGHT THE FOGLETS WOULD NOT RETURN. YET THEY RETURNED.
THEY *KILLED* ELA'S BOY, THEN VANISHED ONCE MORE. I WAS *WRONG*.
SEEING MY VILLAGE'S CHILD DISAPPEAR *UPSETS* ME GREATLY. SURELY YOU UNDERSTAND.
THAT I UNDERSTAND.
WHAT I *DON'T* UNDERSTAND IS HOW, AFTER ALL THAT, YOU *STILL* WANT TO TELL ME WHAT TO DO.
I SIMPLY *KNOW BEST* WHAT TO TELL MY PEOPLE SO THEY FEEL *SAFE*. AND HOW *YOU* SHOULD BEHAVE SO THEY *DO NOT WORRY*.
YOU KNOW HOW PEOPLE FEEL ABOUT *WITCHERS*...
NOT HERE TO MAKE FRIENDS.
NEED TO TALK TO THE *MOTHER* WHOSE CHILD WAS KILLED. NEED TO BE *CERTAIN* OF SOMETHING.
YOU SUSPECT *MAGIC*, YES, I REMEMBER. DO NOT WORRY, OUR *MAGE* HAS ASSURED ME IT IS *NOT* THAT.
AS FOR ELA, SHE'S DEEP IN *MOURNING*. LEAVE HER *ALONE*, SHE MUST REST.
YOU ARE SKILLED AT *KILLING* MONSTERS, SO IF THEY APPEAR, *KILL THEM*.
IF THEY DO NOT, IT WILL BE THE *EASIEST* COIN YOU'VE EVER EARNED.

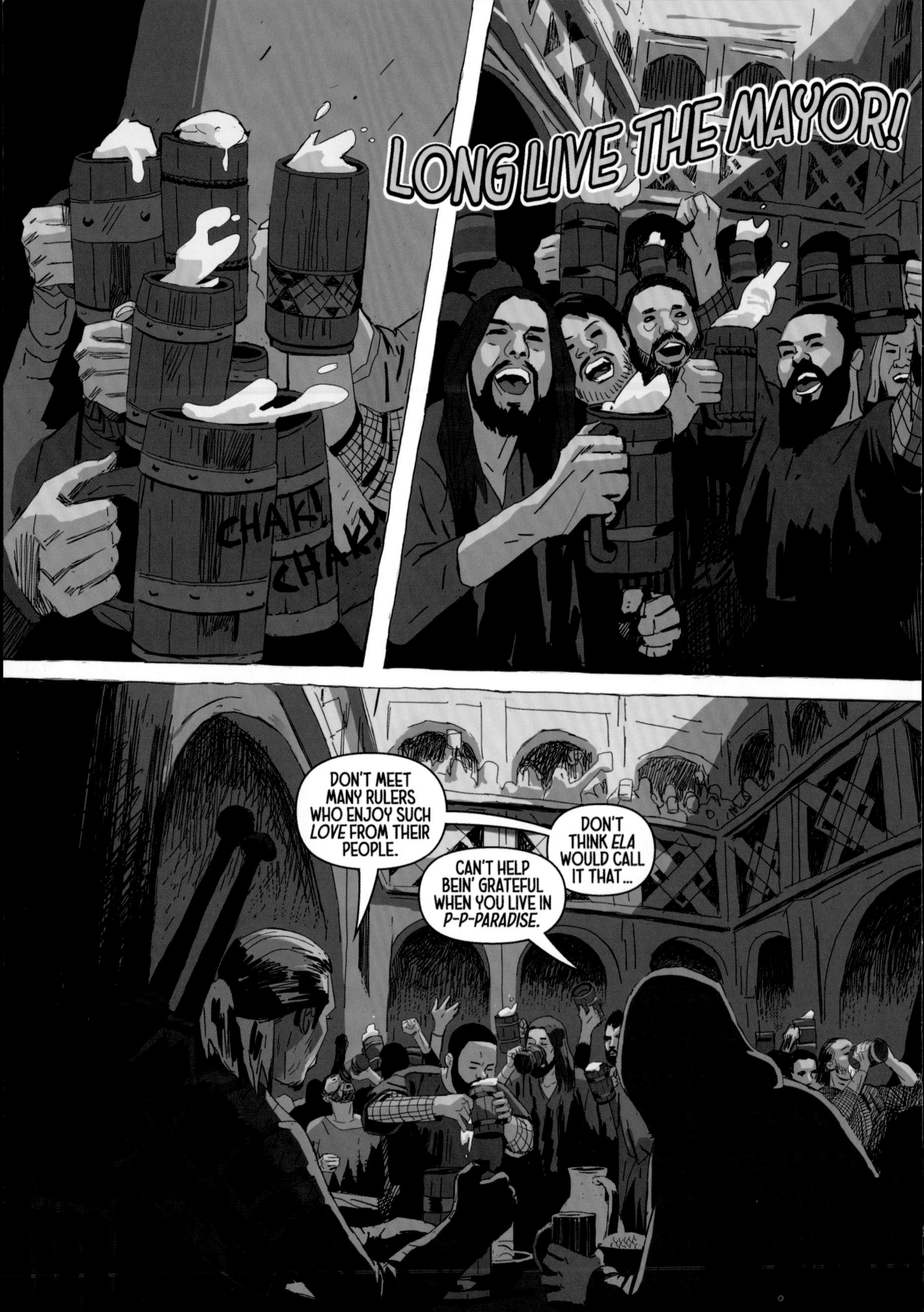
CHAK!
CHAK!
LONG LIVE THE MAYOR!
DON'T MEET MANY RULERS WHO ENJOY SUCH *LOVE* FROM THEIR PEOPLE.
DON'T THINK *ELA* WOULD CALL IT THAT...
CAN'T HELP BEIN' GRATEFUL WHEN YOU LIVE IN *P-P-PARADISE.*

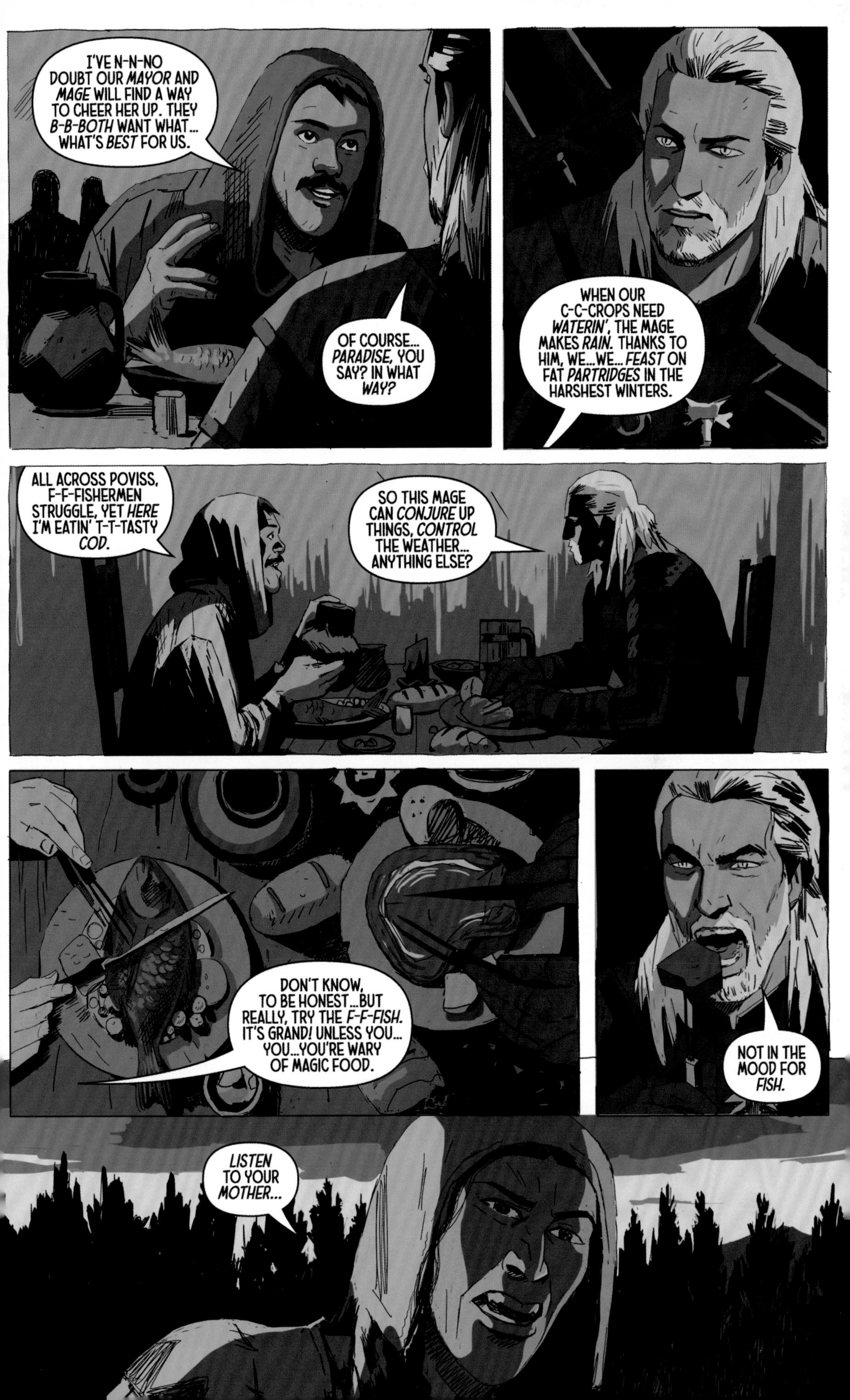
I'VE N-N-NO DOUBT OUR *MAYOR* AND *MAGE* WILL FIND A WAY TO CHEER HER UP. THEY *B-B-BOTH* WANT WHAT... WHAT'S *BEST* FOR US.
OF COURSE... *PARADISE,* YOU SAY? IN WHAT *WAY?*
WHEN OUR C-C-CROPS NEED *WATERIN',* THE MAGE MAKES *RAIN.* THANKS TO HIM, WE...WE... *FEAST* ON FAT *PARTRIDGES* IN THE HARSHEST WINTERS.
ALL ACROSS POVISS, F-F-FISHERMEN STRUGGLE, YET *HERE* I'M EATIN' T-T-TASTY *COD.*
SO THIS MAGE CAN *CONJURE* UP THINGS, *CONTROL* THE WEATHER... ANYTHING ELSE?
DON'T KNOW, TO BE HONEST...BUT REALLY, TRY THE *F-F-FISH.* IT'S GRAND! UNLESS YOU... YOU...YOU'RE WARY OF MAGIC FOOD.
NOT IN THE MOOD FOR *FISH.*
LISTEN TO YOUR *MOTHER...*

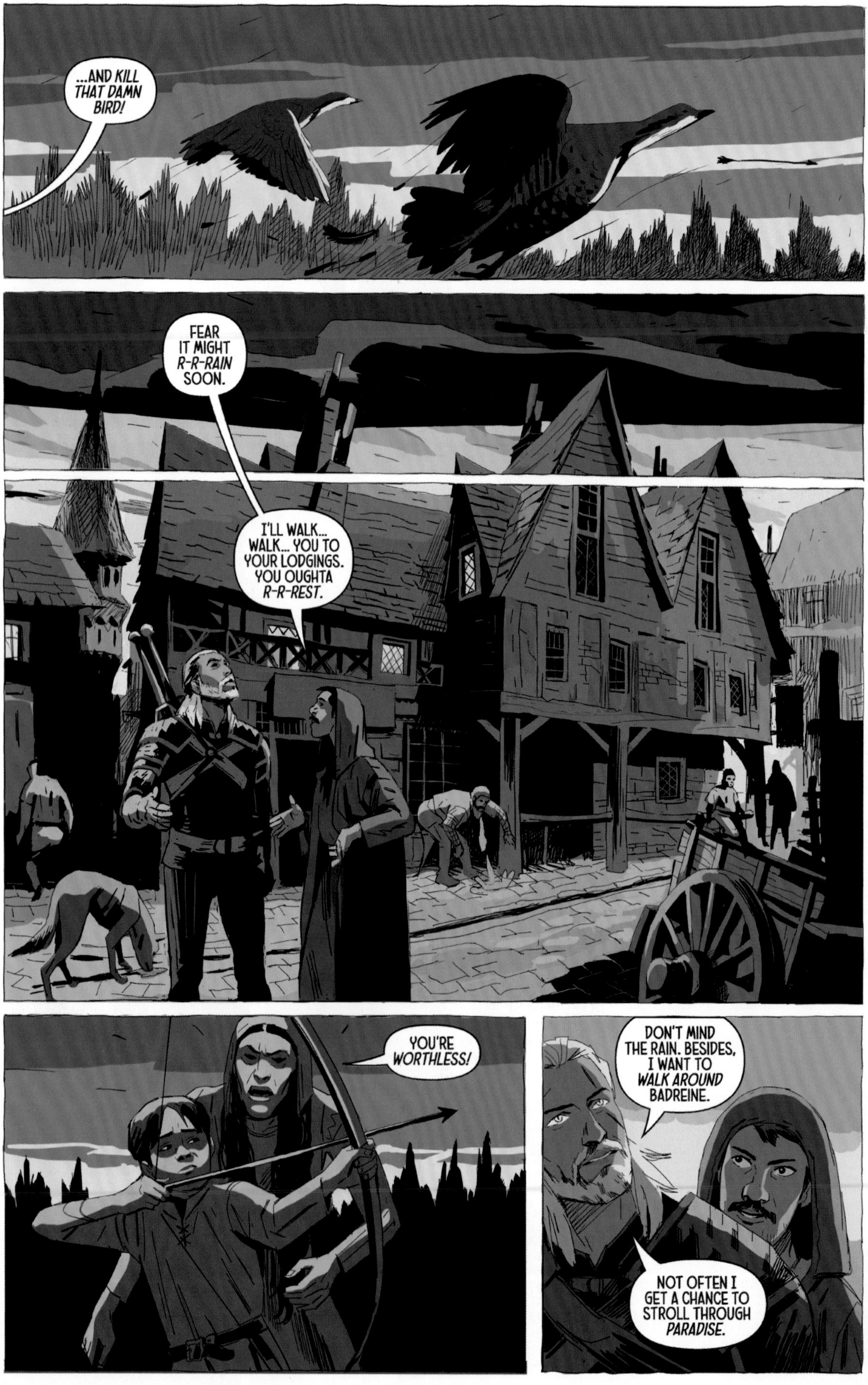
...AND KILL THAT DAMN BIRD!
FEAR IT MIGHT R-R-RAIN SOON.
I'LL WALK... WALK... YOU TO YOUR LODGINGS. YOU OUGHTA R-R-REST.
YOU'RE WORTHLESS!
DON'T MIND THE RAIN. BESIDES, I WANT TO WALK AROUND BADREINE.
NOT OFTEN I GET A CHANCE TO STROLL THROUGH PARADISE.

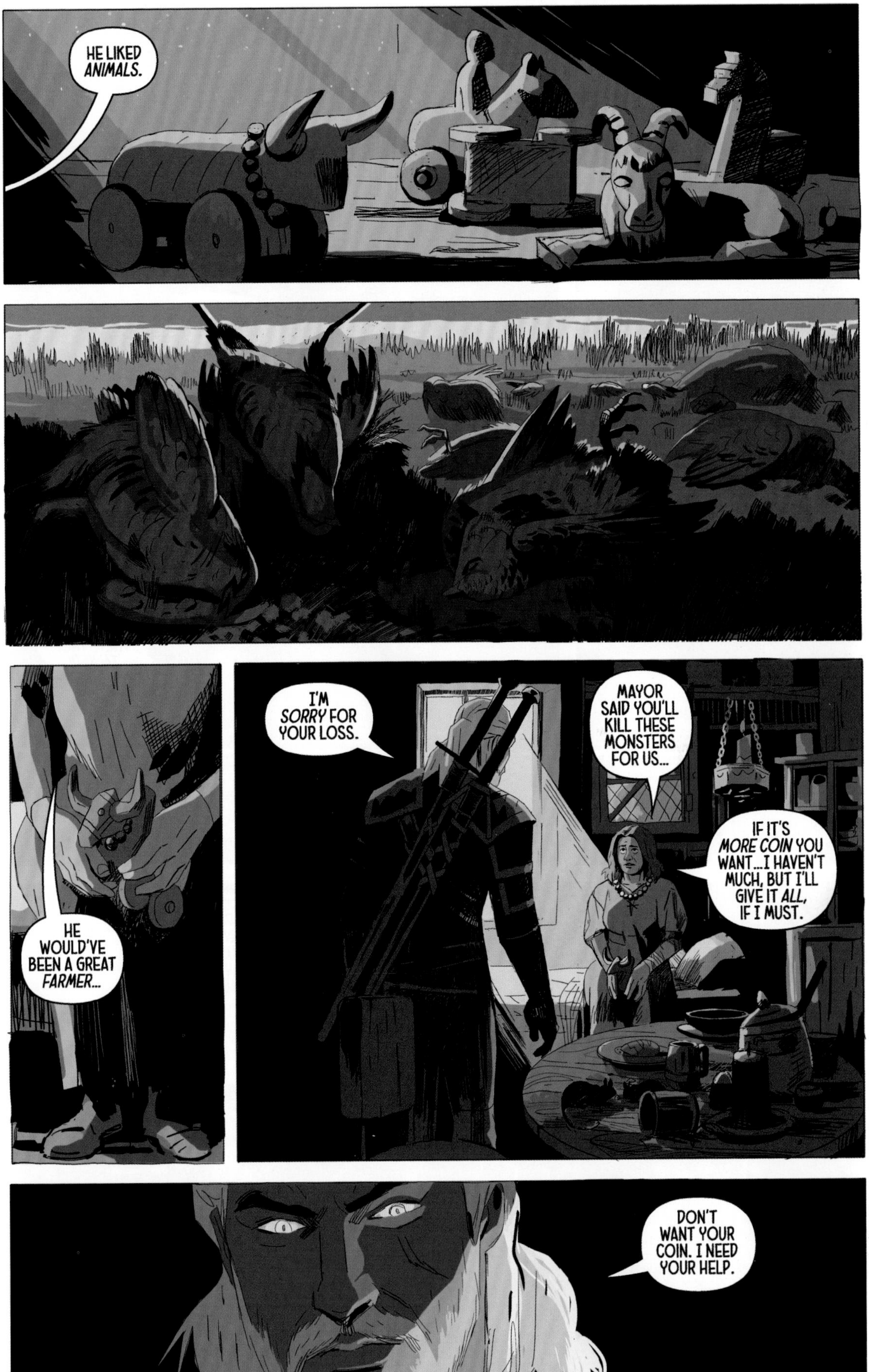
HE LIKED ANIMALS.
HE WOULD'VE BEEN A GREAT FARMER...
I'M SORRY FOR YOUR LOSS.
MAYOR SAID YOU'LL KILL THESE MONSTERS FOR US...
IF IT'S MORE COIN YOU WANT...I HAVEN'T MUCH, BUT I'LL GIVE IT ALL, IF I MUST.
DON'T WANT YOUR COIN. I NEED YOUR HELP.

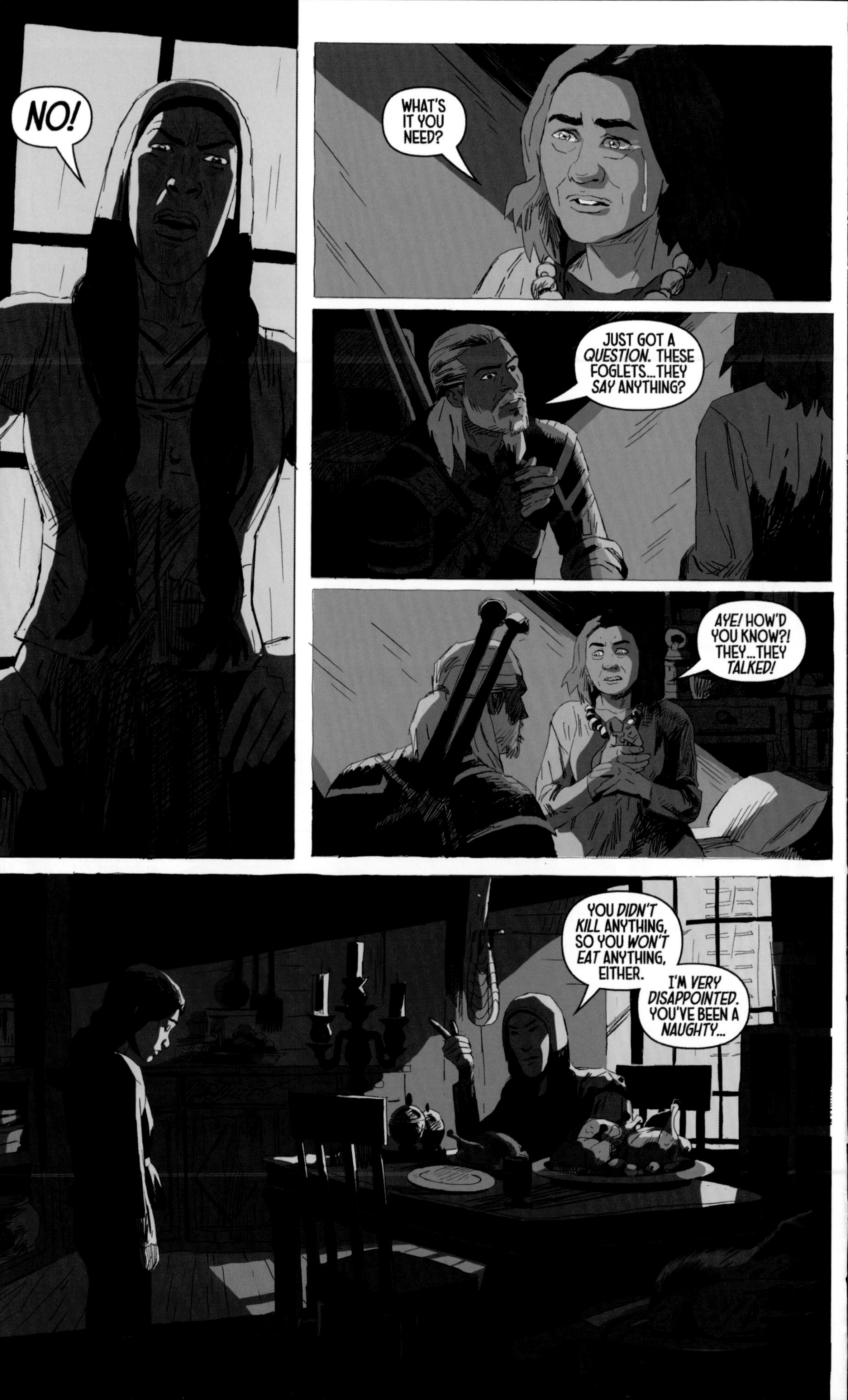
NO!
WHAT'S IT YOU NEED?
JUST GOT A *QUESTION.* THESE FOGLETS... THEY *SAY* ANYTHING?
AYE! HOW'D YOU KNOW?! THEY... THEY *TALKED!*
YOU *DIDN'T KILL* ANYTHING, SO YOU *WON'T EAT* ANYTHING, EITHER.
I'M *VERY DISAPPOINTED.* YOU'VE BEEN A *NAUGHTY*...

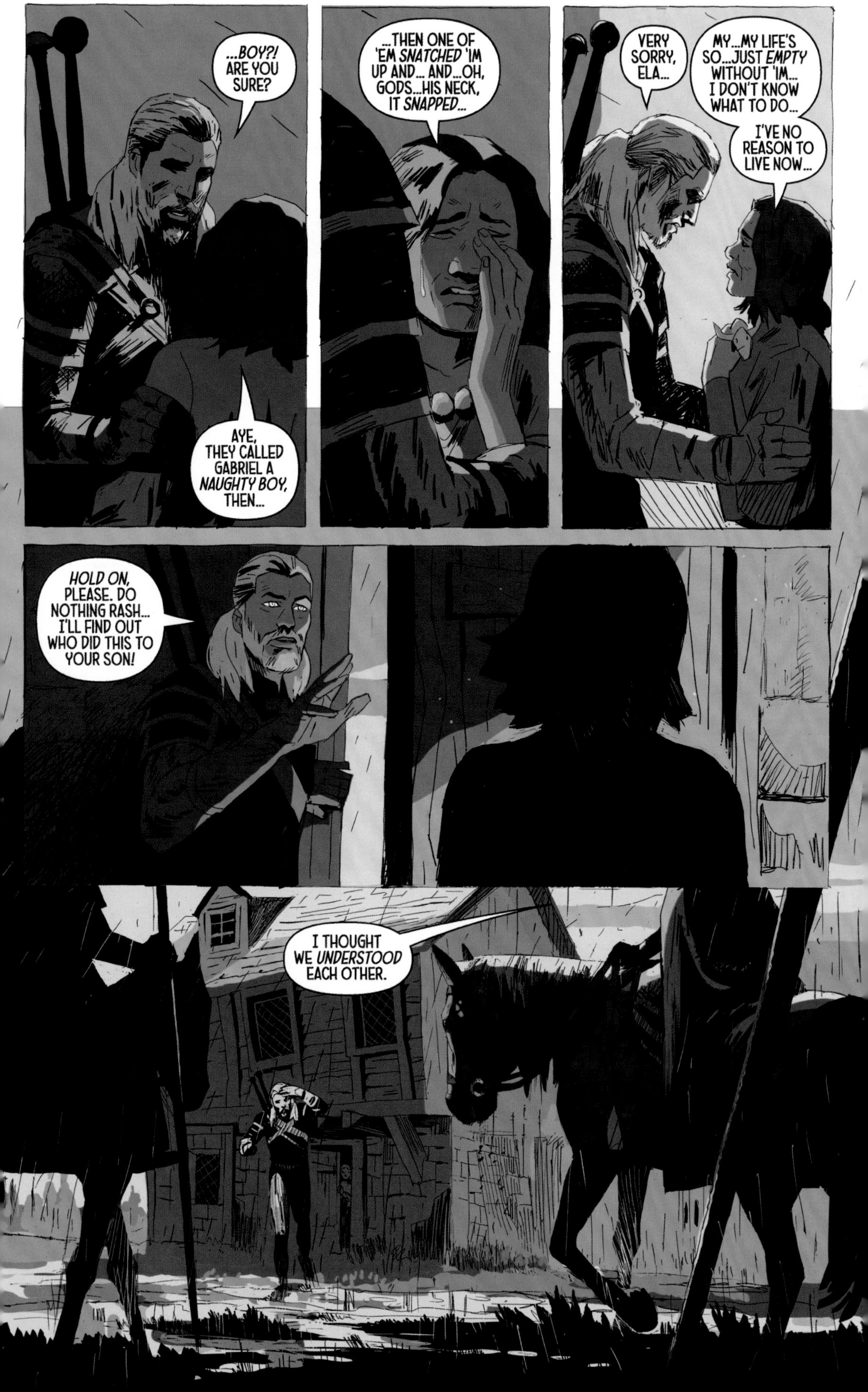
...BOY?! ARE YOU SURE?
AYE, THEY CALLED GABRIEL A NAUGHTY BOY, THEN...
...THEN ONE OF 'EM SNATCHED 'IM UP AND... AND...OH, GODS...HIS NECK, IT SNAPPED...
VERY SORRY, ELA...
MY...MY LIFE'S SO...JUST EMPTY WITHOUT 'IM... I DON'T KNOW WHAT TO DO...
I'VE NO REASON TO LIVE NOW...
HOLD ON, PLEASE. DO NOTHING RASH... I'LL FIND OUT WHO DID THIS TO YOUR SON!
I THOUGHT WE UNDERSTOOD EACH OTHER.

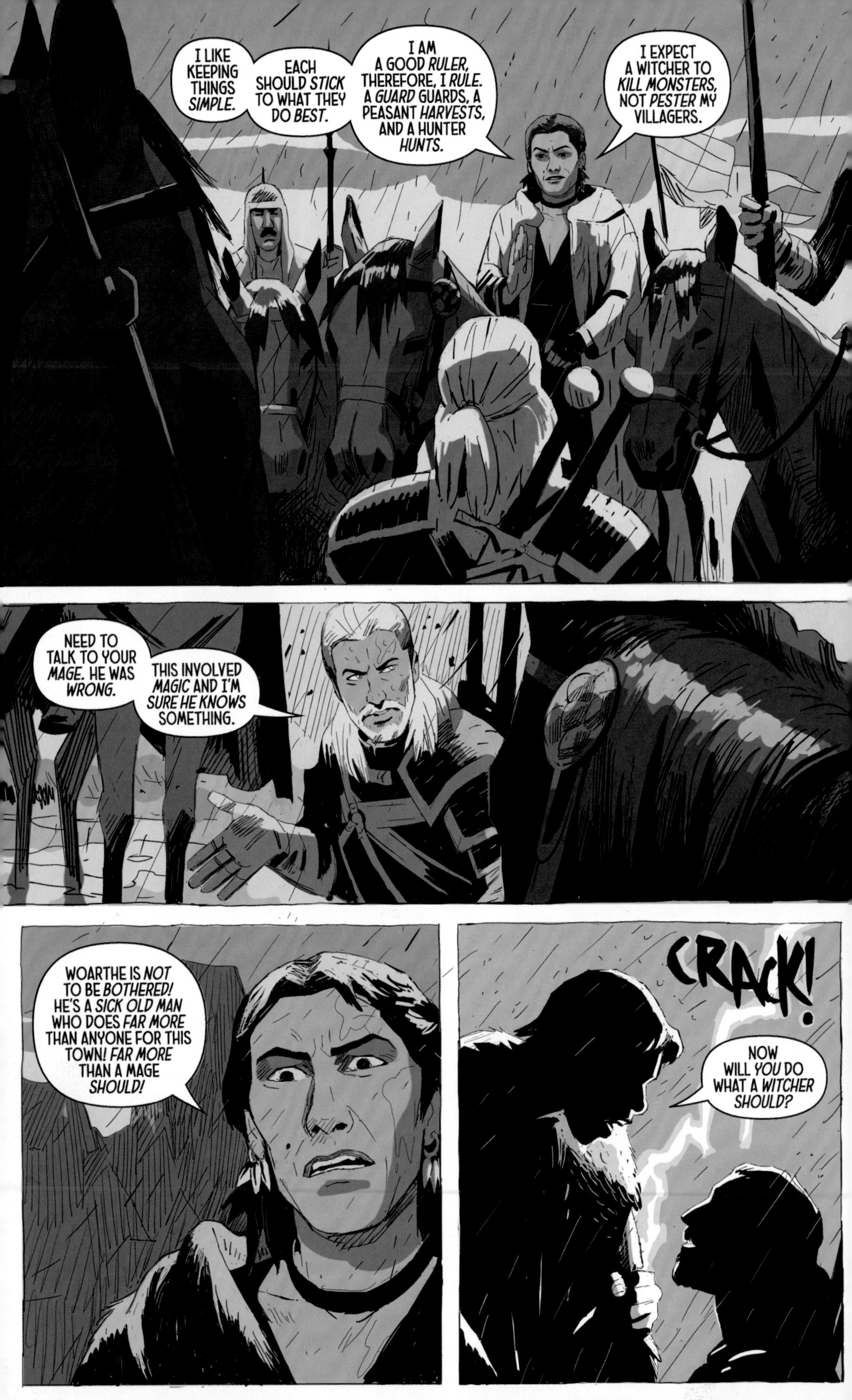
I LIKE KEEPING THINGS *SIMPLE*.
EACH SHOULD *STICK* TO WHAT THEY DO *BEST*.
I AM A GOOD *RULER*, THEREFORE, I *RULE*. A *GUARD* GUARDS, A PEASANT *HARVESTS*, AND A HUNTER *HUNTS*.
I EXPECT A WITCHER TO *KILL MONSTERS*, NOT *PESTER* MY VILLAGERS.
NEED TO TALK TO YOUR *MAGE*. HE WAS *WRONG*.
THIS INVOLVED *MAGIC* AND I'M *SURE HE KNOWS* SOMETHING.
WOARTHE IS *NOT* TO BE *BOTHERED!* HE'S A *SICK OLD MAN* WHO DOES *FAR MORE* THAN ANYONE FOR THIS TOWN! *FAR MORE* THAN A MAGE *SHOULD!*
CRACK!
NOW WILL *YOU* DO WHAT A *WITCHER SHOULD?*

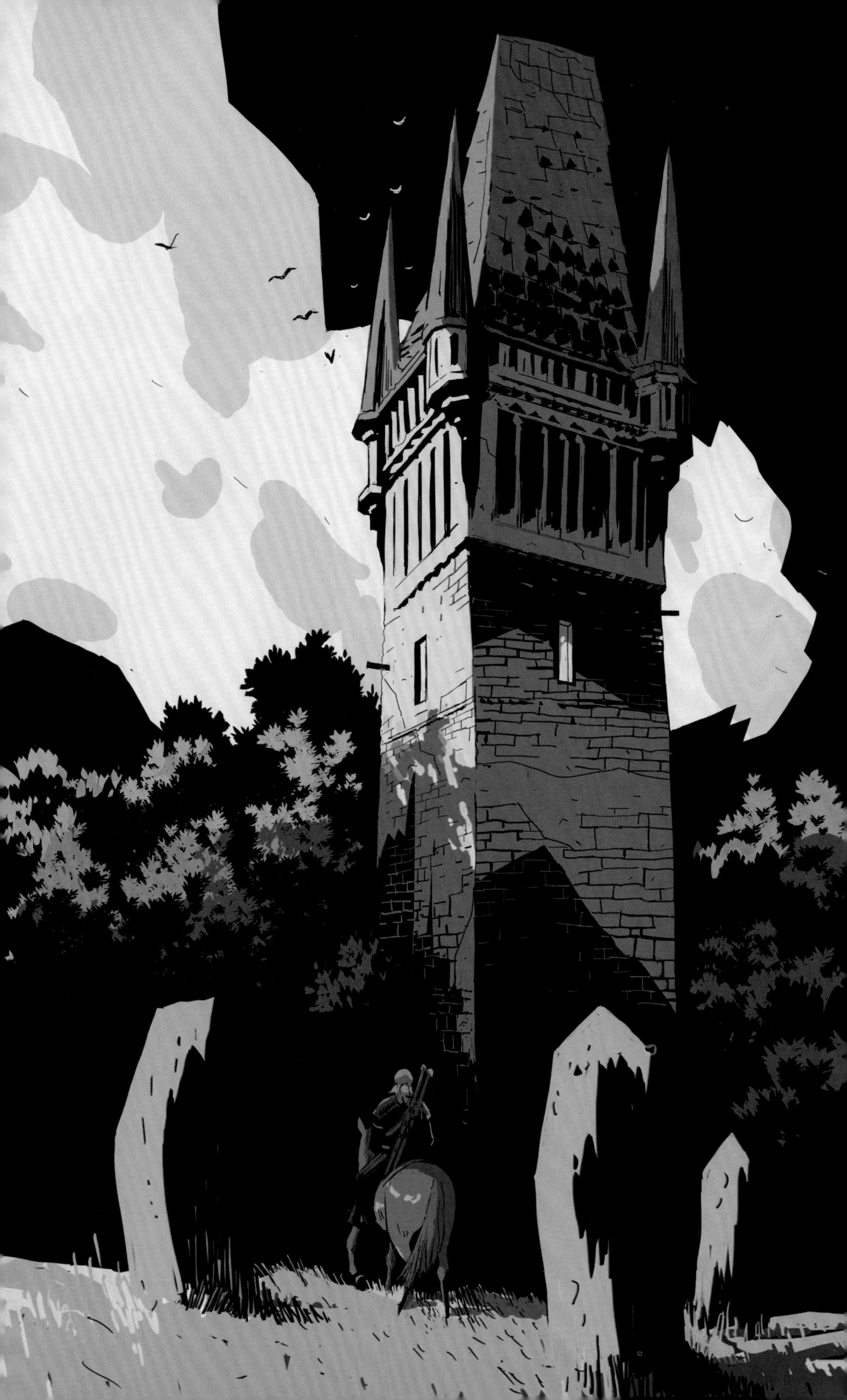

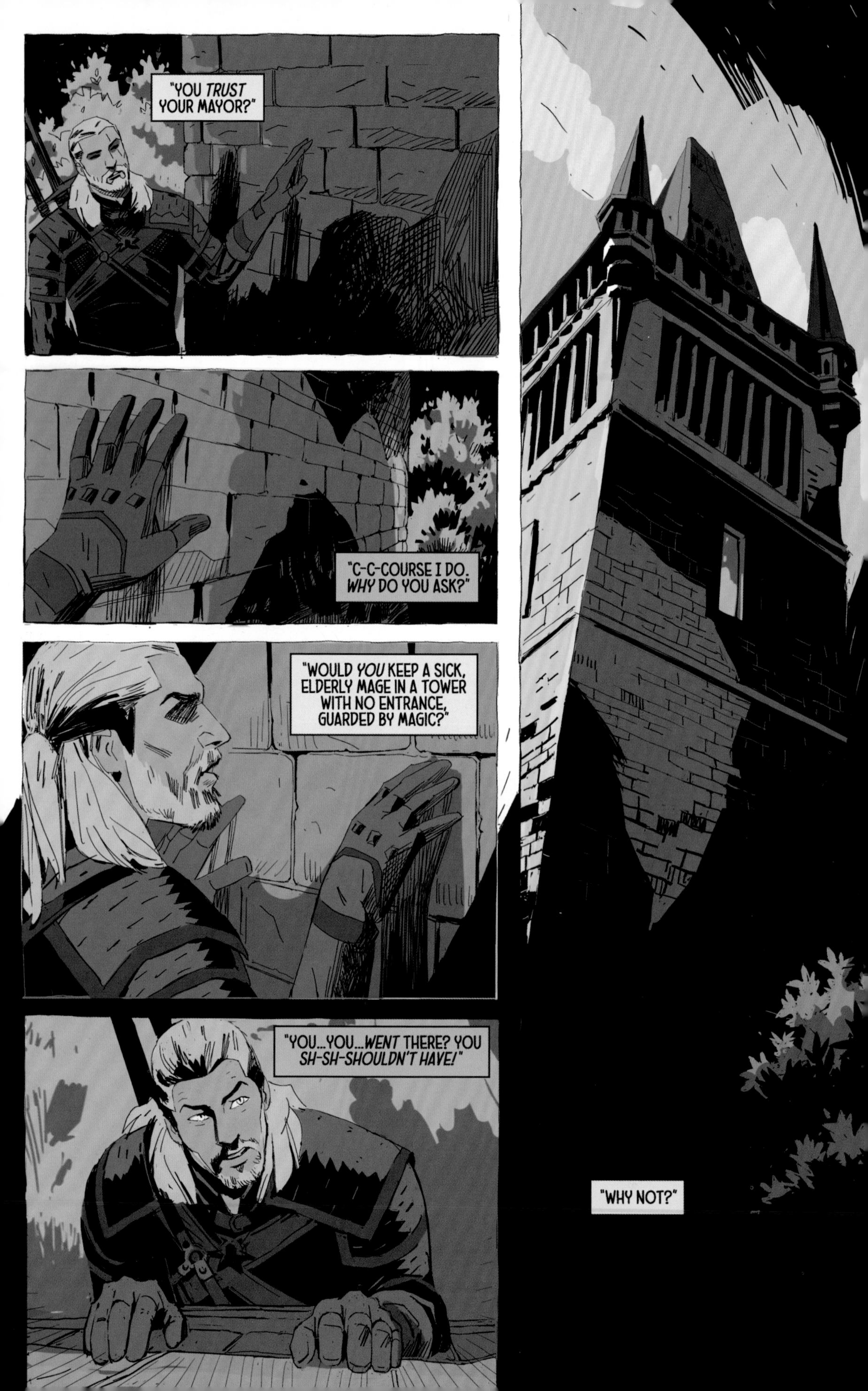
"YOU *TRUST* YOUR MAYOR?"
"C-C-COURSE I DO. *WHY* DO YOU ASK?"
"WOULD *YOU* KEEP A SICK, ELDERLY MAGE IN A TOWER WITH NO ENTRANCE, GUARDED BY MAGIC?"
"YOU...YOU...*WENT* THERE? YOU *SH-SH-SHOULDN'T HAVE!*"
"WHY NOT?"

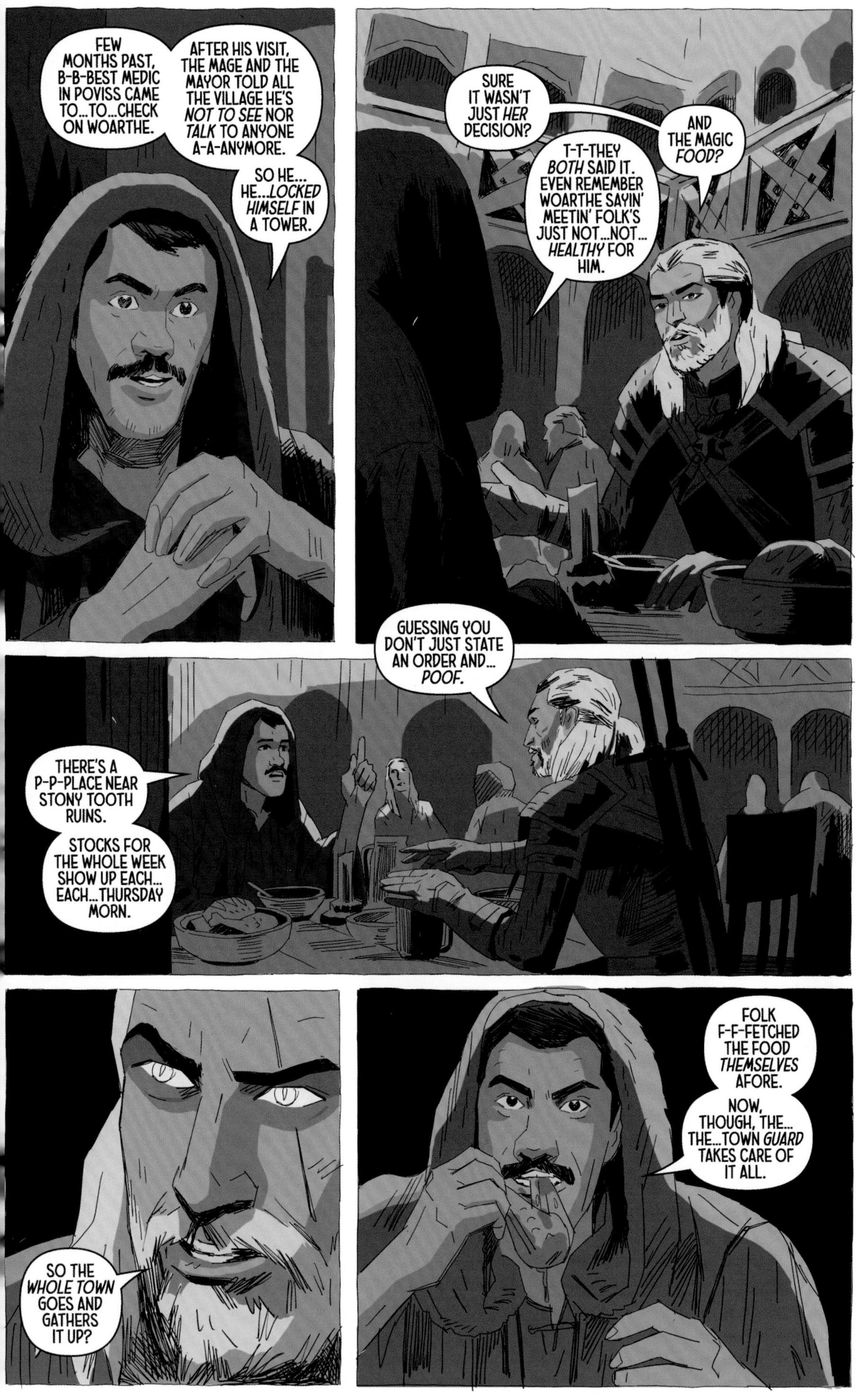
FEW MONTHS PAST, B-B-BEST MEDIC IN POVISS CAME TO...TO...CHECK ON WOARTHE.
AFTER HIS VISIT, THE MAGE AND THE MAYOR TOLD ALL THE VILLAGE HE'S *NOT TO SEE* NOR *TALK* TO ANYONE A-A-ANYMORE.
SO HE... HE...*LOCKED HIMSELF* IN A TOWER.
SURE IT WASN'T JUST *HER* DECISION?
T-T-THEY *BOTH* SAID IT. EVEN REMEMBER WOARTHE SAYIN' MEETIN' FOLK'S JUST NOT...NOT... *HEALTHY* FOR HIM.
AND THE MAGIC *FOOD?*
GUESSING YOU DON'T JUST STATE AN ORDER AND... *POOF.*
THERE'S A P-P-PLACE NEAR STONY TOOTH RUINS.
STOCKS FOR THE WHOLE WEEK SHOW UP EACH... EACH...THURSDAY MORN.
SO THE *WHOLE TOWN* GOES AND GATHERS IT UP?
FOLK F-F-FETCHED THE FOOD *THEMSELVES* AFORE.
NOW, THOUGH, THE... THE...TOWN *GUARD* TAKES CARE OF IT ALL.

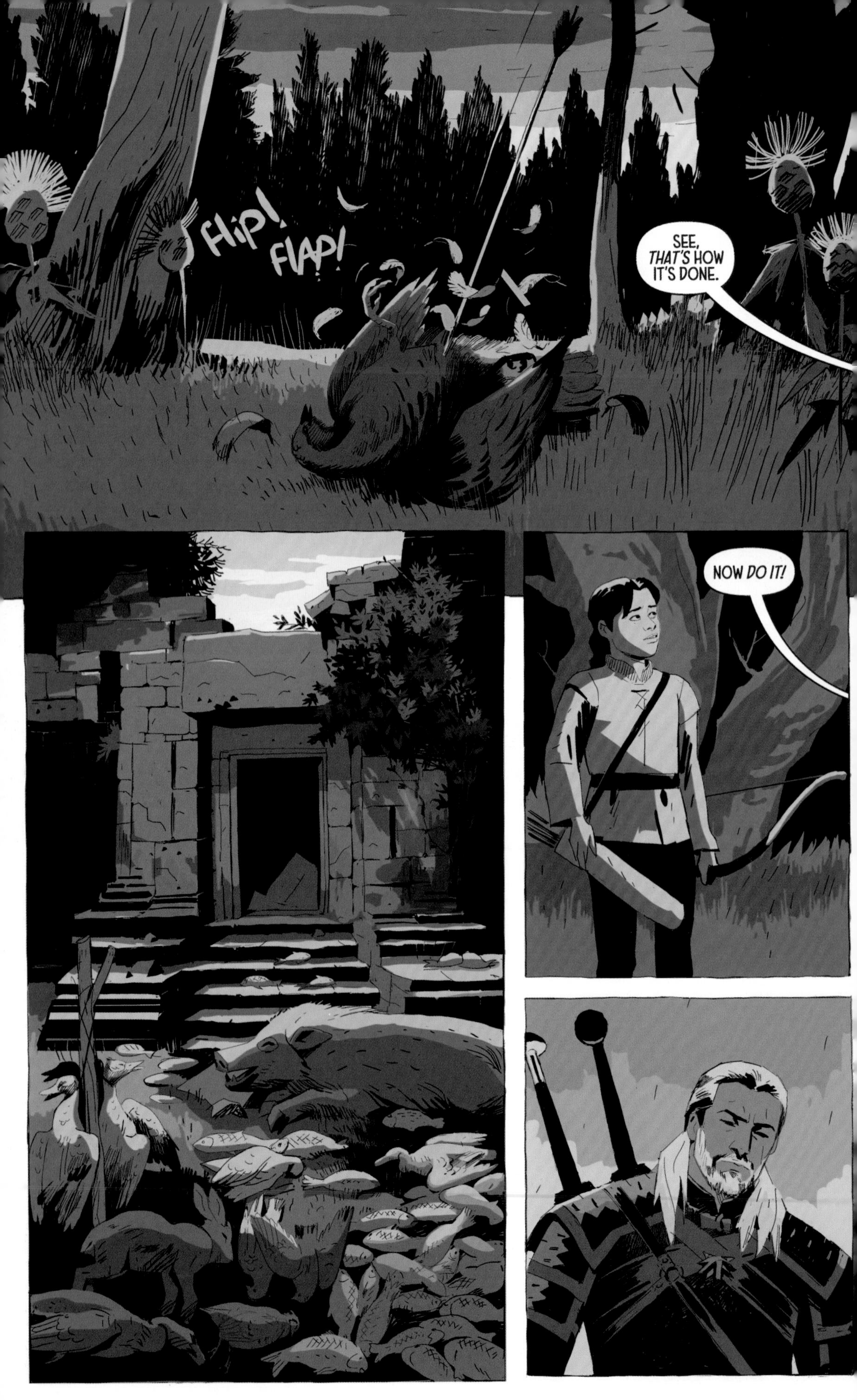
FLIP! FLAP!
SEE, THAT'S HOW IT'S DONE.
NOW DO IT!

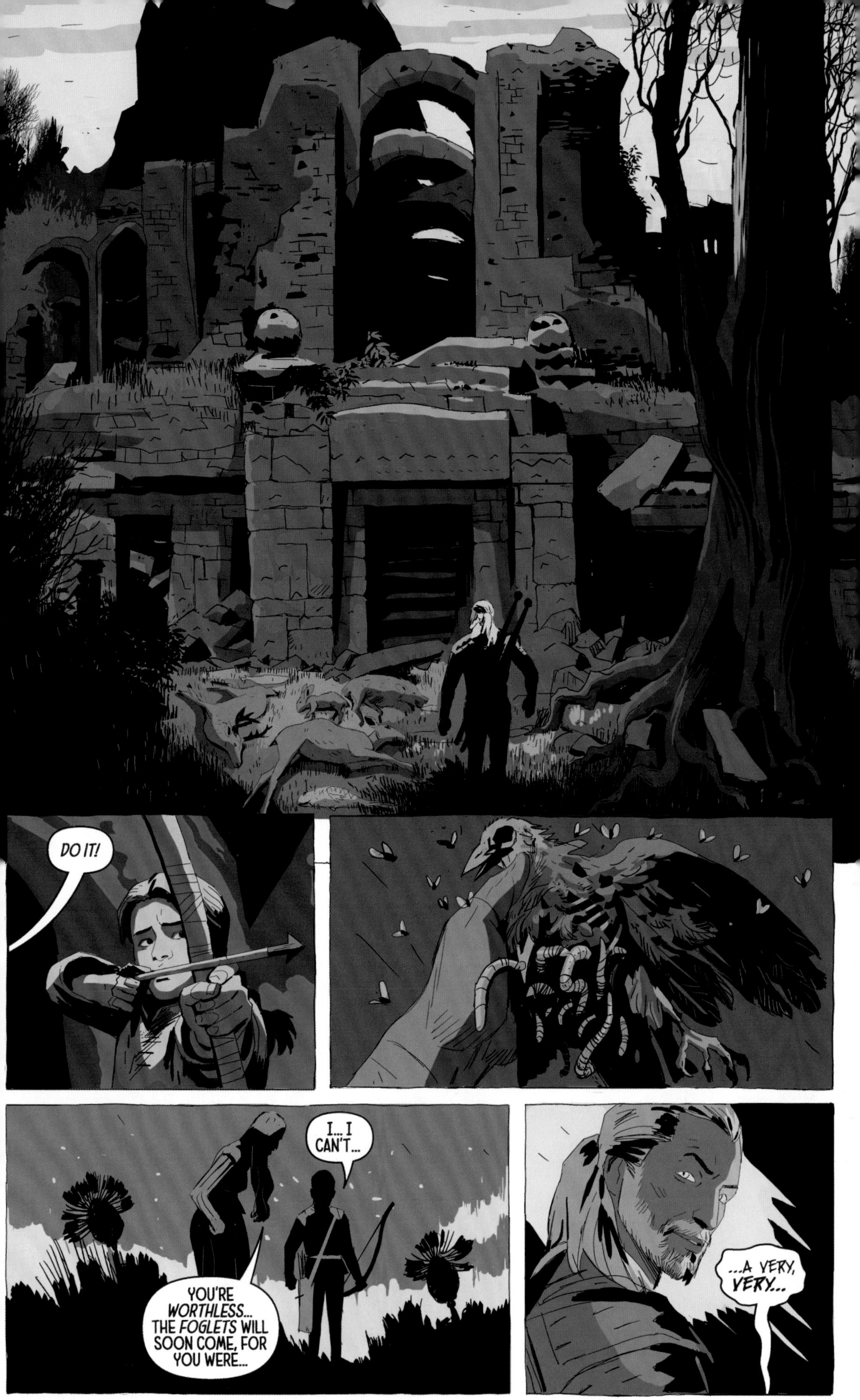
DO IT!
I... I CAN'T...
YOU'RE WORTHLESS... THE FOGLETS WILL SOON COME, FOR YOU WERE...
...A VERY, VERY...

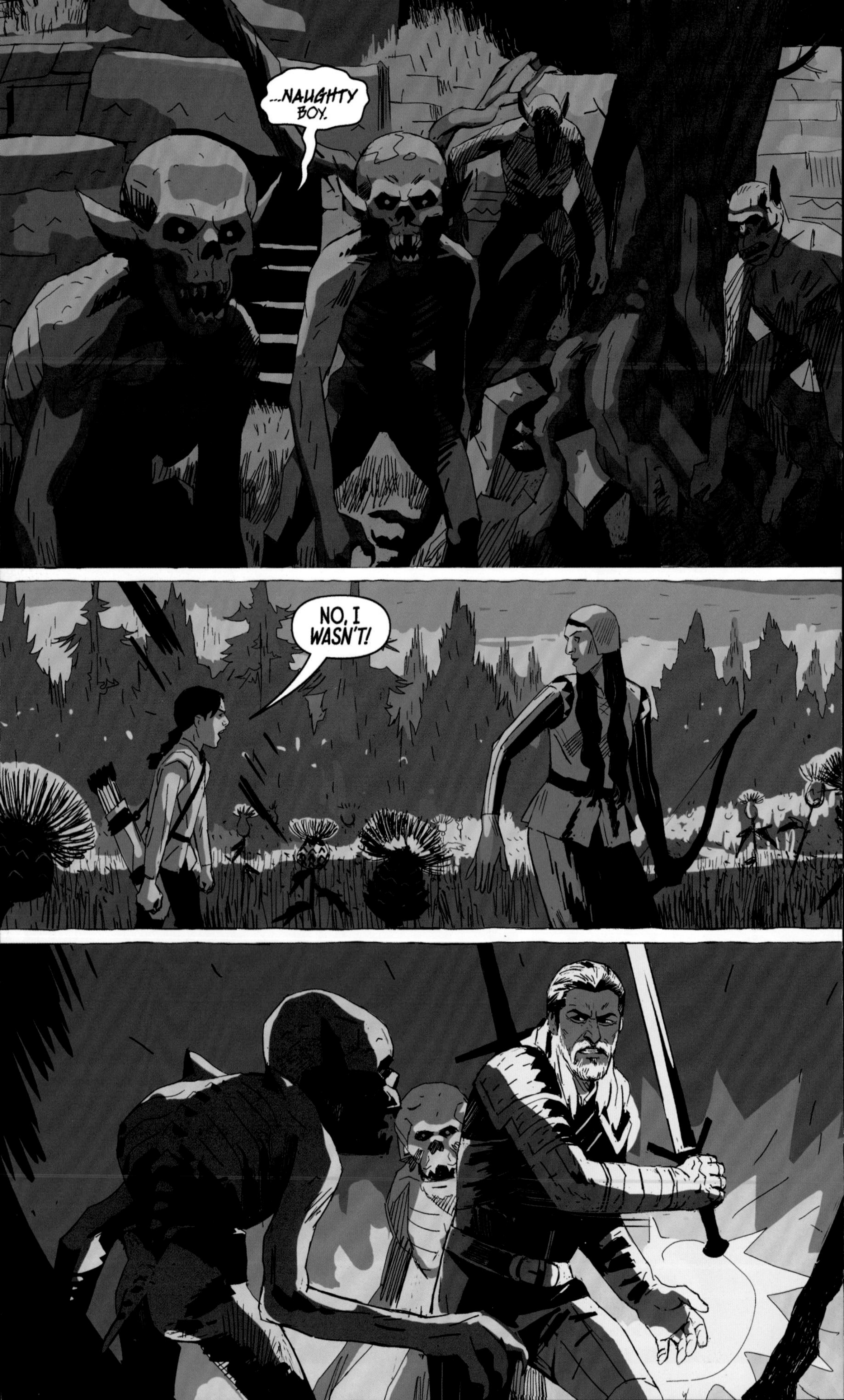
...NAUGHTY BOY.
NO, I WASN'T!

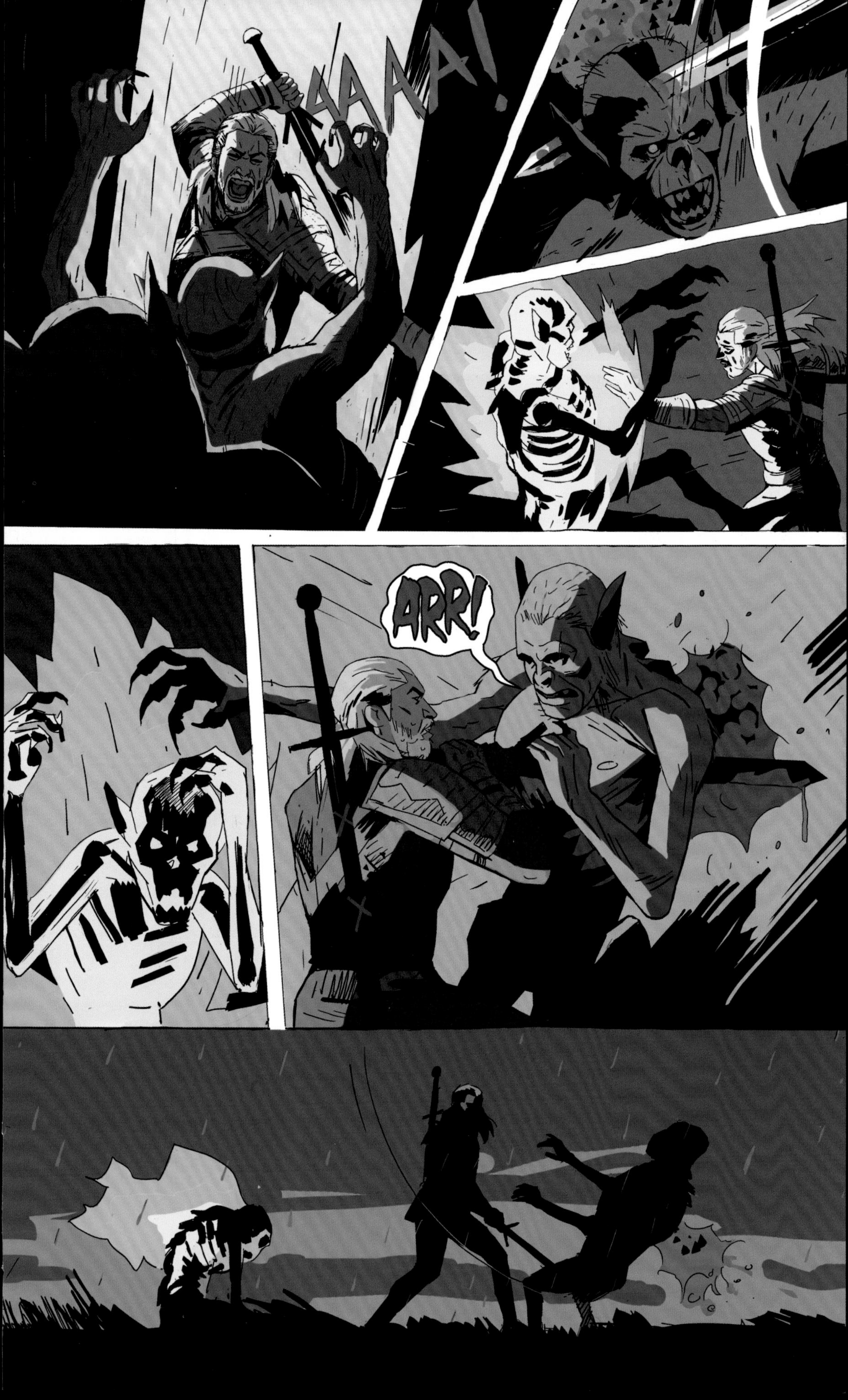
AAAA!
ARR!

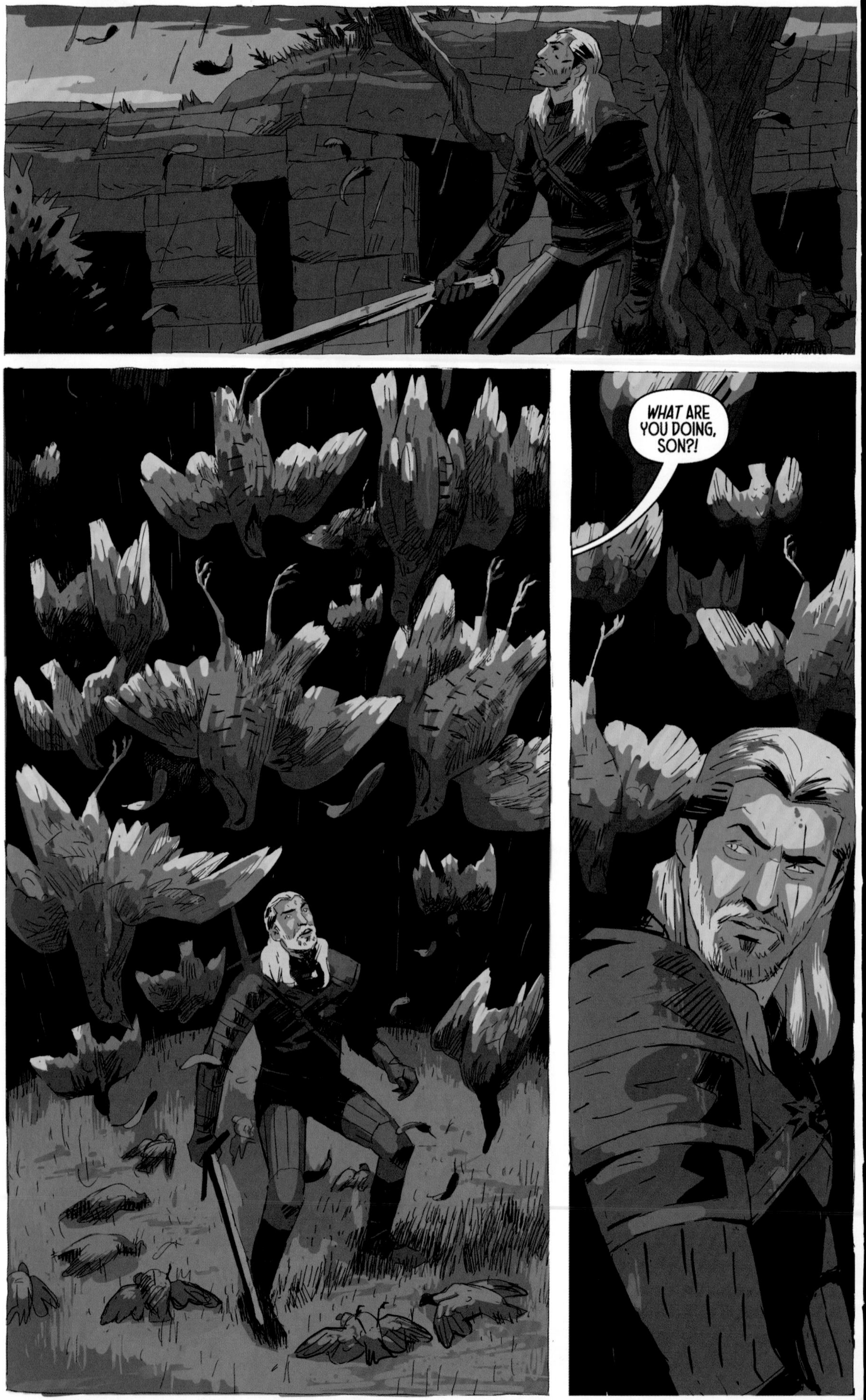
WHAT ARE YOU DOING, SON?!

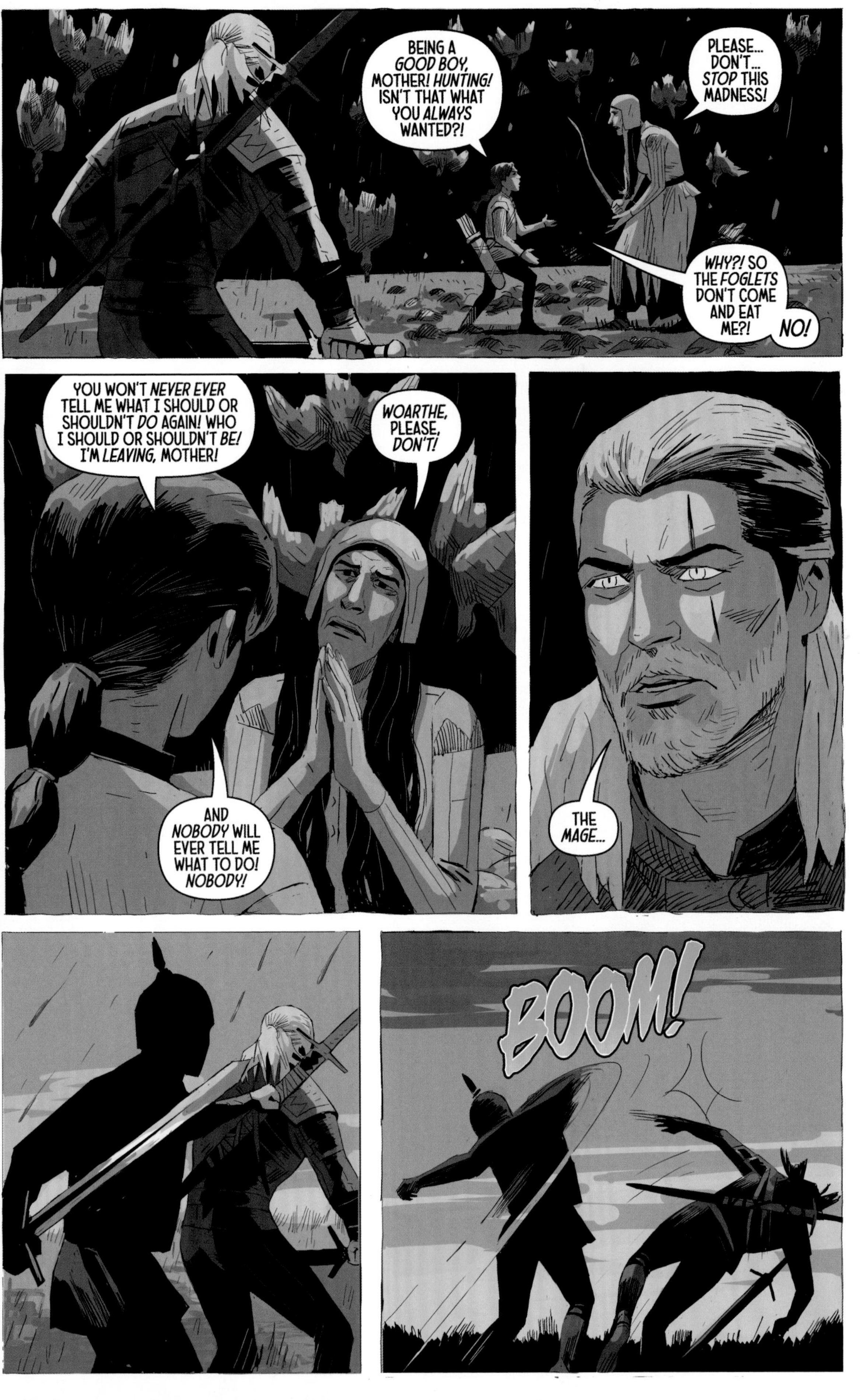
BEING A GOOD BOY, MOTHER! HUNTING! ISN'T THAT WHAT YOU ALWAYS WANTED?!
PLEASE... DON'T... STOP THIS MADNESS!
WHY?! SO THE FOGLETS DON'T COME AND EAT ME?!
NO!
YOU WON'T NEVER EVER TELL ME WHAT I SHOULD OR SHOULDN'T DO AGAIN! WHO I SHOULD OR SHOULDN'T BE! I'M LEAVING, MOTHER!
WOARTHE, PLEASE, DON'T!
AND NOBODY WILL EVER TELL ME WHAT TO DO! NOBODY!
THE MAGE...
BOOM!

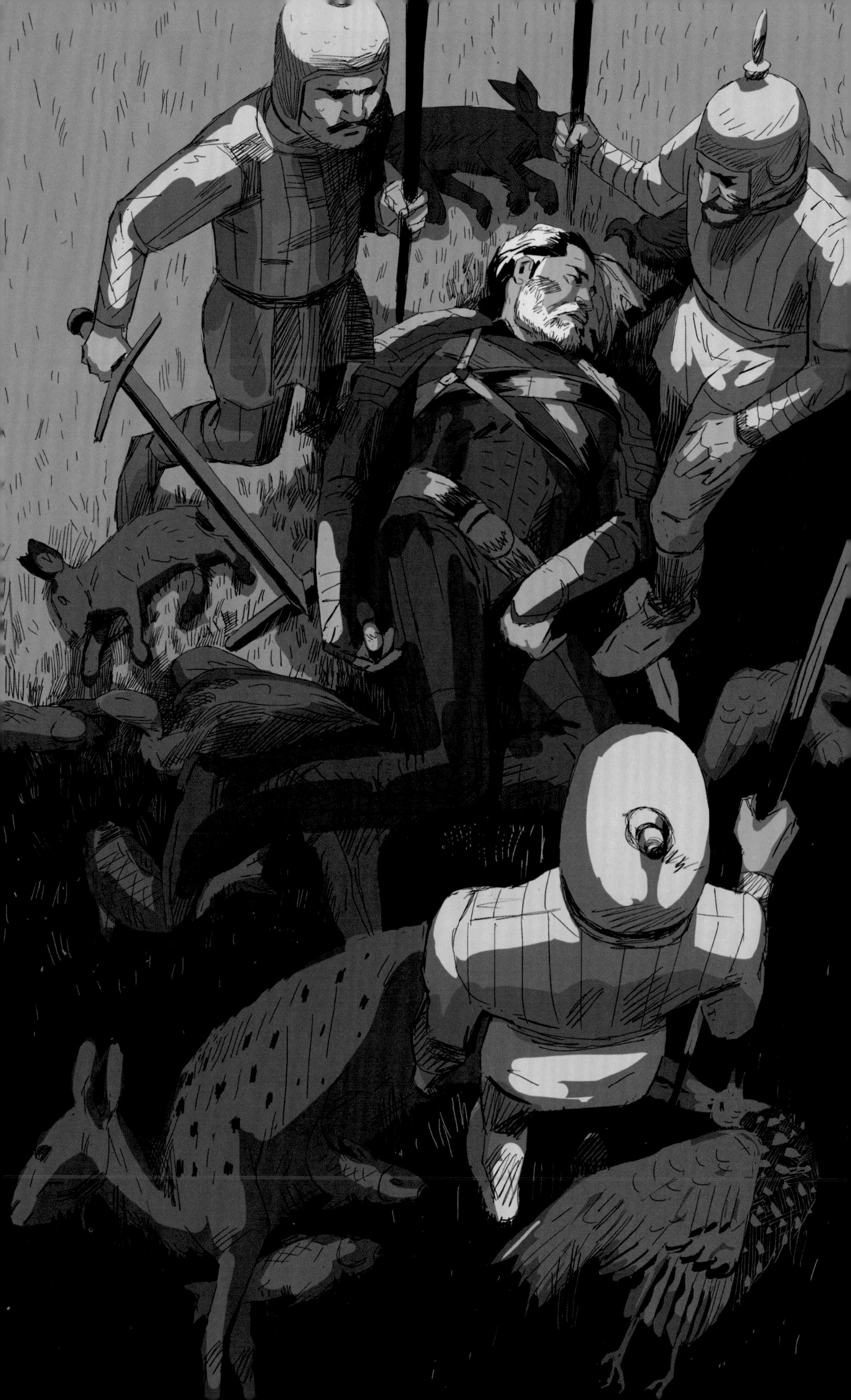

CHAPTER THREE

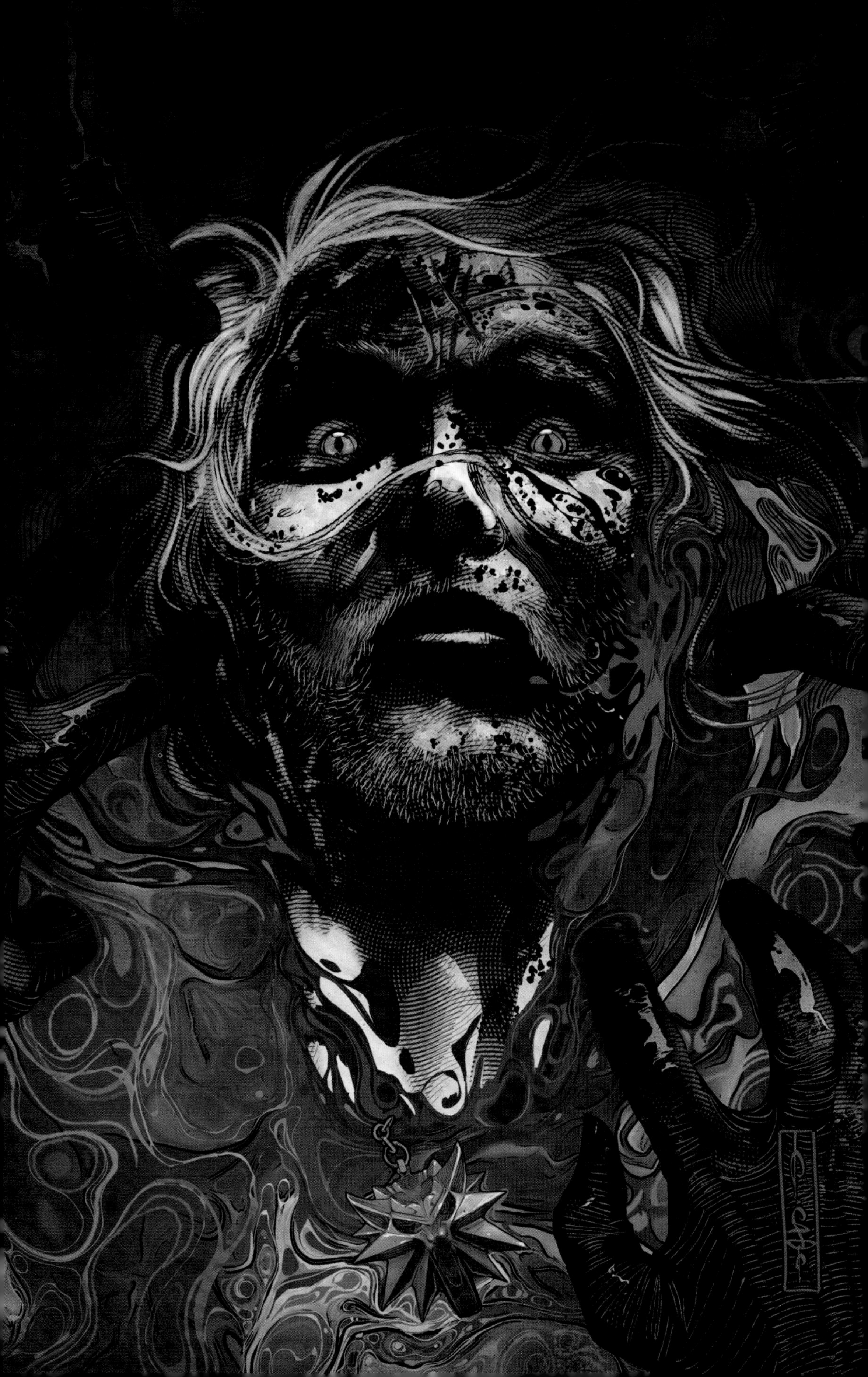

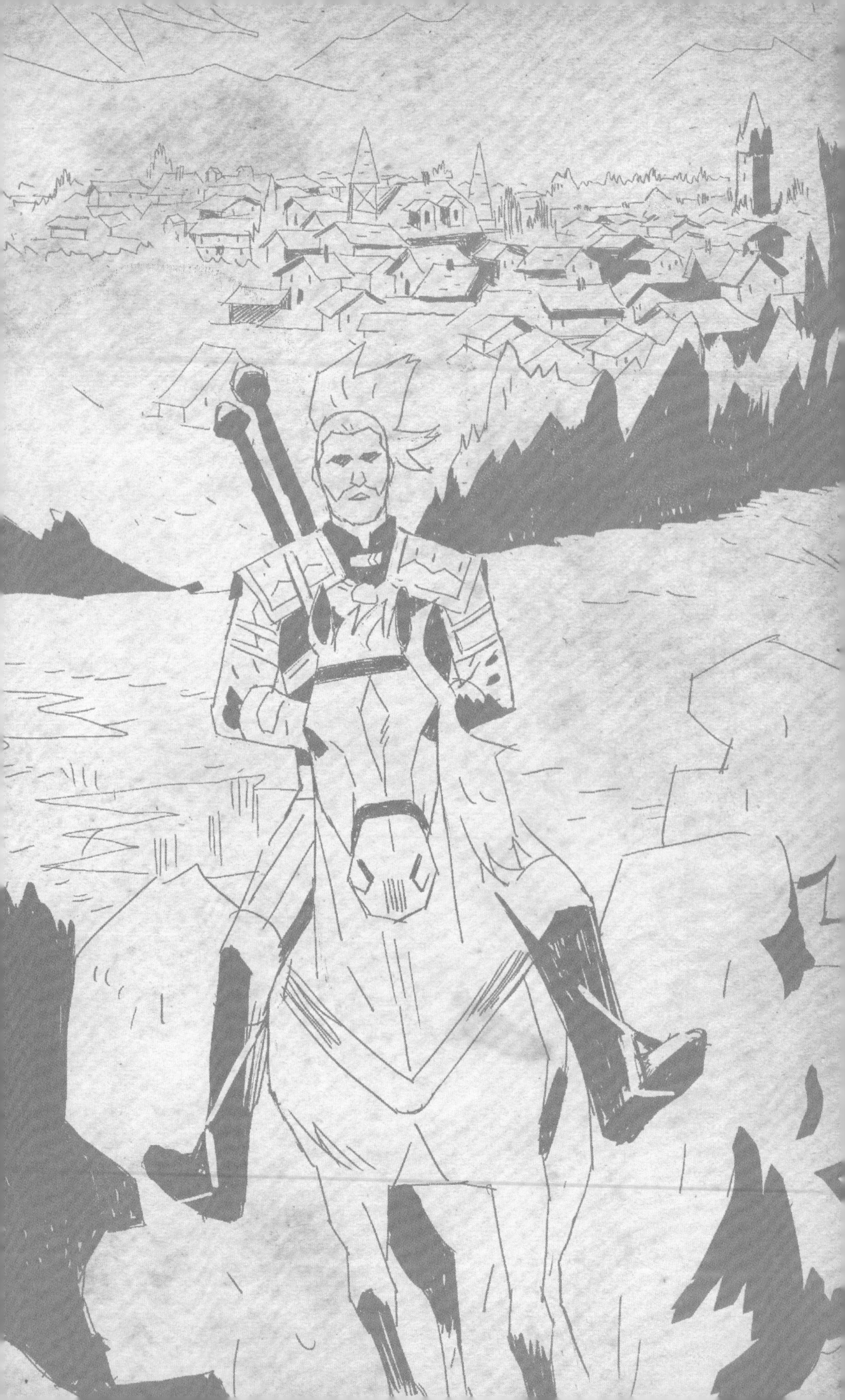

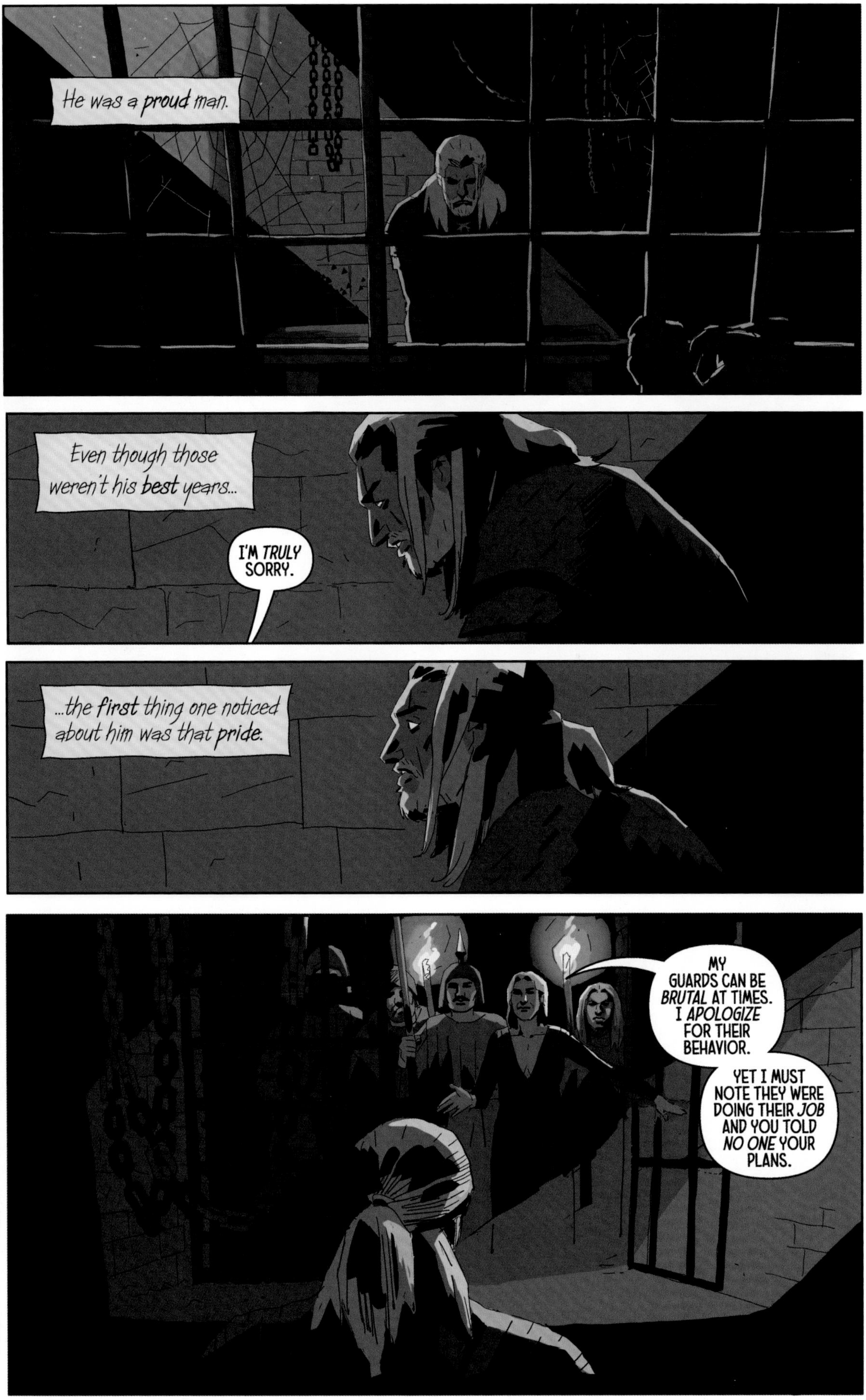
He was a proud man.
Even though those weren't his best years...
I'M TRULY SORRY.
...the first thing one noticed about him was that pride.
MY GUARDS CAN BE BRUTAL AT TIMES. I APOLOGIZE FOR THEIR BEHAVIOR.
YET I MUST NOTE THEY WERE DOING THEIR JOB AND YOU TOLD NO ONE YOUR PLANS.

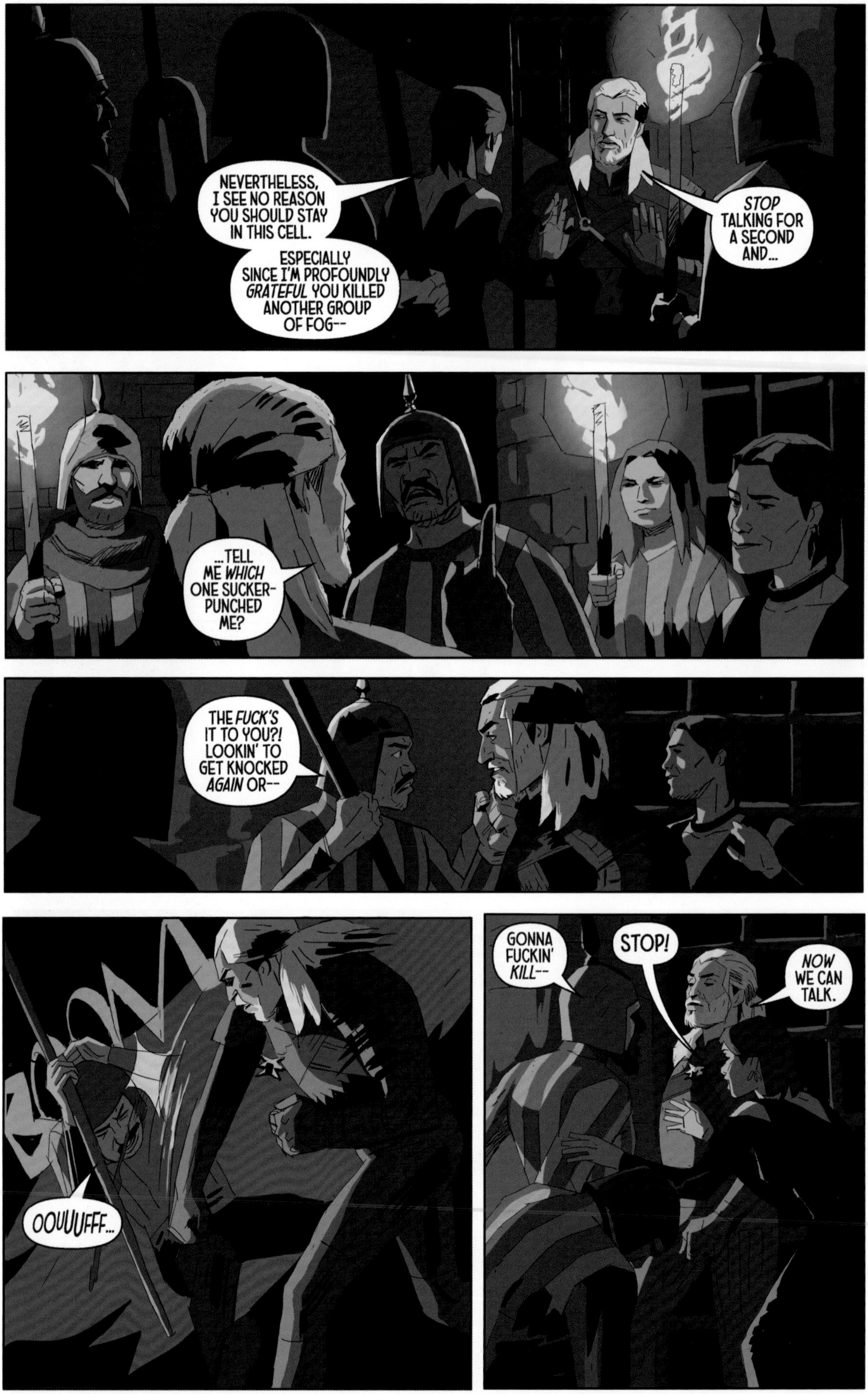
NEVERTHELESS, I SEE NO REASON YOU SHOULD STAY IN THIS CELL.
ESPECIALLY SINCE I'M PROFOUNDLY *GRATEFUL* YOU KILLED ANOTHER GROUP OF FOG--
STOP TALKING FOR A SECOND AND...
...TELL ME *WHICH* ONE SUCKER-PUNCHED ME?
THE *FUCK'S* IT TO YOU?! LOOKIN' TO GET KNOCKED *AGAIN* OR--
OOUUUFFF...
GONNA FUCKIN' *KILL*--
STOP!
NOW WE CAN TALK.

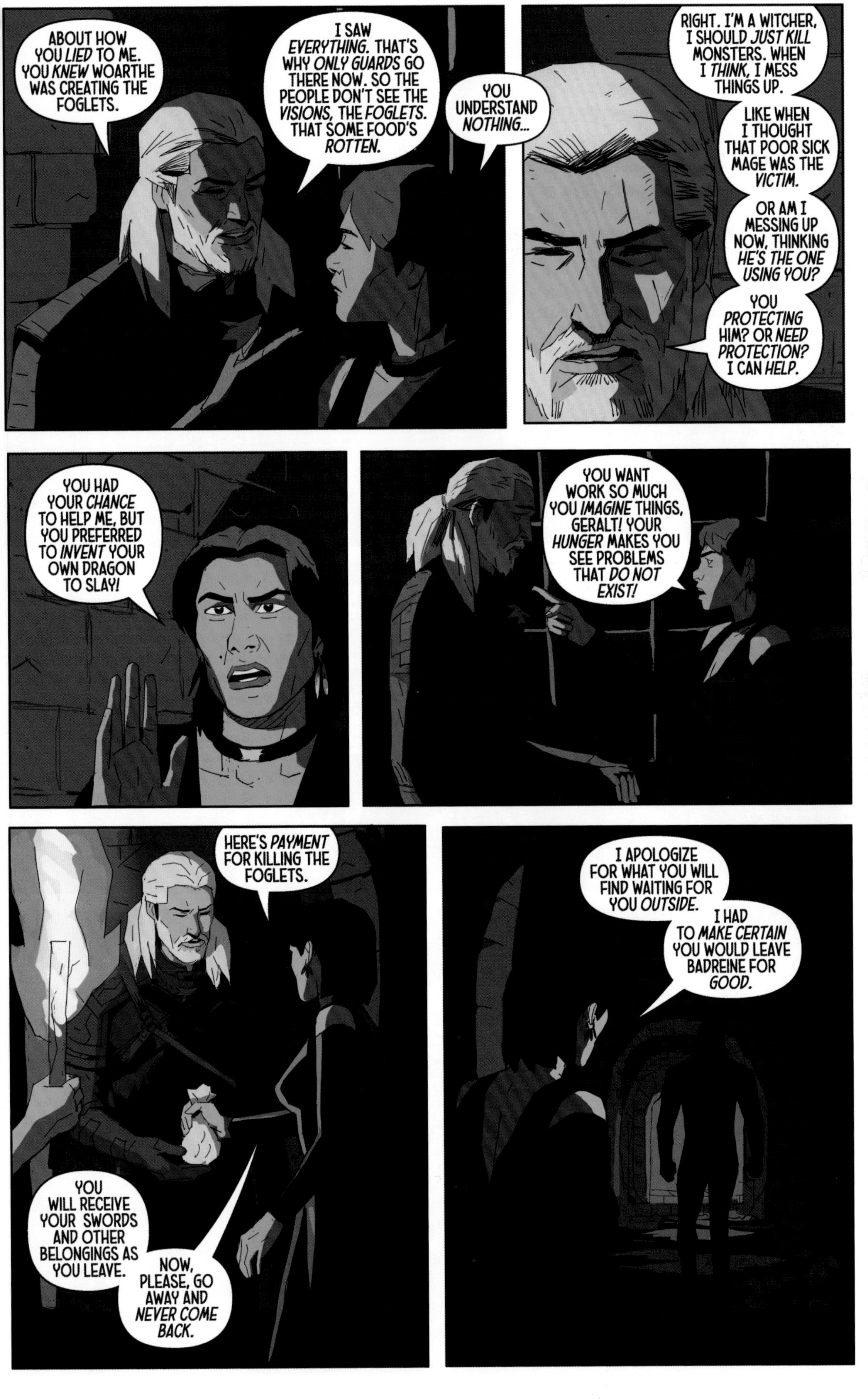
ABOUT HOW YOU *LIED* TO ME. YOU *KNEW* WOARTHE WAS CREATING THE FOGLETS.
I SAW *EVERYTHING*. THAT'S WHY *ONLY GUARDS* GO THERE NOW. SO THE PEOPLE DON'T SEE THE *VISIONS*, THE *FOGLETS*. THAT SOME FOOD'S *ROTTEN*.
YOU UNDERSTAND *NOTHING*...
RIGHT. I'M A WITCHER, I SHOULD *JUST KILL* MONSTERS. WHEN I *THINK*, I MESS THINGS UP.
LIKE WHEN I THOUGHT THAT POOR SICK MAGE WAS THE *VICTIM*.
OR AM I MESSING UP NOW, THINKING *HE'S THE ONE USING YOU?*
YOU *PROTECTING* HIM? OR *NEED PROTECTION?* I CAN *HELP*.
YOU HAD YOUR *CHANCE* TO HELP ME, BUT YOU PREFERRED TO *INVENT* YOUR OWN DRAGON TO SLAY!
YOU WANT WORK SO MUCH YOU *IMAGINE* THINGS, GERALT! YOUR *HUNGER* MAKES YOU SEE PROBLEMS THAT *DO NOT EXIST!*
HERE'S *PAYMENT* FOR KILLING THE FOGLETS.
YOU WILL RECEIVE YOUR SWORDS AND OTHER BELONGINGS AS YOU LEAVE.
NOW, PLEASE, GO AWAY AND *NEVER COME BACK*.
I APOLOGIZE FOR WHAT YOU WILL FIND WAITING FOR YOU *OUTSIDE*.
I HAD TO *MAKE CERTAIN* YOU WOULD LEAVE BADREINE FOR *GOOD*.

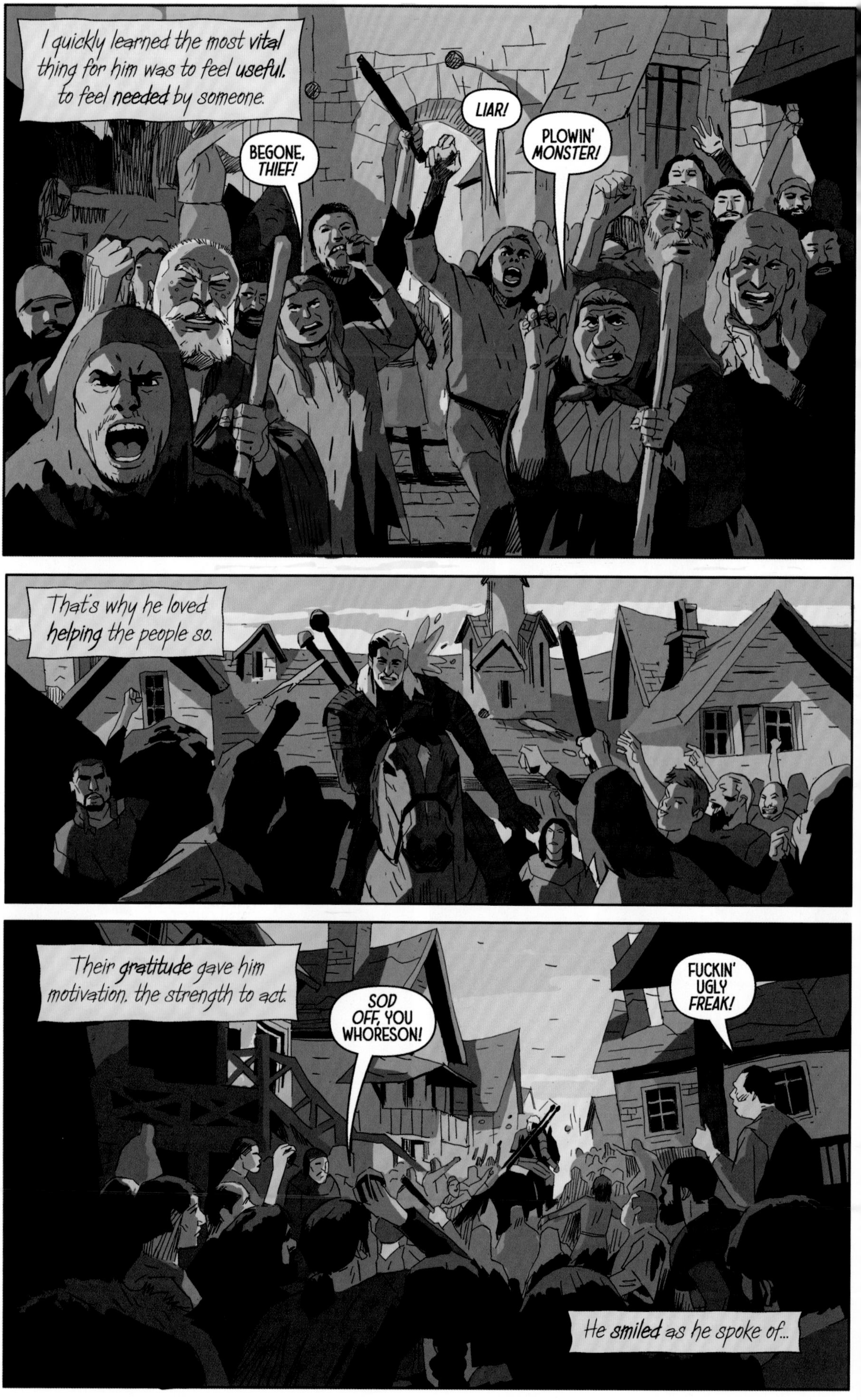
I quickly learned the most vital thing for him was to feel useful. to feel needed by someone.
BEGONE, THIEF!
LIAR!
PLOWIN' MONSTER!
That's why he loved helping the people so.
Their gratitude gave him motivation. the strength to act.
SOD OFF, YOU WHORESON!
FUCKIN' UGLY FREAK!
He smiled as he spoke of...

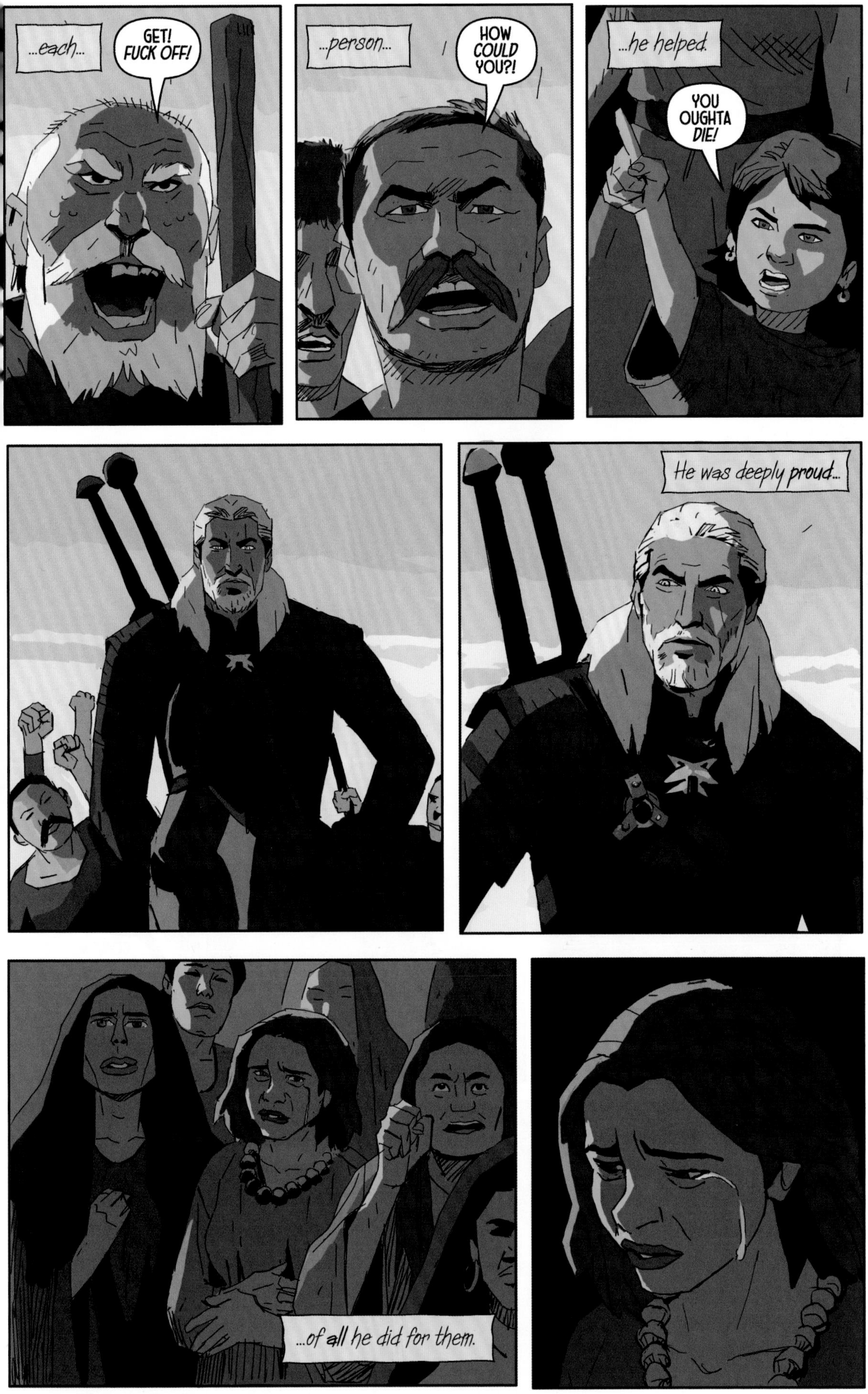
...each...
GET! FUCK OFF!
...person...
HOW COULD YOU?!
...he helped.
YOU OUGHTA DIE!
He was deeply proud...
...of all he did for them.

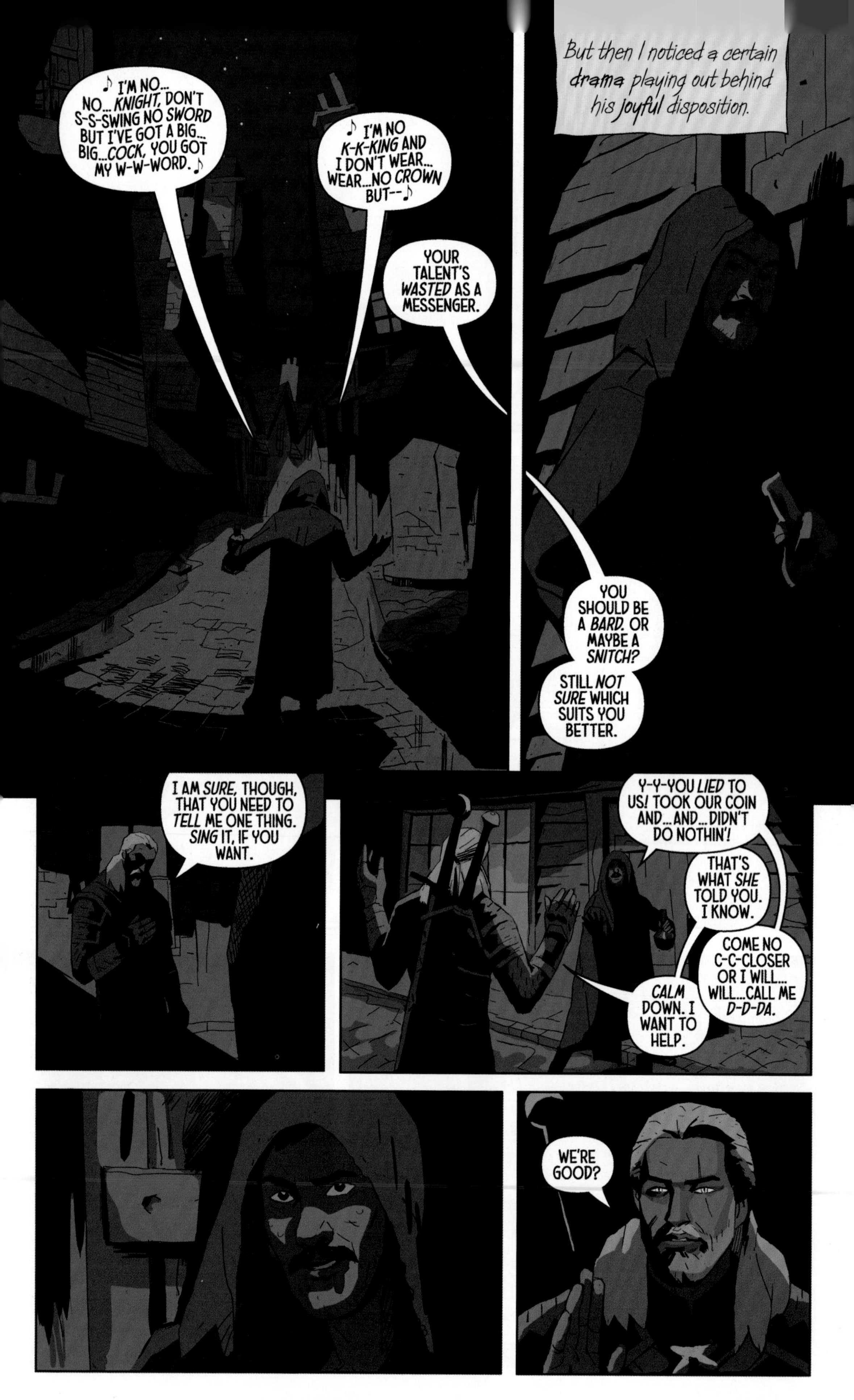
♪ I'M NO... NO... KNIGHT, DON'T S-S-SWING NO SWORD BUT I'VE GOT A BIG... BIG...COCK, YOU GOT MY W-W-WORD. ♪
♪ I'M NO K-K-KING AND I DON'T WEAR... WEAR...NO CROWN BUT-- ♪
YOUR TALENT'S WASTED AS A MESSENGER.
But then I noticed a certain drama playing out behind his joyful disposition.
YOU SHOULD BE A BARD. OR MAYBE A SNITCH?
STILL NOT SURE WHICH SUITS YOU BETTER.
I AM SURE, THOUGH, THAT YOU NEED TO TELL ME ONE THING. SING IT, IF YOU WANT.
Y-Y-YOU LIED TO US! TOOK OUR COIN AND... AND... DIDN'T DO NOTHIN'!
THAT'S WHAT SHE TOLD YOU. I KNOW.
COME NO C-C-CLOSER OR I WILL... WILL...CALL ME D-D-DA.
CALM DOWN. I WANT TO HELP.
WE'RE GOOD?

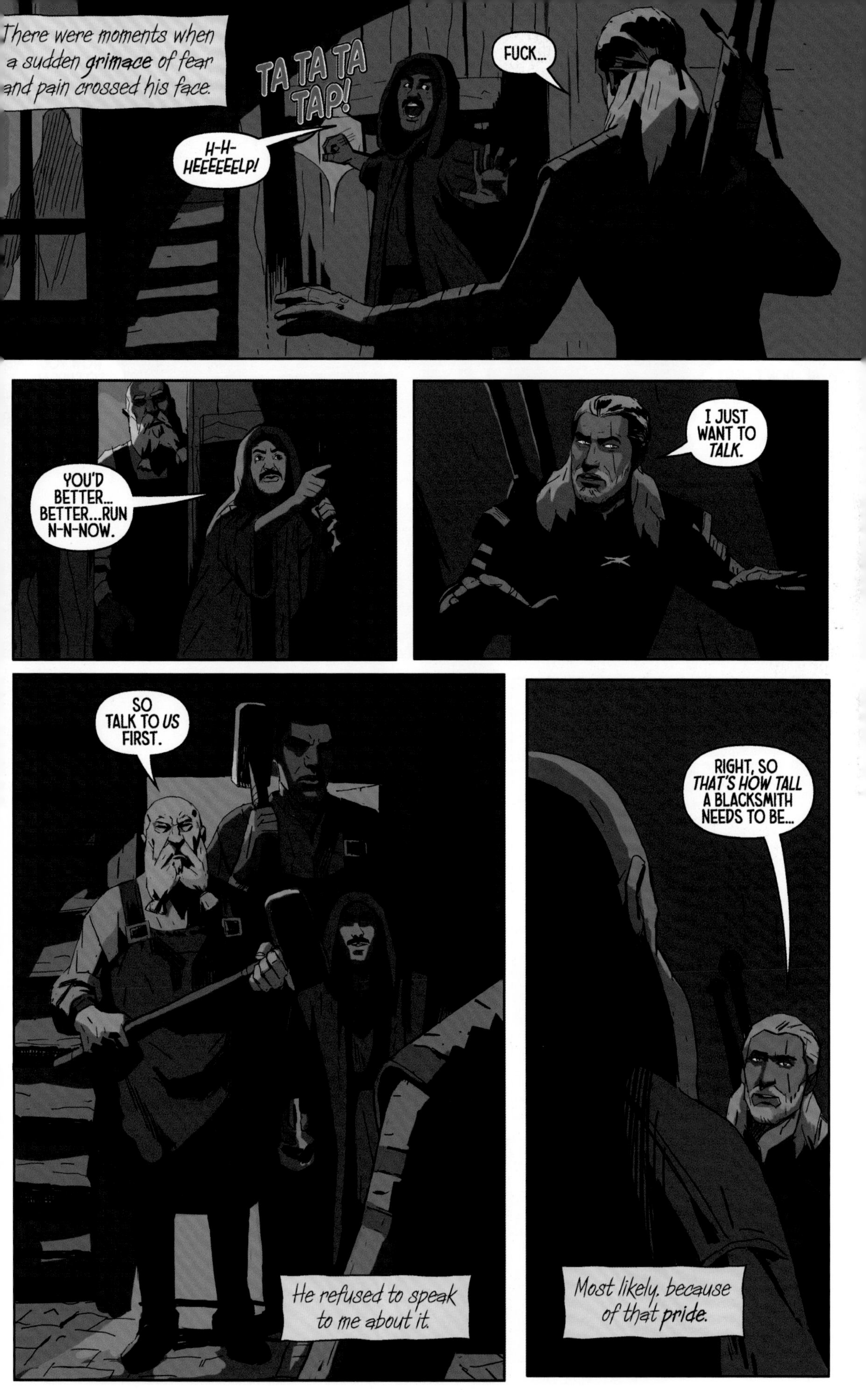
There were moments when a sudden grimace of fear and pain crossed his face.
TA TA TA TAP!
FUCK...
H-H-HEEEEEELP!
YOU'D BETTER... BETTER...RUN N-N-NOW.
I JUST WANT TO TALK.
SO TALK TO US FIRST.
He refused to speak to me about it.
RIGHT, SO THAT'S HOW TALL A BLACKSMITH NEEDS TO BE...
Most likely, because of that pride.

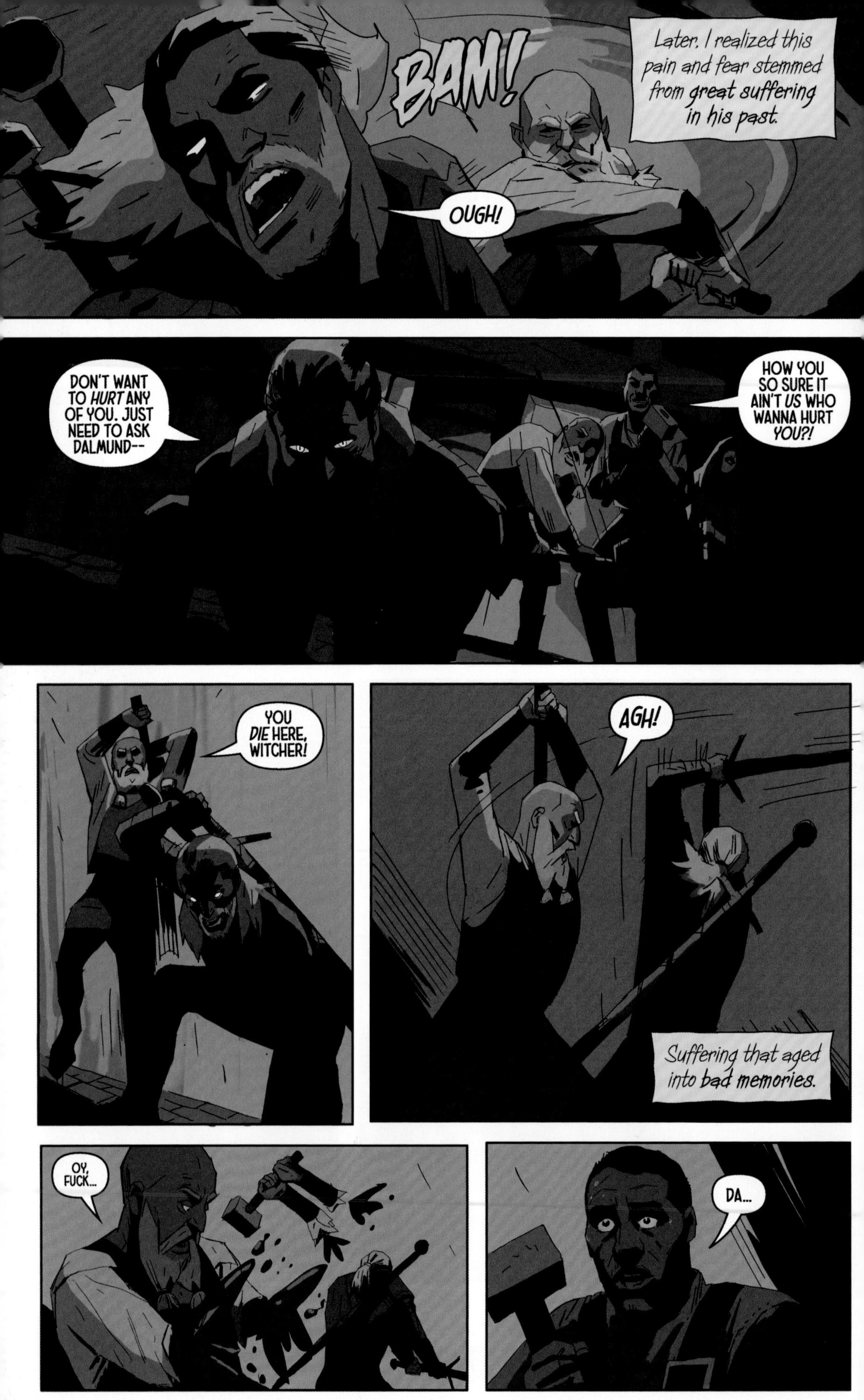
BAM!
Later, I realized this pain and fear stemmed from great suffering in his past.
OUGH!
DON'T WANT TO HURT ANY OF YOU. JUST NEED TO ASK DALMUND--
HOW YOU SO SURE IT AIN'T US WHO WANNA HURT YOU?!
YOU DIE HERE, WITCHER!
AGH!
Suffering that aged into bad memories.
OY, FUCK...
DA...

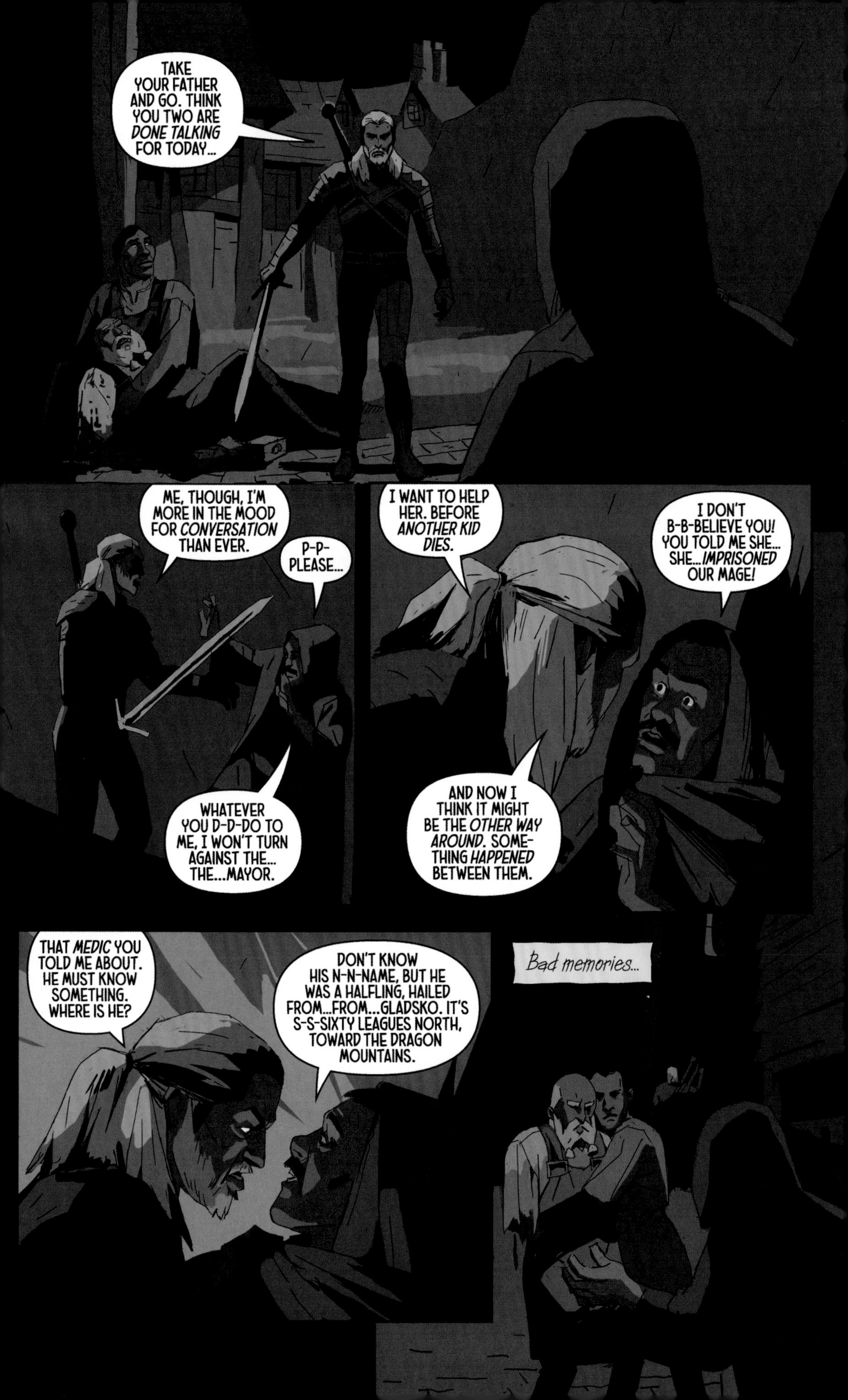
TAKE YOUR FATHER AND GO. THINK YOU TWO ARE *DONE TALKING* FOR TODAY...
ME, THOUGH, I'M MORE IN THE MOOD FOR *CONVERSATION* THAN EVER.
P-P-PLEASE...
WHATEVER YOU D-D-DO TO ME, I WON'T TURN AGAINST THE... THE...MAYOR.
I WANT TO HELP HER. BEFORE *ANOTHER KID DIES.*
I DON'T B-B-BELIEVE YOU! YOU TOLD ME SHE... SHE...*IMPRISONED* OUR MAGE!
AND NOW I THINK IT MIGHT BE THE *OTHER WAY AROUND.* SOMETHING *HAPPENED* BETWEEN THEM.
THAT *MEDIC* YOU TOLD ME ABOUT. HE MUST KNOW SOMETHING. WHERE IS HE?
DON'T KNOW HIS N-N-NAME, BUT HE WAS A HALFLING, HAILED FROM...FROM...GLADSKO. IT'S S-S-SIXTY LEAGUES NORTH, TOWARD THE DRAGON MOUNTAINS.
Bad memories...

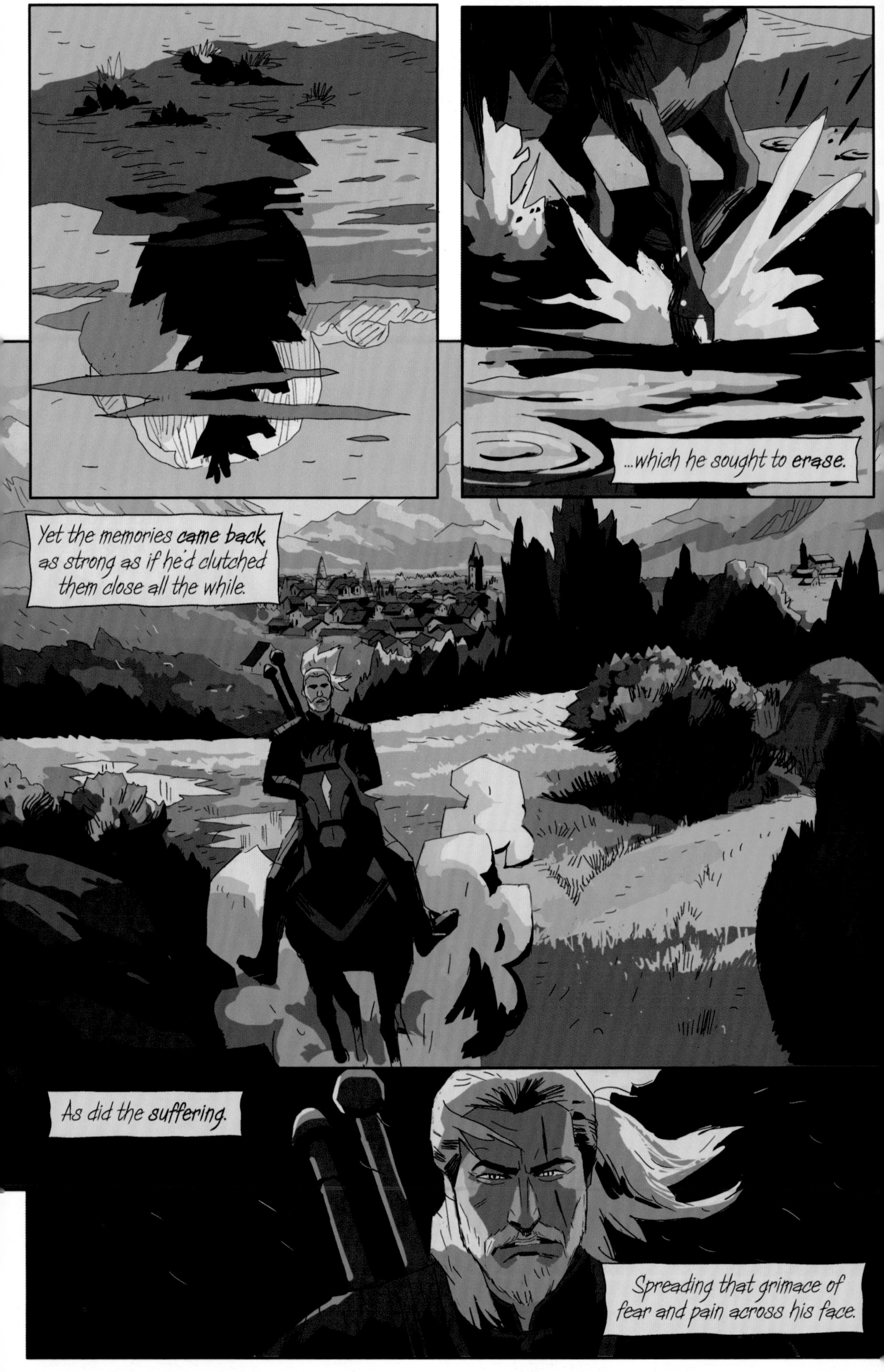
...which he sought to erase.
Yet the memories came back, as strong as if he'd clutched them close all the while.
As did the suffering.
Spreading that grimace of fear and pain across his face.

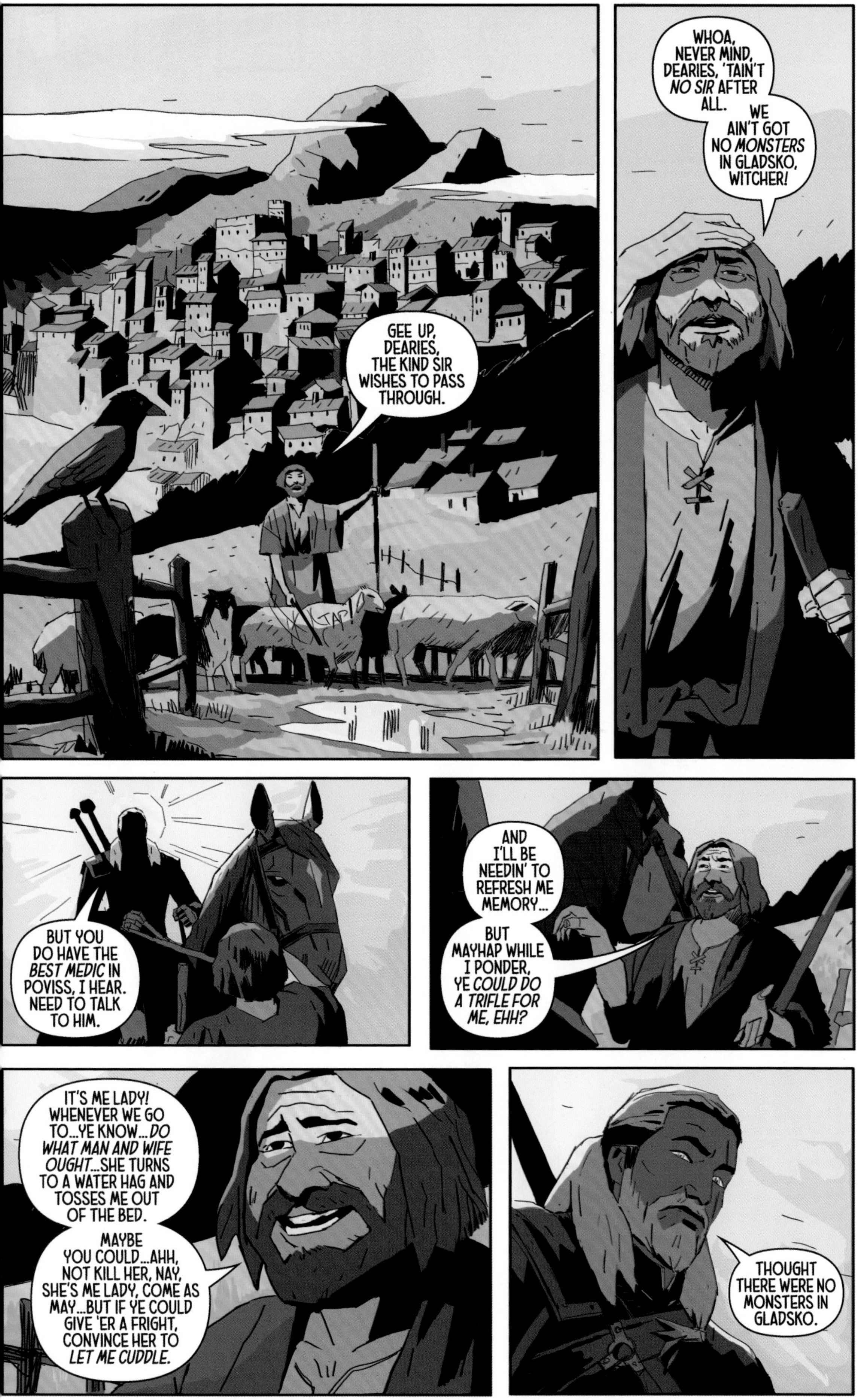
GEE UP, DEARIES, THE KIND SIR WISHES TO PASS THROUGH.
TAP
WHOA, NEVER MIND, DEARIES, 'TAIN'T *NO SIR* AFTER ALL.
WE AIN'T GOT NO *MONSTERS* IN GLADSKO, WITCHER!
BUT YOU DO HAVE THE *BEST MEDIC* IN POVISS, I HEAR. NEED TO TALK TO HIM.
AND I'LL BE NEEDIN' TO REFRESH ME MEMORY...
BUT MAYHAP WHILE I PONDER, YE *COULD DO A TRIFLE FOR ME, EHH?*
IT'S ME LADY! WHENEVER WE GO TO...YE KNOW...*DO WHAT MAN AND WIFE OUGHT*...SHE TURNS TO A WATER HAG AND TOSSES ME OUT OF THE BED.
MAYBE YOU COULD...AHH, NOT KILL HER, NAY, SHE'S ME LADY, COME AS MAY...BUT IF YE COULD GIVE 'ER A FRIGHT, CONVINCE HER TO *LET ME CUDDLE.*
THOUGHT THERE WERE NO MONSTERS IN GLADSKO.

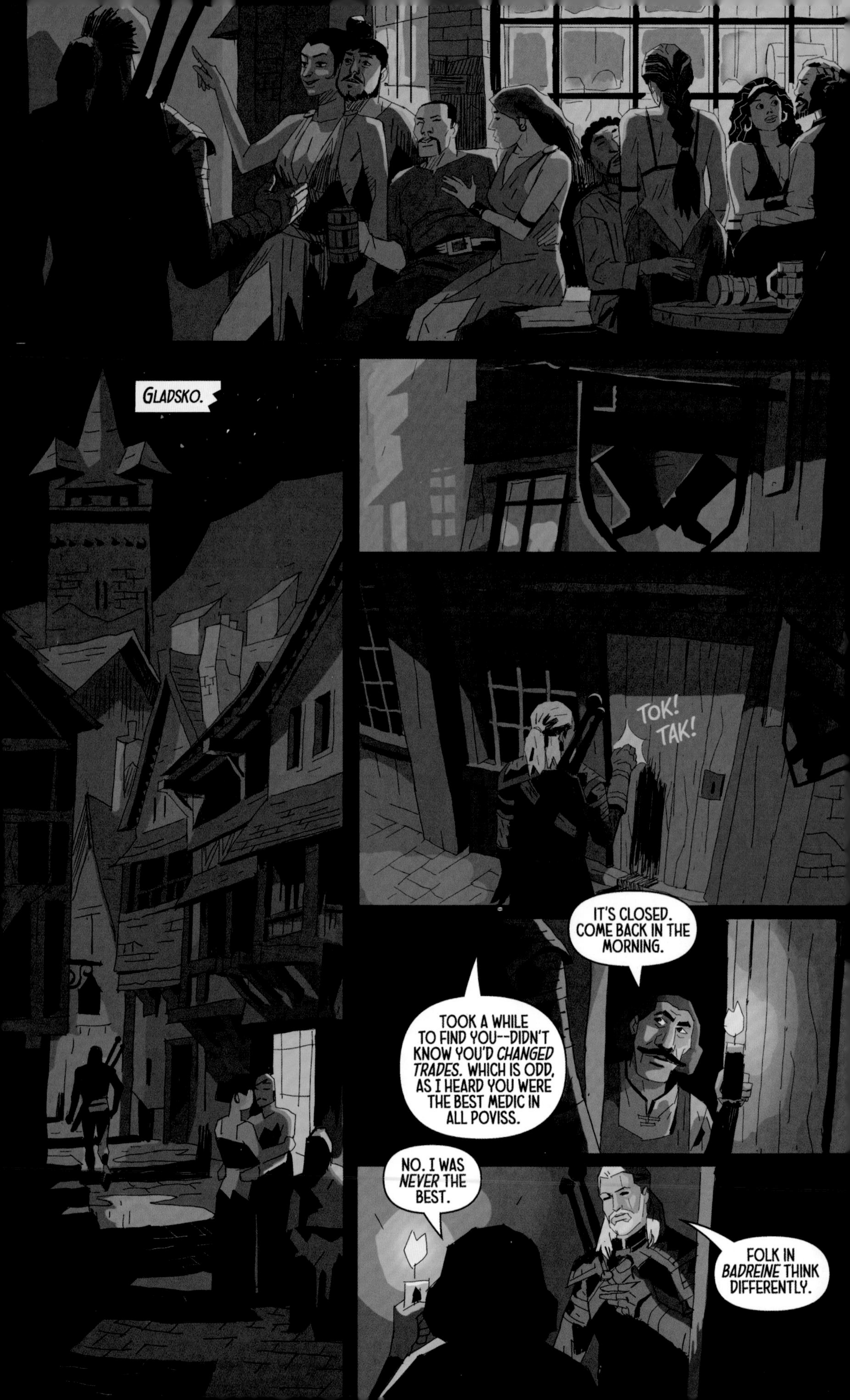
GLADSKO.
TOK!
TAK!
IT'S CLOSED. COME BACK IN THE MORNING.
TOOK A WHILE TO FIND YOU--DIDN'T KNOW YOU'D *CHANGED TRADES.* WHICH IS ODD, AS I HEARD YOU WERE THE BEST MEDIC IN ALL POVISS.
NO. I WAS *NEVER* THE BEST.
FOLK IN *BADREINE* THINK DIFFERENTLY.

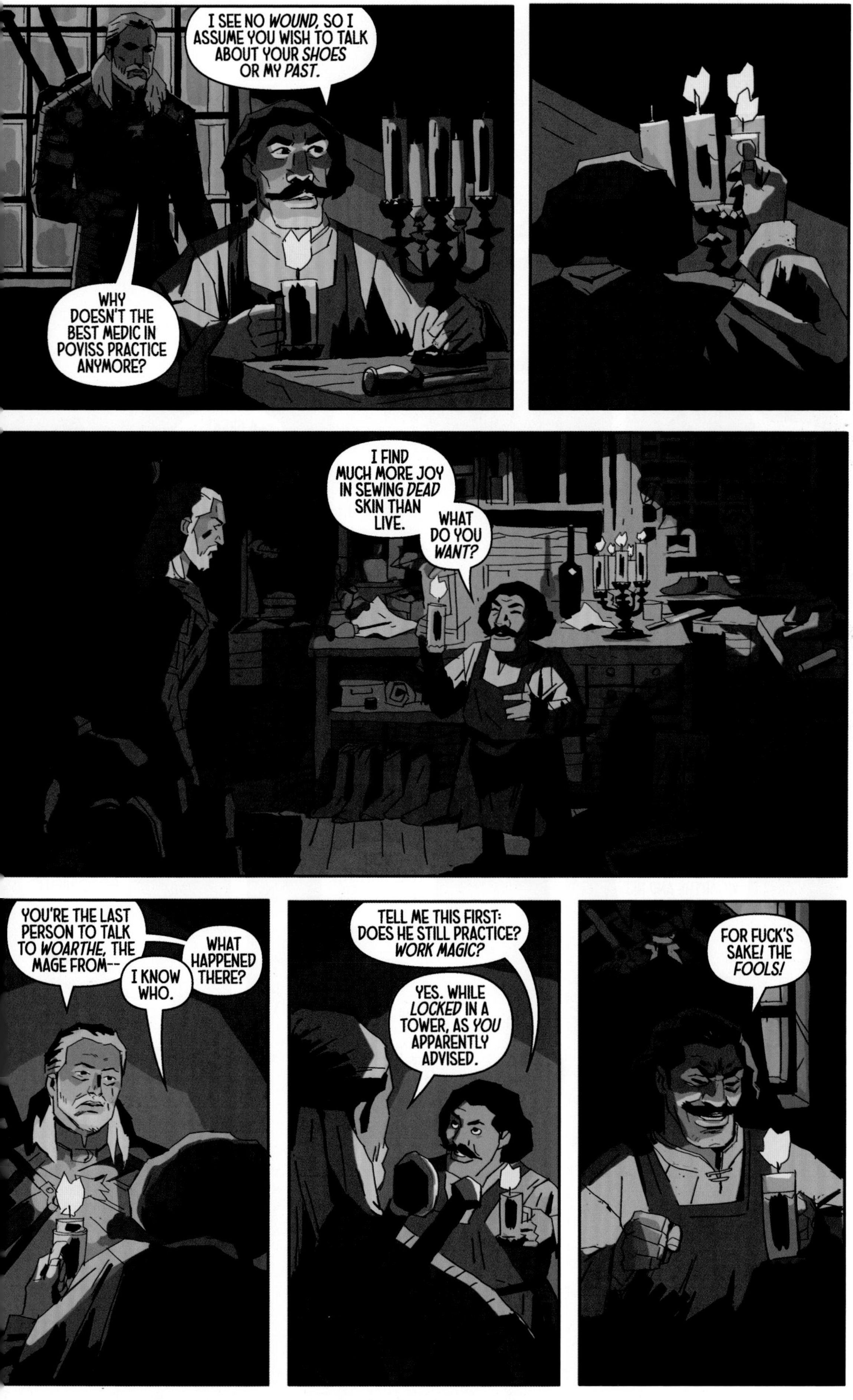
I SEE NO *WOUND*, SO I ASSUME YOU WISH TO TALK ABOUT YOUR *SHOES* OR MY *PAST*.
WHY DOESN'T THE BEST MEDIC IN POVISS PRACTICE ANYMORE?
I FIND MUCH MORE JOY IN SEWING *DEAD* SKIN THAN LIVE.
WHAT DO YOU *WANT?*
YOU'RE THE LAST PERSON TO TALK TO *WOARTHE*, THE MAGE FROM--
I KNOW WHO.
WHAT HAPPENED THERE?
TELL ME THIS FIRST: DOES HE STILL PRACTICE? *WORK MAGIC?*
YES. WHILE *LOCKED* IN A TOWER, AS *YOU* APPARENTLY ADVISED.
FOR FUCK'S SAKE! THE *FOOLS!*

EXACTLY WHY I *QUIT* THE MEDIC'S TRADE. FOLK *NEVER LISTEN*, THEY FEEL THEY KNOW BEST, YET WHEN SOMEONE DIES, IT'S ALL *YOUR FAULT* AND *YOUR HEAD* THEY WANT!

BLAST ALL THAT! NOBODY EVER CALLED FOR MY HEAD OVER A *SHOE*!

THE ILLUSION WOARTHE CREATED *KILLED* A YOUNG BOY...I REALLY NEED TO *KNOW* WHAT HAPPENED THERE, WHOSE *FAULT* IT IS...

OH, NO...I KNEW IT WOULD HAPPEN SOMEDAY... I TOLD THEM BOTH HE SHOULD *NEVER WORK MAGIC* AGAIN.

WHAT'S *WRONG* WITH HIM?

WAIT ONE MOMENT.

A GREAT DEAL...THERE'S A *GREAT DEAL* WRONG WITH HIM...

HERE'S ALL I GATHERED ABOUT WOARTHE AND HIS *CONDITION.*

I quickly learned the most vital thing for him was to feel useful. to feel needed by someone.

YOU CAN HAVE IT, BUT PLEASE, *GO.* NOW.

That's why he loved help, the people s... The gratitu...

MY *OLD LIFE* BRINGS ME ONLY FRUSTRATION. I WOULD VERY MUCH LIKE TO *FORGET* IT.

GOOD NIGHT.

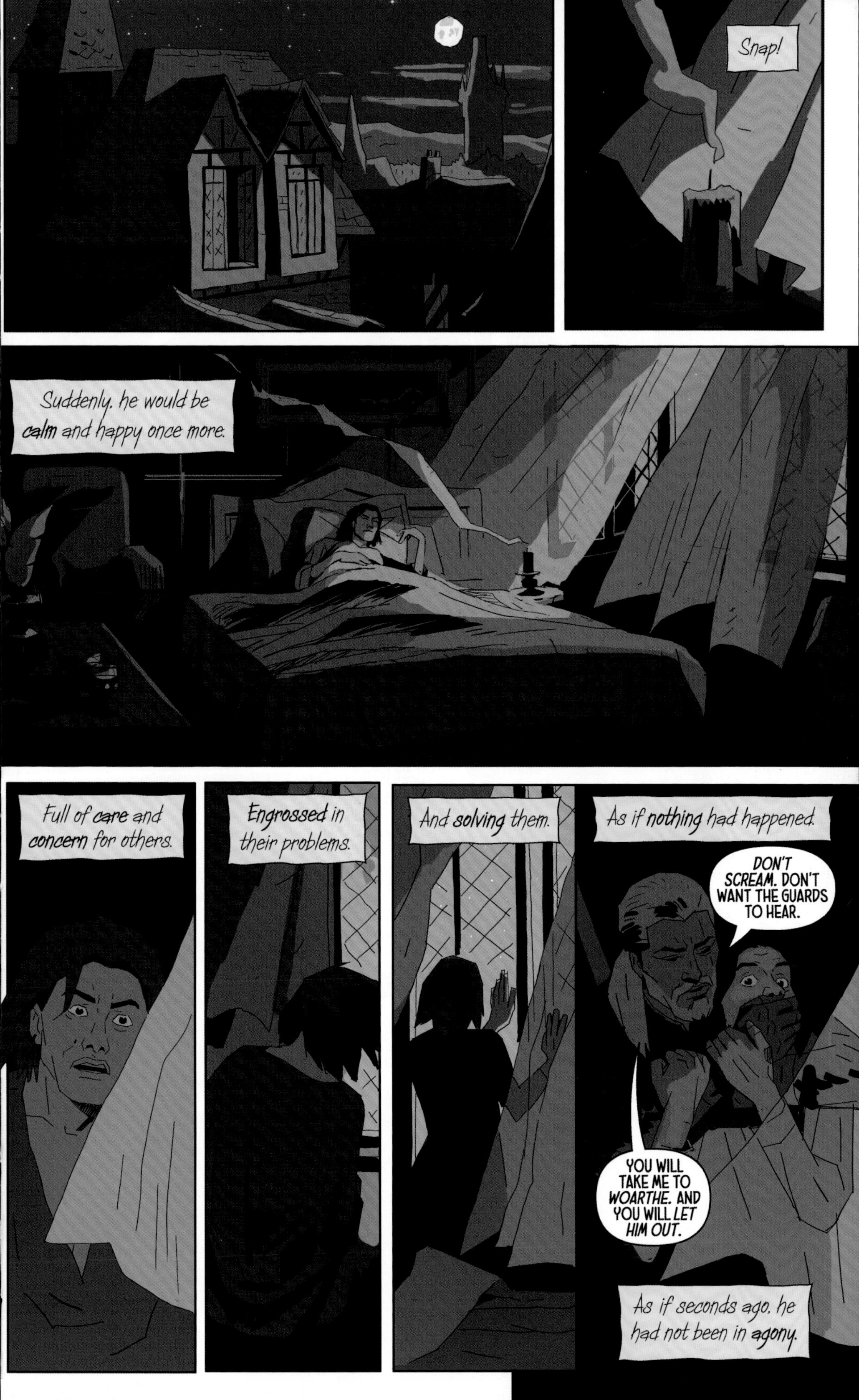
Snap!
Suddenly, he would be calm and happy once more.
Full of care and concern for others.
Engrossed in their problems.
And solving them.
As if nothing had happened.
DON'T SCREAM. DON'T WANT THE GUARDS TO HEAR.
YOU WILL TAKE ME TO WOARTHE. AND YOU WILL LET HIM OUT.
As if seconds ago, he had not been in agony.

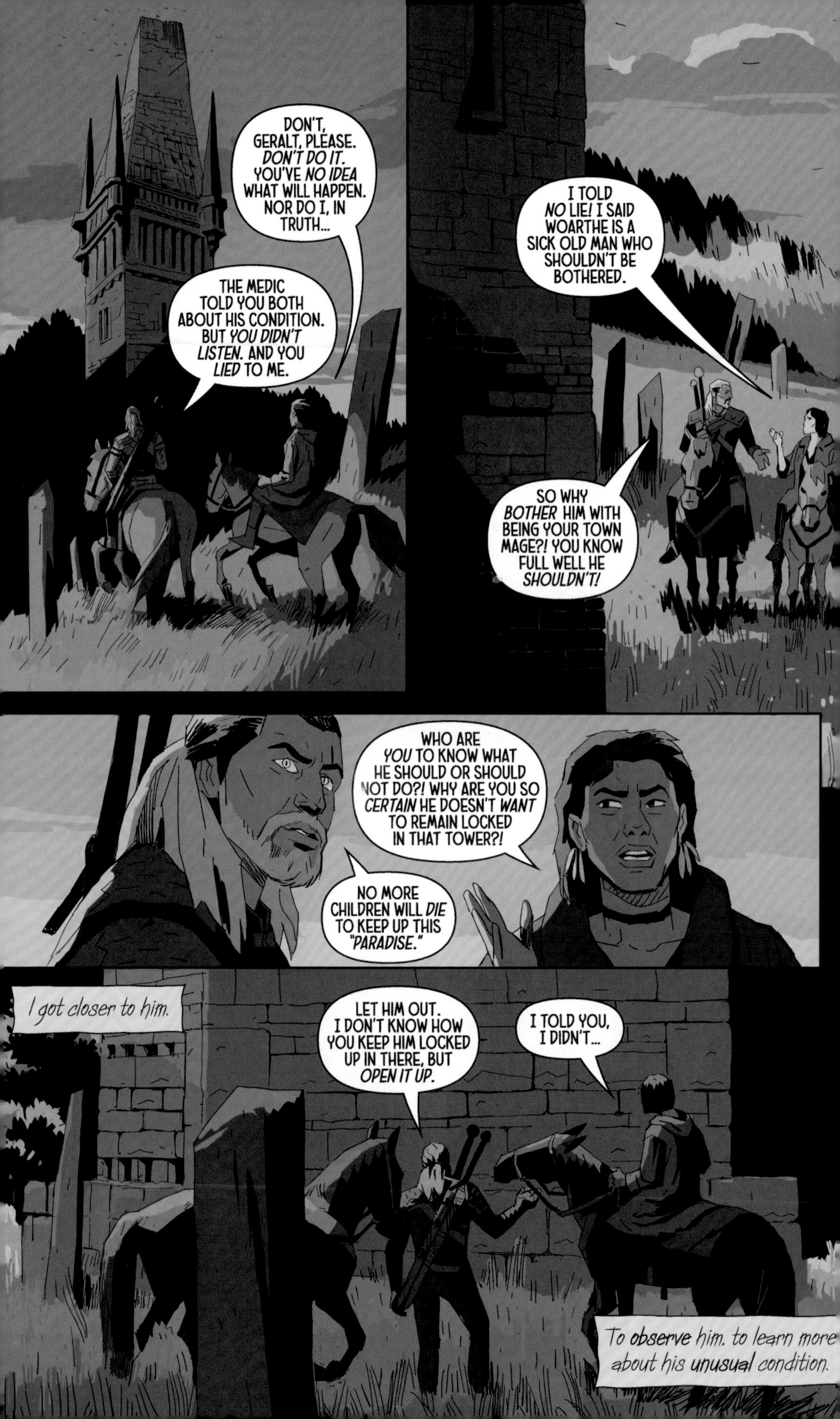

DON'T, GERALT, PLEASE. *DON'T DO IT*. YOU'VE *NO IDEA* WHAT WILL HAPPEN. NOR DO I, IN TRUTH...
THE MEDIC TOLD YOU BOTH ABOUT HIS CONDITION. BUT *YOU DIDN'T LISTEN*. AND YOU *LIED* TO ME.
I TOLD *NO LIE!* I SAID WOARTHE IS A SICK OLD MAN WHO SHOULDN'T BE BOTHERED.
SO WHY *BOTHER* HIM WITH BEING YOUR TOWN MAGE?! YOU KNOW FULL WELL HE *SHOULDN'T!*
WHO ARE *YOU* TO KNOW WHAT HE SHOULD OR SHOULD NOT DO?! WHY ARE YOU SO *CERTAIN* HE DOESN'T *WANT* TO REMAIN LOCKED IN THAT TOWER?!
NO MORE CHILDREN WILL *DIE* TO KEEP UP THIS "*PARADISE*."
I got closer to him.
LET HIM OUT. I DON'T KNOW HOW YOU KEEP HIM LOCKED UP IN THERE, BUT *OPEN IT UP*.
I TOLD YOU, I DIDN'T...
To observe him, to learn more about his unusual condition.

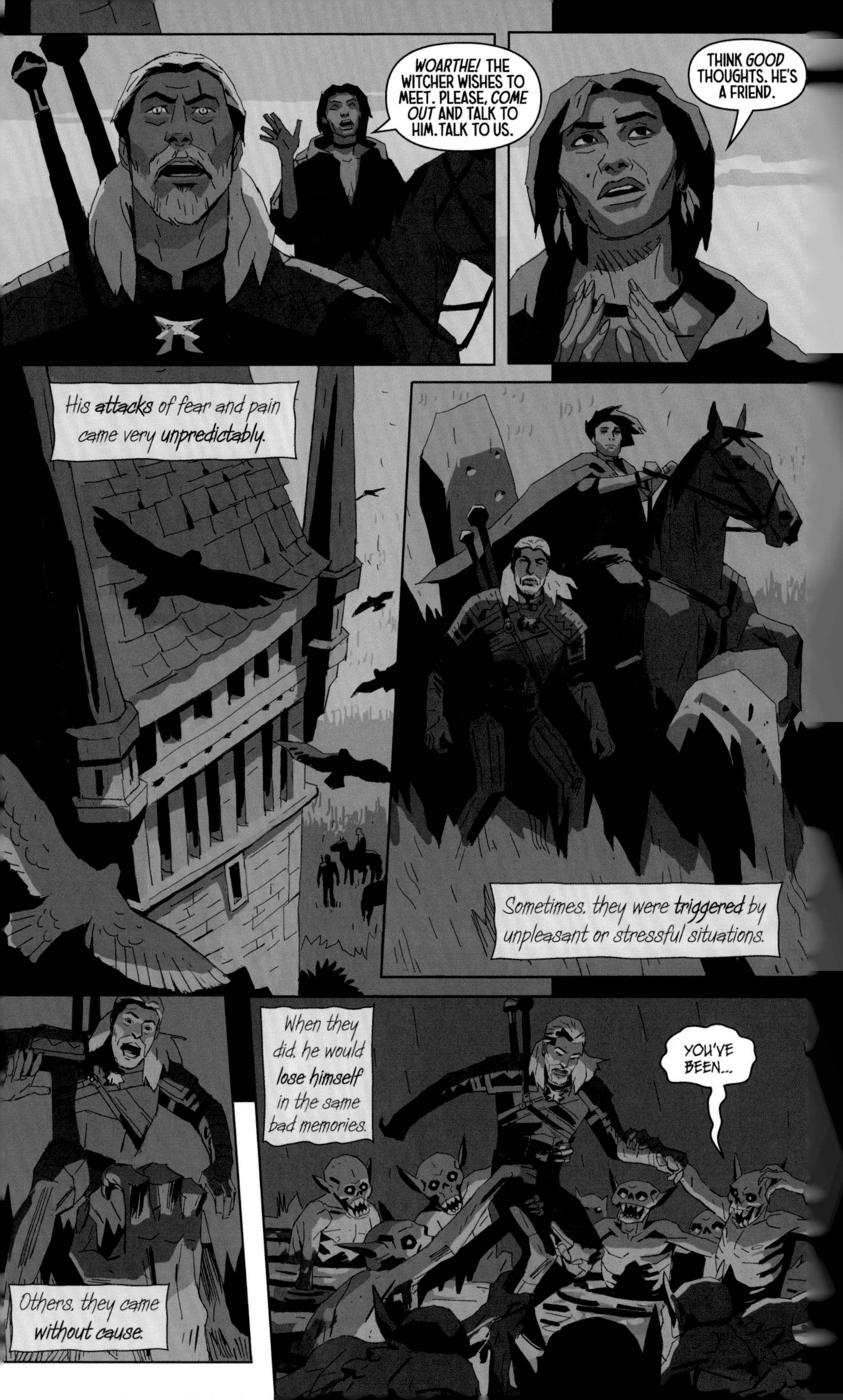
WOARTHE! THE WITCHER WISHES TO MEET. PLEASE, COME OUT AND TALK TO HIM.TALK TO US.
THINK GOOD THOUGHTS. HE'S A FRIEND.
His attacks of fear and pain came very unpredictably.
Sometimes, they were triggered by unpleasant or stressful situations.
Others, they came without cause.
When they did, he would lose himself in the same bad memories.
YOU'VE BEEN...

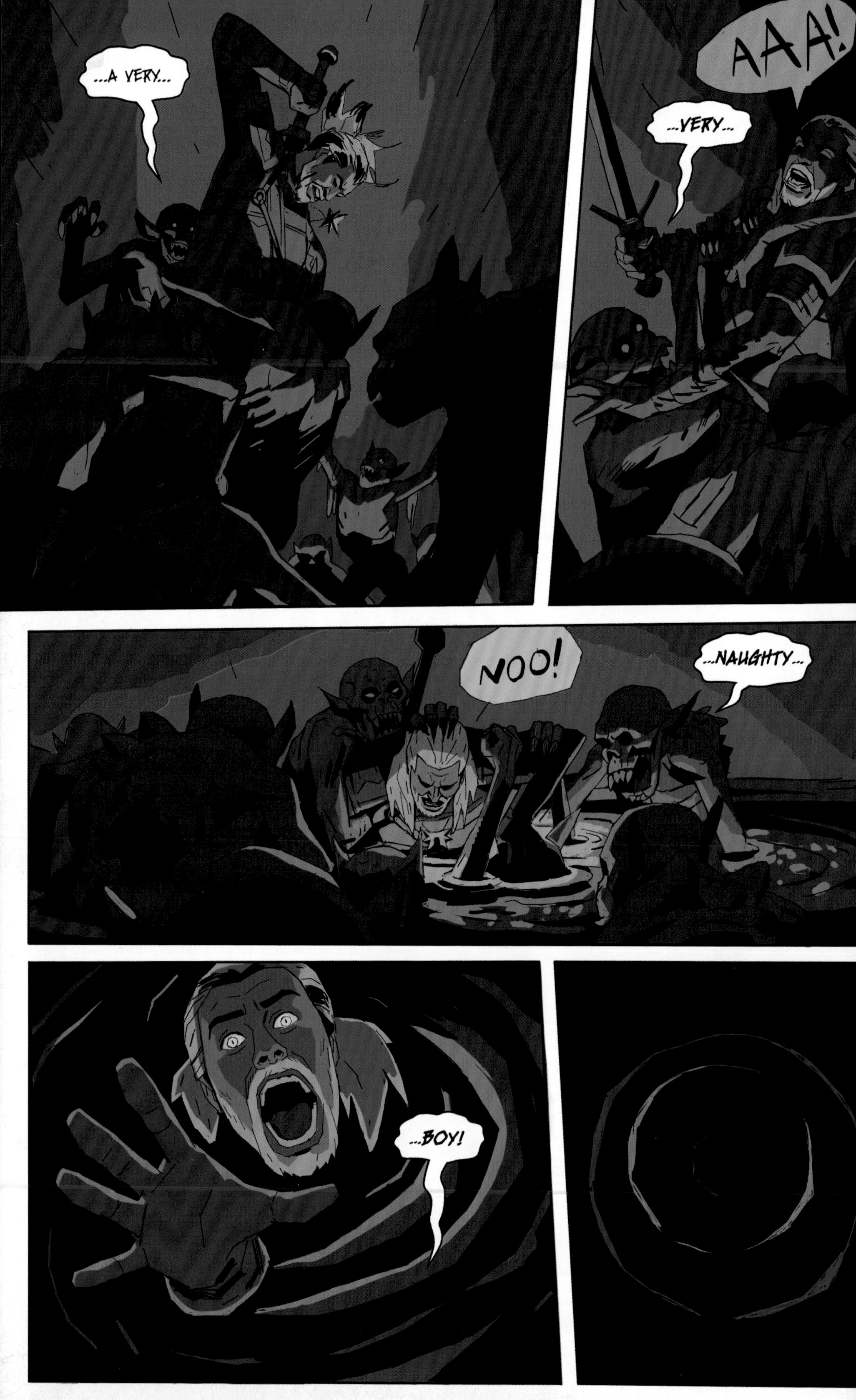

...A VERY...
AAA!
...VERY...
NOO!
...NAUGHTY...
...BOY!

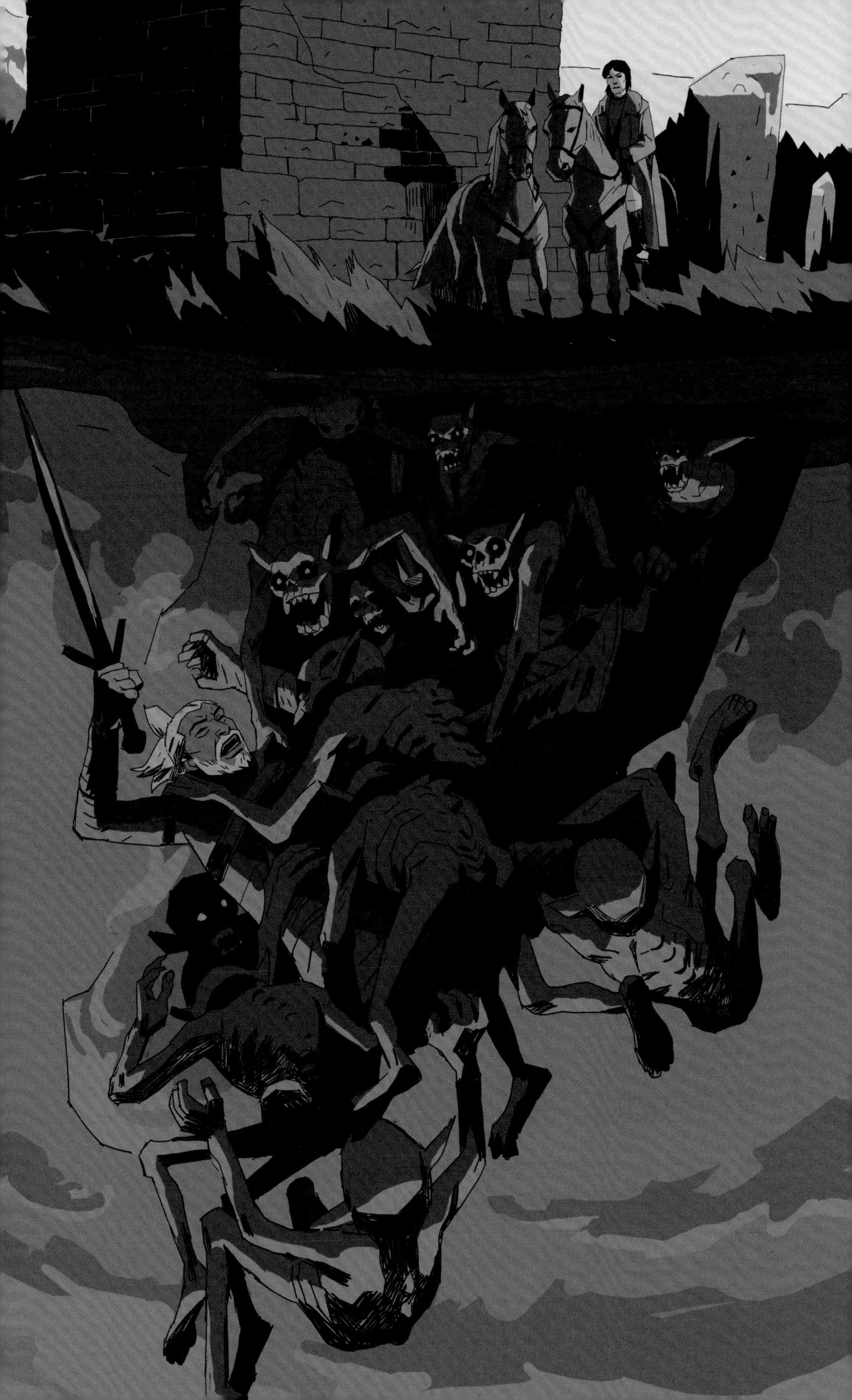

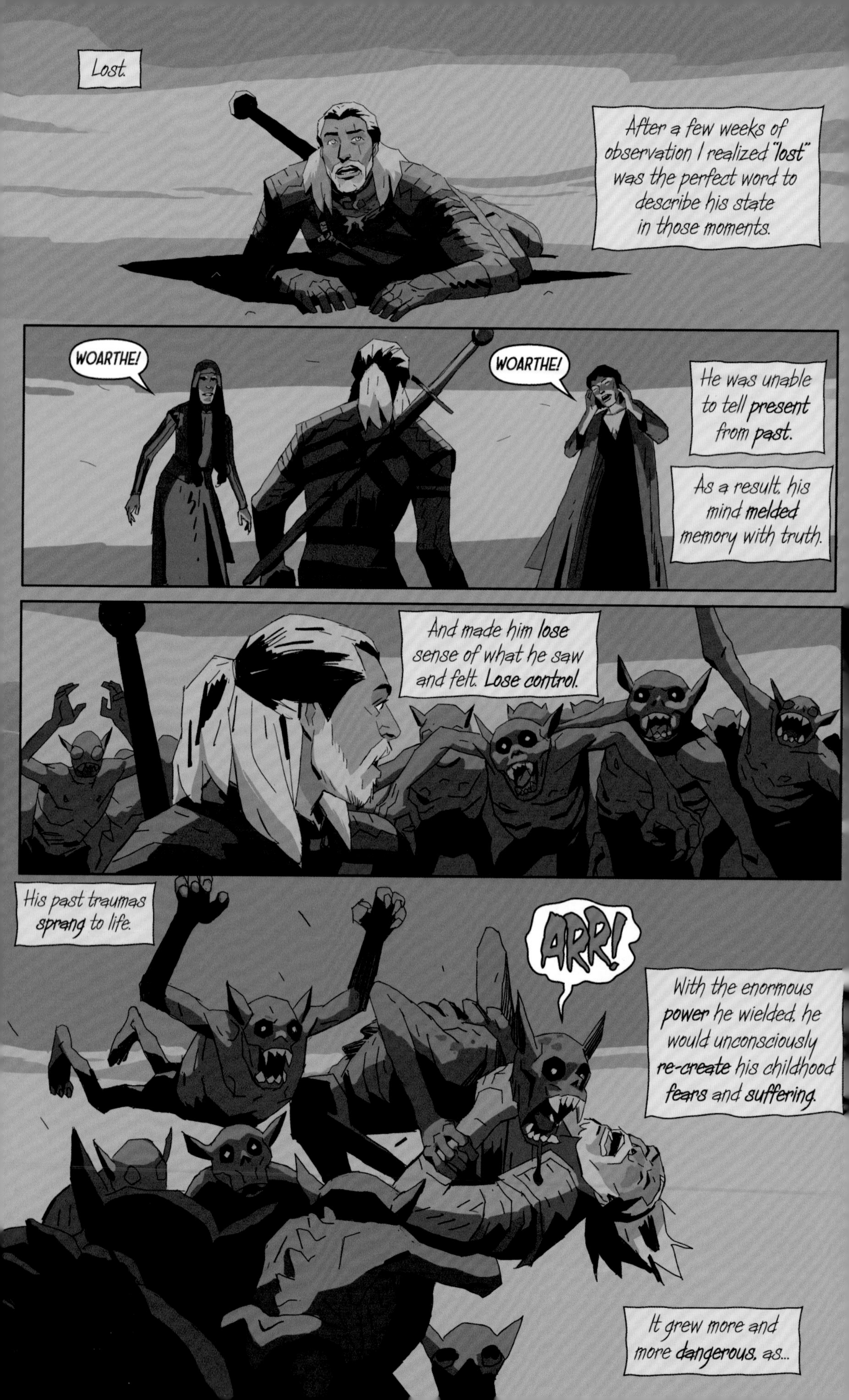
Lost.
After a few weeks of observation I realized "lost" was the perfect word to describe his state in those moments.
WOARTHE!
WOARTHE!
He was unable to tell present from past.
As a result, his mind melded memory with truth.
And made him lose sense of what he saw and felt. Lose control.
His past traumas sprang to life.
ARR!
With the enormous power he wielded, he would unconsciously re-create his childhood fears and suffering.
It grew more and more dangerous, as...

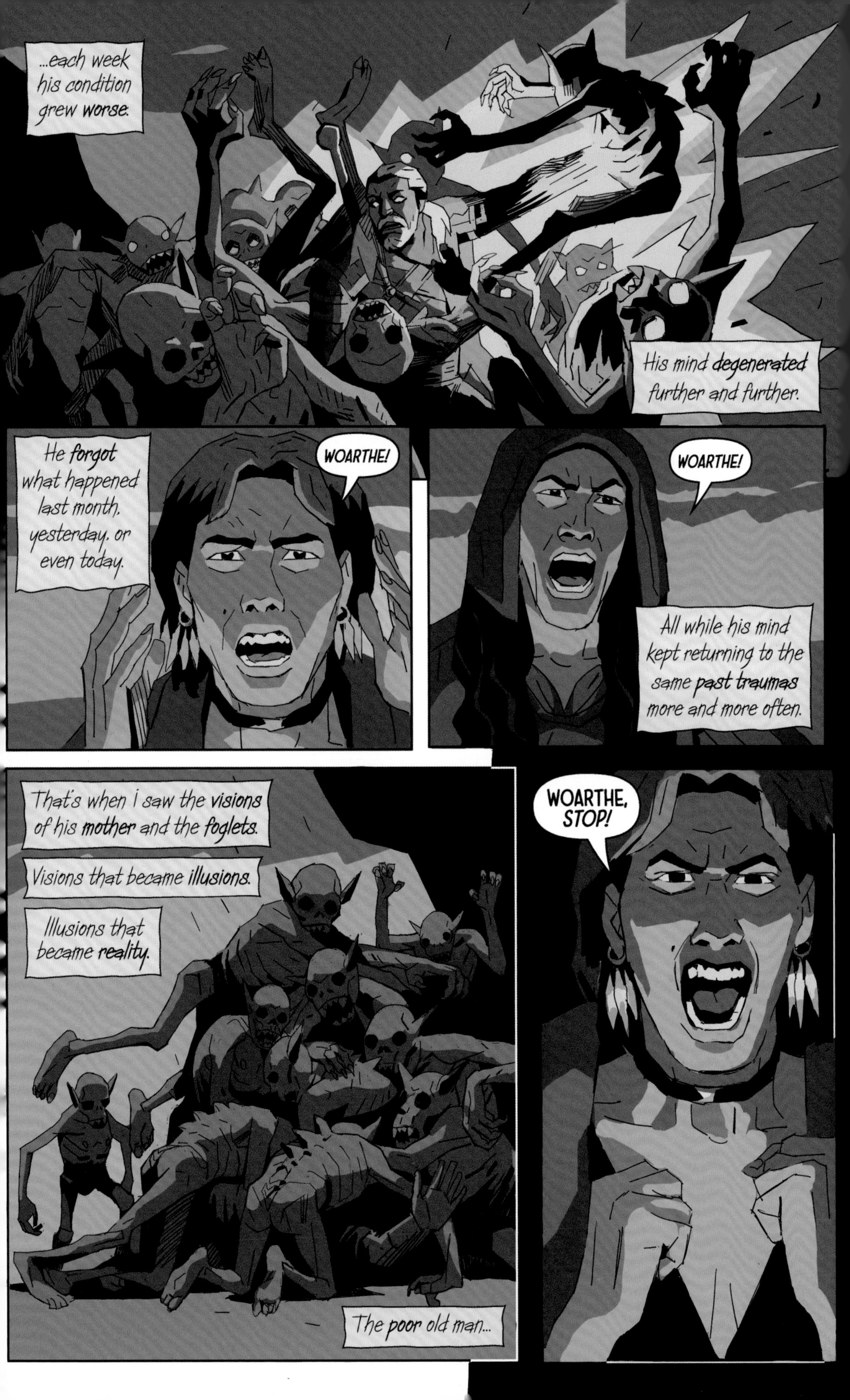
...each week his condition grew worse.
His mind degenerated further and further.
He forgot what happened last month, yesterday, or even today.
WOARTHE!
WOARTHE!
All while his mind kept returning to the same past traumas more and more often.
That's when I saw the visions of his mother and the foglets.
Visions that became illusions.
Illusions that became reality.
The poor old man...
WOARTHE, STOP!

When he returned to his *normal self*, his mind clear once more, he would *destroy* his unconscious creations.

ARE YOU *UNHARMED*, GERALT? I'M SORRY...

TO BE *HONEST*, YOUR TOWN'S *NOT* THE PARADISE THEY SAY.

But there were days when he *couldn't remember* events from moments before. I feared one day he would *forget to remove* what his unraveled mind had wrought.

WOARTHE!

HOW DO YOU *FEEL?*

I had never seen such a disease, but it seemed as though his *mind was slowly dying* and its last wish was to hurt him by bringing back his life's greatest pain...

WOARTHE? TALK TO ME, PLEASE...

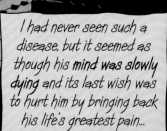

W-WHO... WHO ARE YOU?

...and making all the other memories fade.

CHAPTER FOUR

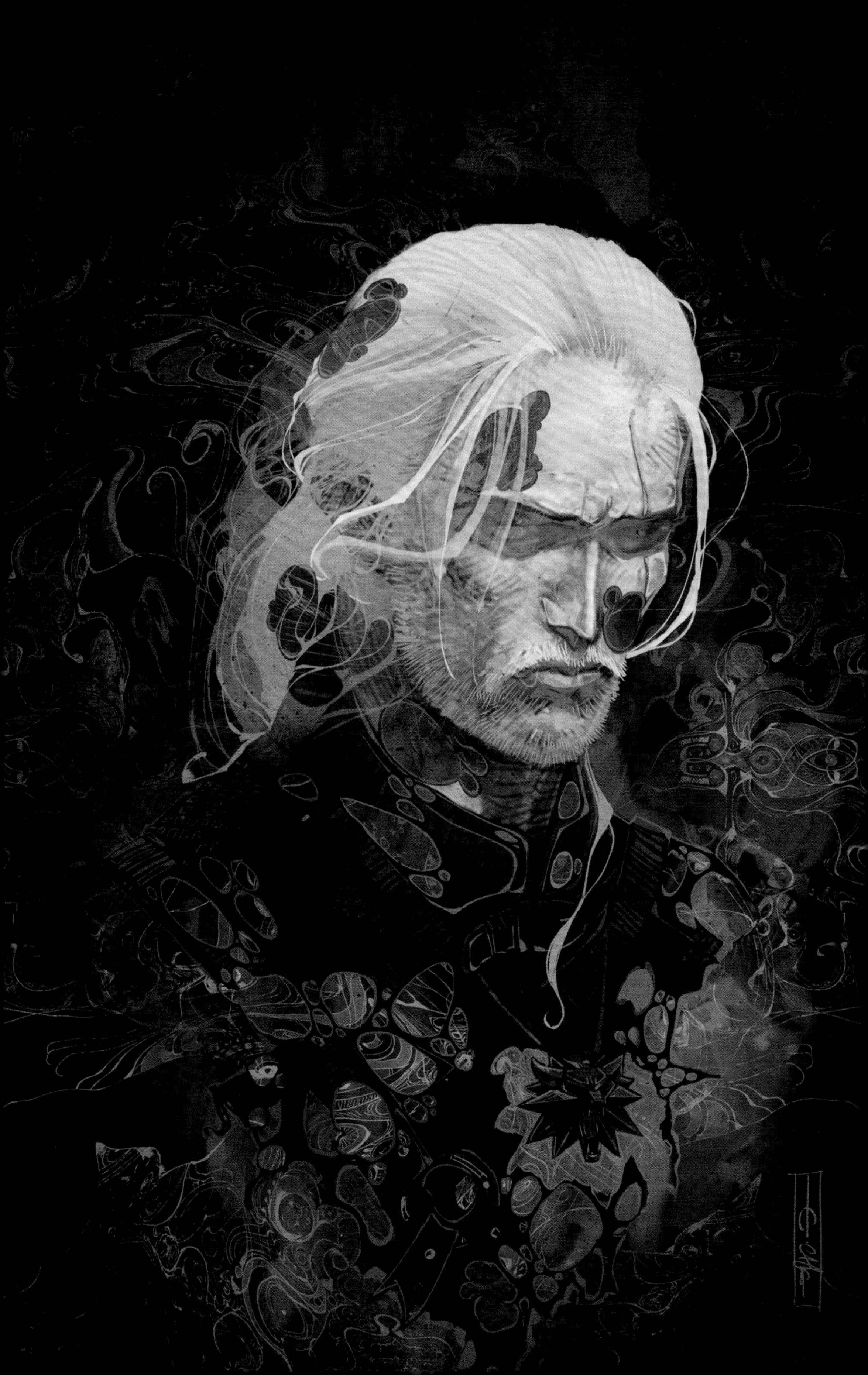

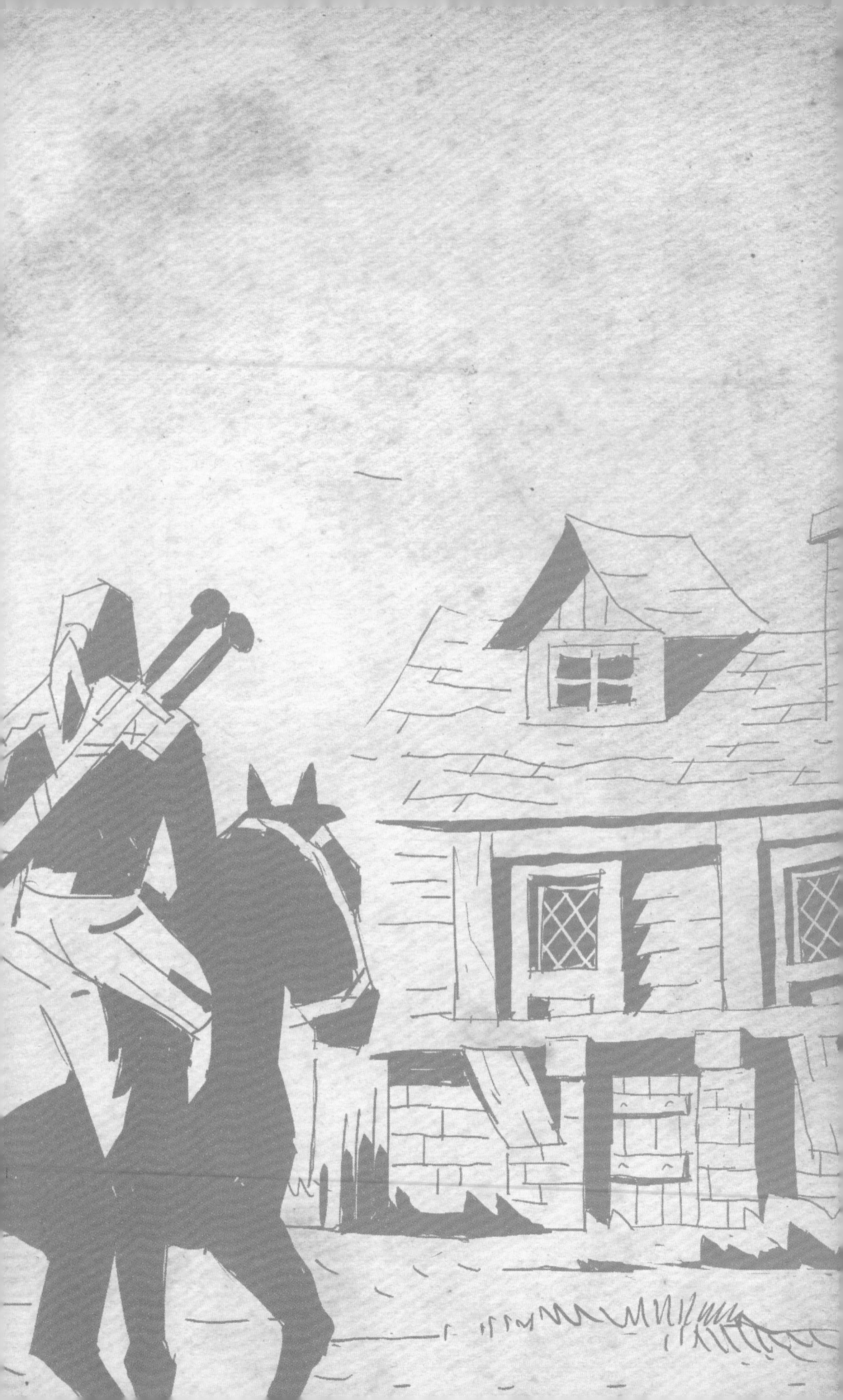

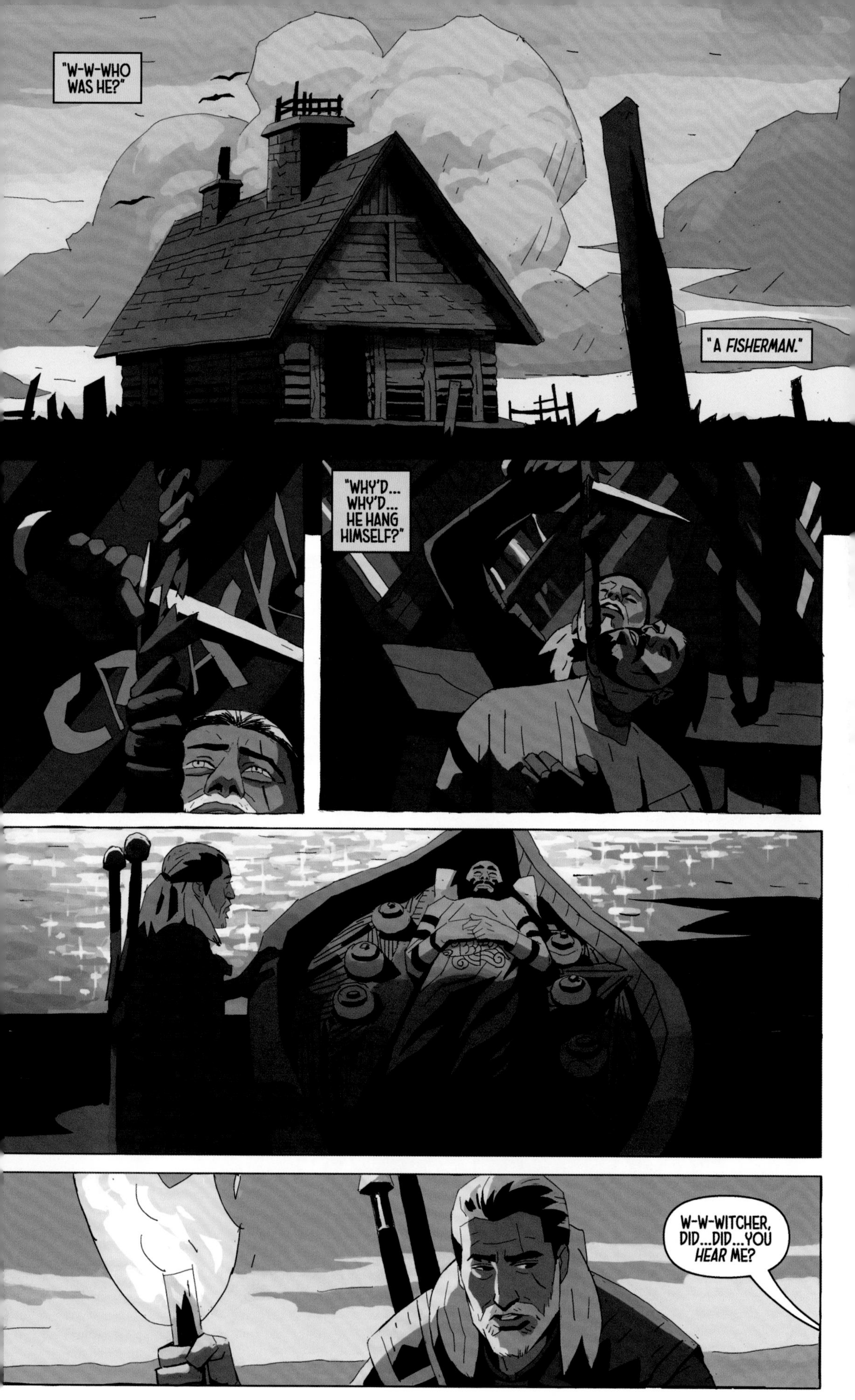
"W-W-WHO WAS HE?"
"A FISHERMAN."
"WHY'D... WHY'D... HE HANG HIMSELF?"
W-W-WITCHER, DID...DID...YOU HEAR ME?

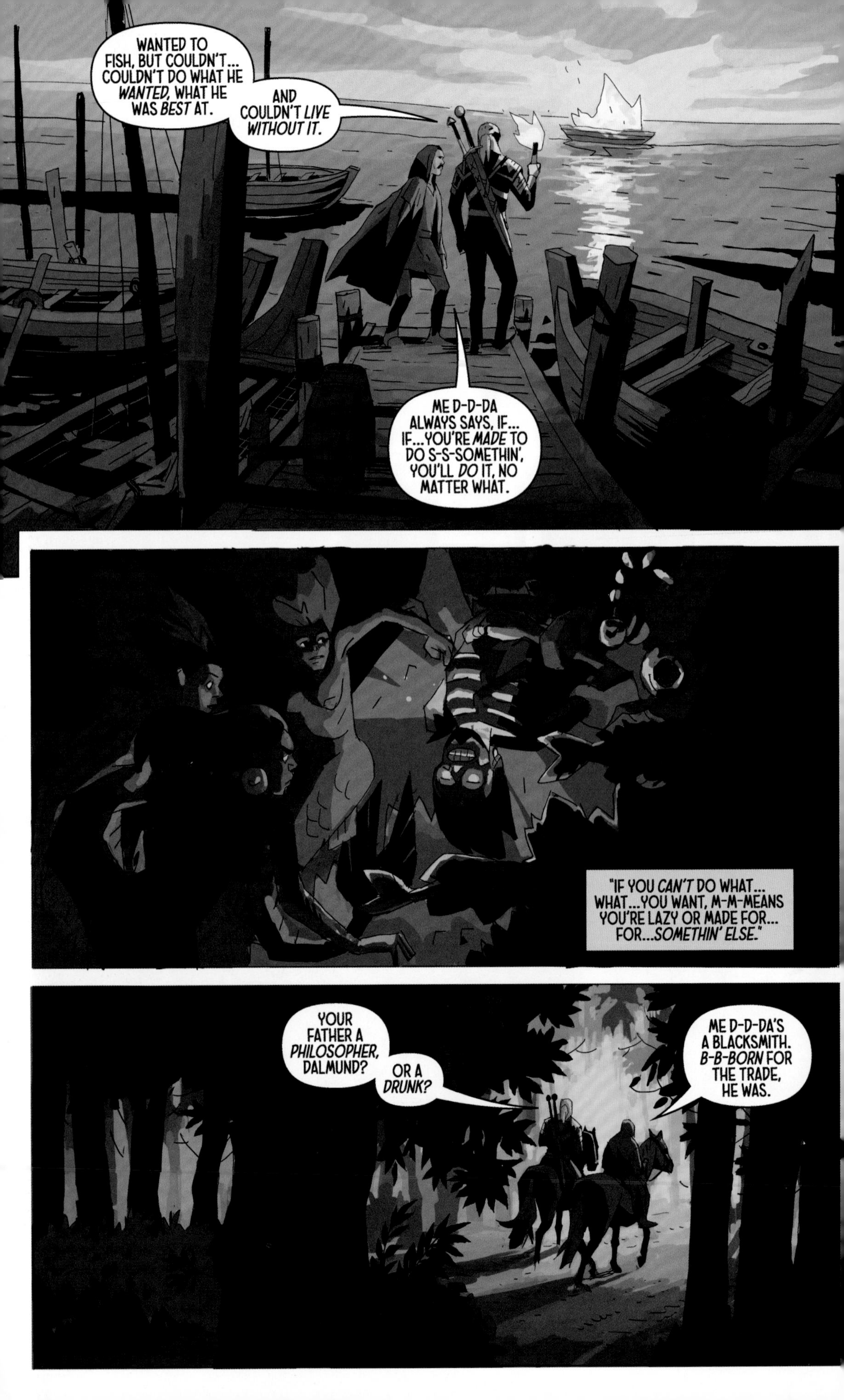
WANTED TO FISH, BUT COULDN'T... COULDN'T DO WHAT HE *WANTED*, WHAT HE WAS *BEST* AT.
AND COULDN'T *LIVE WITHOUT IT.*
ME D-D-DA ALWAYS SAYS, IF... IF...YOU'RE *MADE* TO DO S-S-SOMETHIN', YOU'LL *DO* IT, NO MATTER WHAT.
"IF YOU *CAN'T* DO WHAT... WHAT...YOU WANT, M-M-MEANS YOU'RE LAZY OR MADE FOR... FOR...*SOMETHIN' ELSE.*"
YOUR FATHER A *PHILOSOPHER,* DALMUND?
OR A *DRUNK?*
ME D-D-DA'S A BLACKSMITH. *B-B-BORN* FOR THE TRADE, HE WAS.

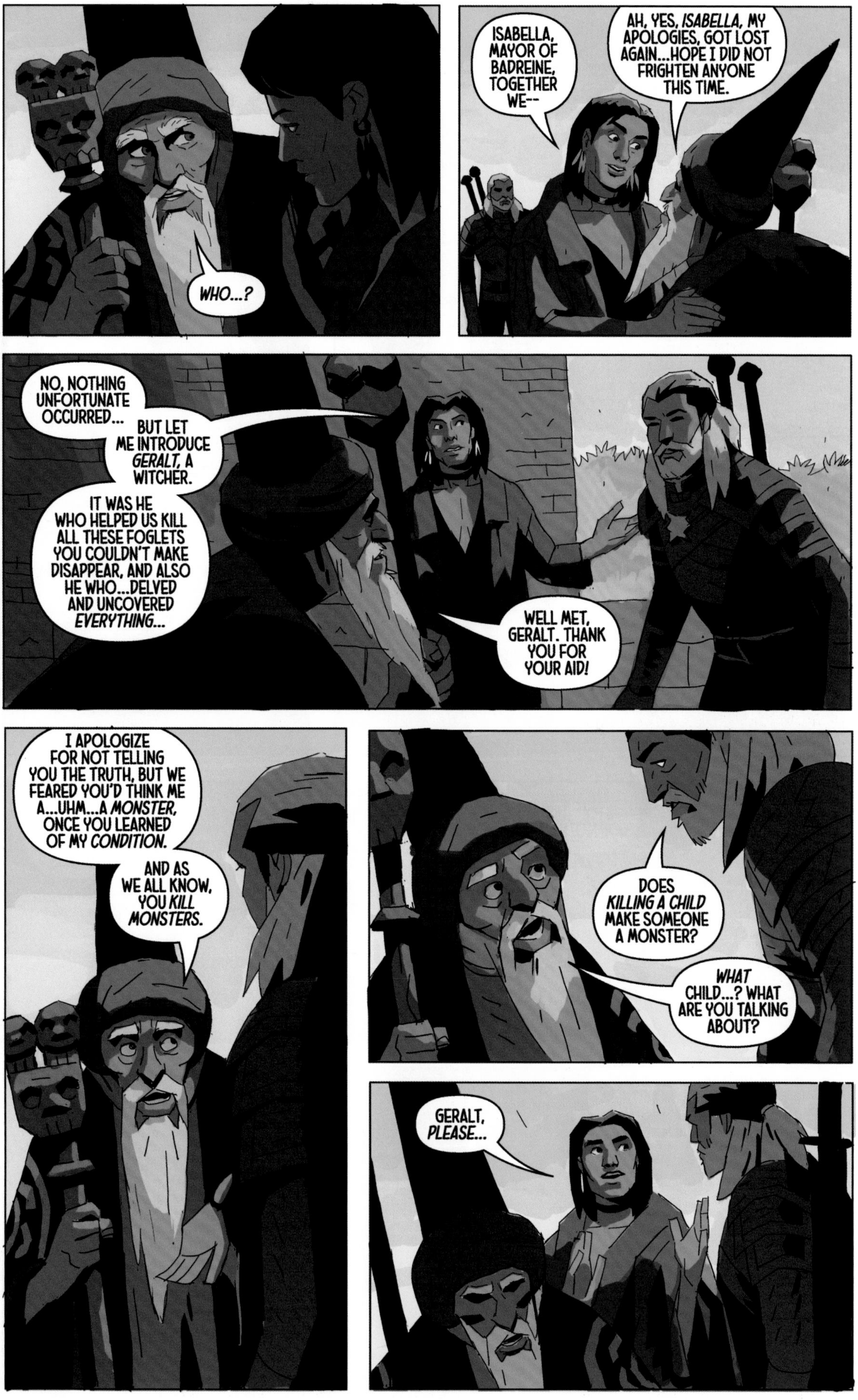
WHO...?
ISABELLA, MAYOR OF BADREINE, TOGETHER WE--
AH, YES, ISABELLA, MY APOLOGIES, GOT LOST AGAIN...HOPE I DID NOT FRIGHTEN ANYONE THIS TIME.
NO, NOTHING UNFORTUNATE OCCURRED...
BUT LET ME INTRODUCE GERALT, A WITCHER.
IT WAS HE WHO HELPED US KILL ALL THESE FOGLETS YOU COULDN'T MAKE DISAPPEAR, AND ALSO HE WHO...DELVED AND UNCOVERED EVERYTHING...
WELL MET, GERALT. THANK YOU FOR YOUR AID!
I APOLOGIZE FOR NOT TELLING YOU THE TRUTH, BUT WE FEARED YOU'D THINK ME A...UHM...A MONSTER, ONCE YOU LEARNED OF MY CONDITION.
AND AS WE ALL KNOW, YOU KILL MONSTERS.
DOES KILLING A CHILD MAKE SOMEONE A MONSTER?
WHAT CHILD...? WHAT ARE YOU TALKING ABOUT?
GERALT, PLEASE...

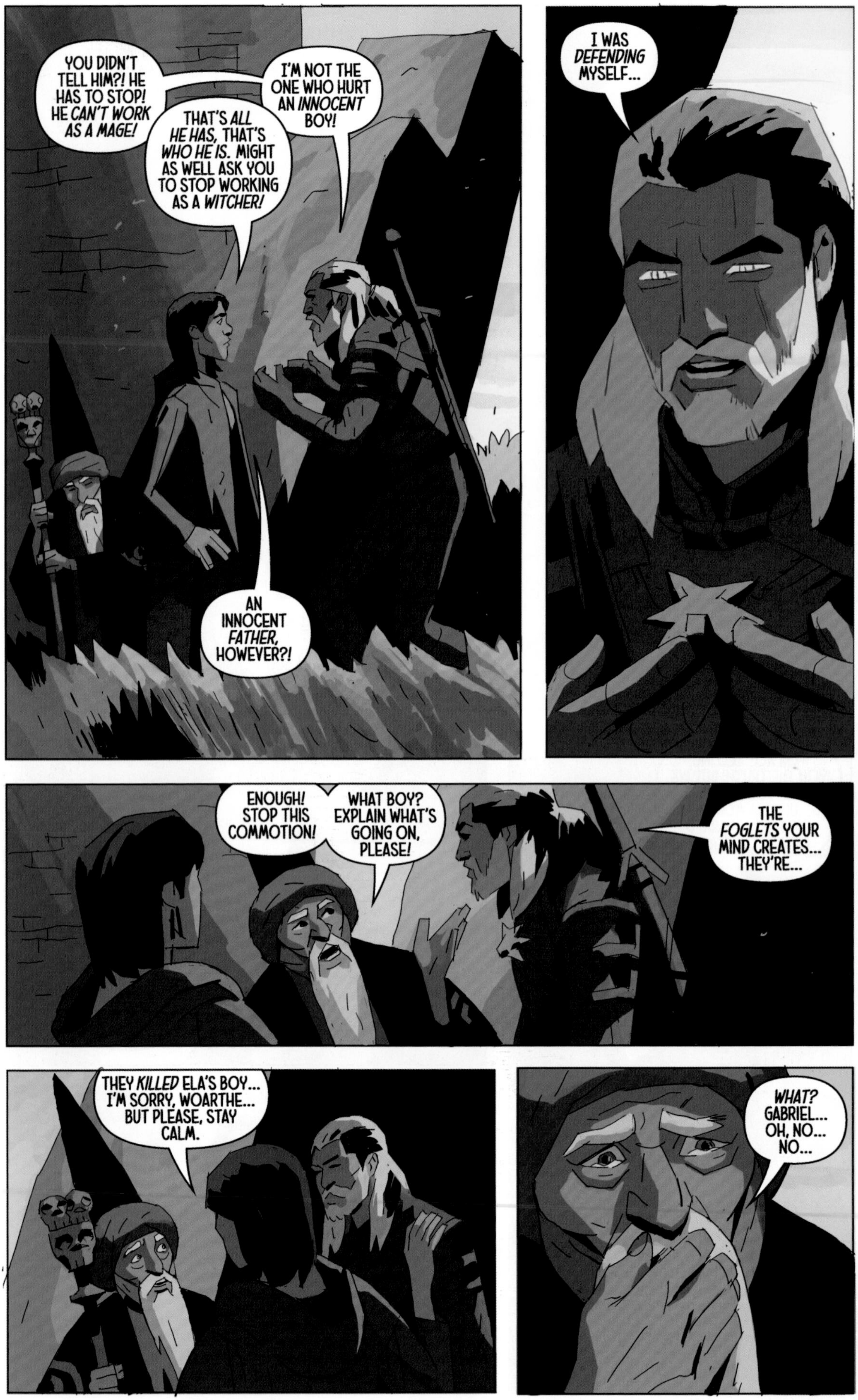
YOU DIDN'T TELL HIM?! HE HAS TO STOP! HE CAN'T WORK AS A MAGE!
I'M NOT THE ONE WHO HURT AN INNOCENT BOY!
THAT'S ALL HE HAS, THAT'S WHO HE IS. MIGHT AS WELL ASK YOU TO STOP WORKING AS A WITCHER!
AN INNOCENT FATHER, HOWEVER?!
I WAS DEFENDING MYSELF...
ENOUGH! STOP THIS COMMOTION!
WHAT BOY? EXPLAIN WHAT'S GOING ON, PLEASE!
THE FOGLETS YOUR MIND CREATES... THEY'RE...
THEY KILLED ELA'S BOY... I'M SORRY, WOARTHE... BUT PLEASE, STAY CALM.
WHAT? GABRIEL... OH, NO... NO...

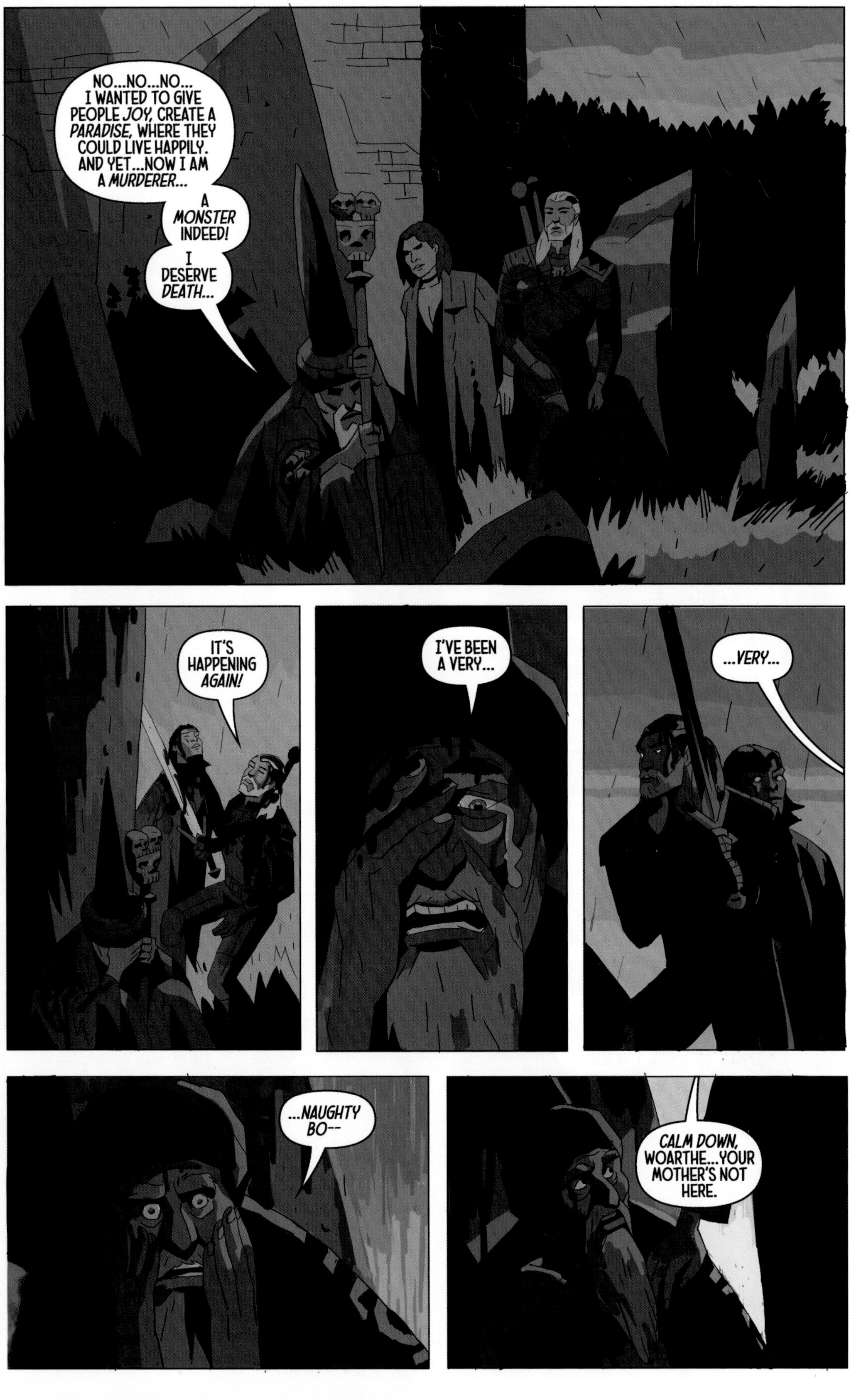
NO...NO...NO... I WANTED TO GIVE PEOPLE *JOY*, CREATE A *PARADISE*, WHERE THEY COULD LIVE HAPPILY. AND YET...NOW I AM A *MURDERER*...
A *MONSTER* INDEED!
I DESERVE *DEATH*...
IT'S HAPPENING *AGAIN!*
I'VE BEEN A VERY...
...*VERY*...
...*NAUGHTY BO--*
CALM DOWN, WOARTHE...YOUR MOTHER'S NOT HERE.

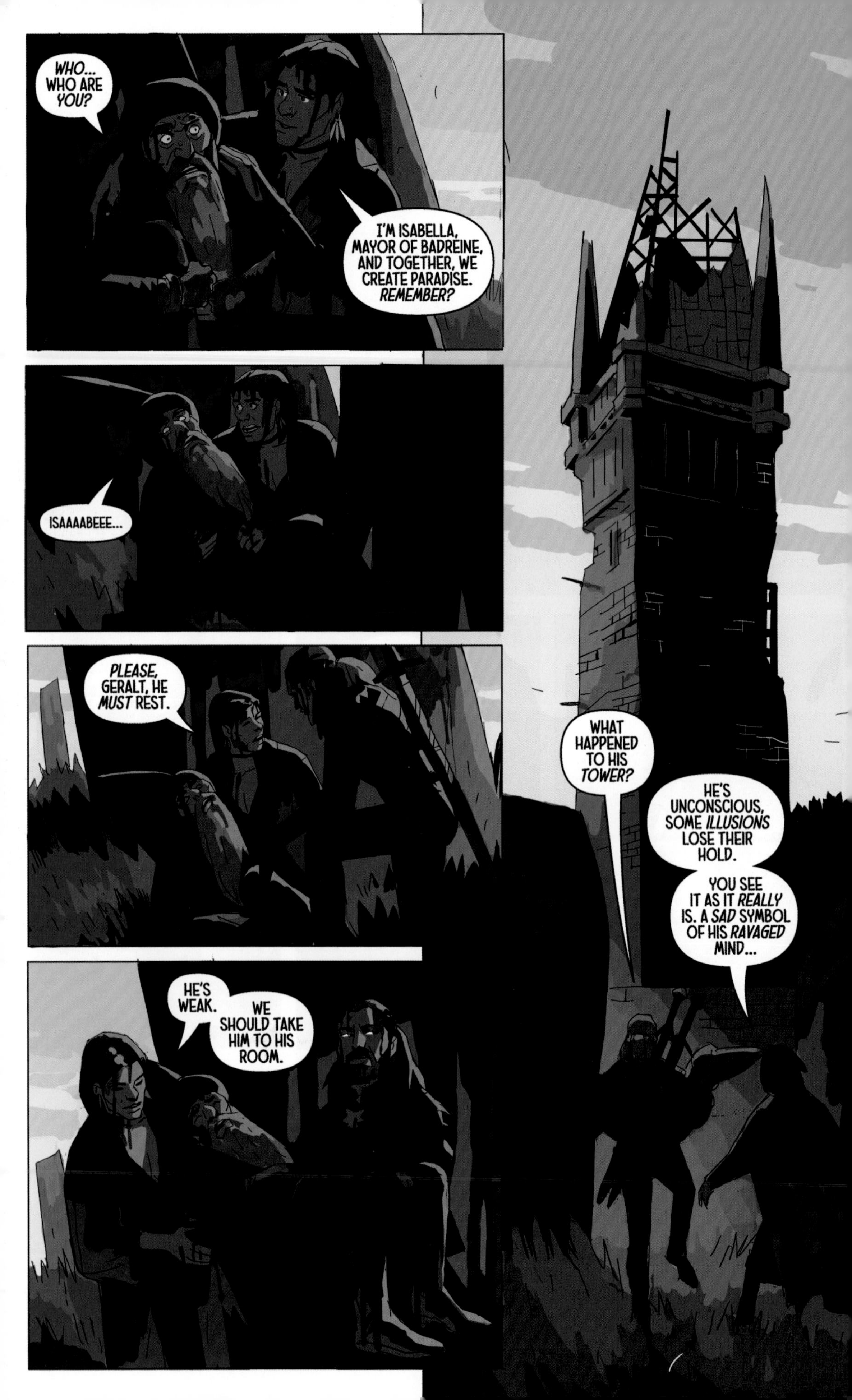
WHO... WHO ARE YOU?
I'M ISABELLA, MAYOR OF BADREINE, AND TOGETHER, WE CREATE PARADISE. REMEMBER?
ISAAAABEEE...
PLEASE, GERALT, HE MUST REST.
HE'S WEAK.
WE SHOULD TAKE HIM TO HIS ROOM.
WHAT HAPPENED TO HIS TOWER?
HE'S UNCONSCIOUS, SOME ILLUSIONS LOSE THEIR HOLD.
YOU SEE IT AS IT REALLY IS. A SAD SYMBOL OF HIS RAVAGED MIND...

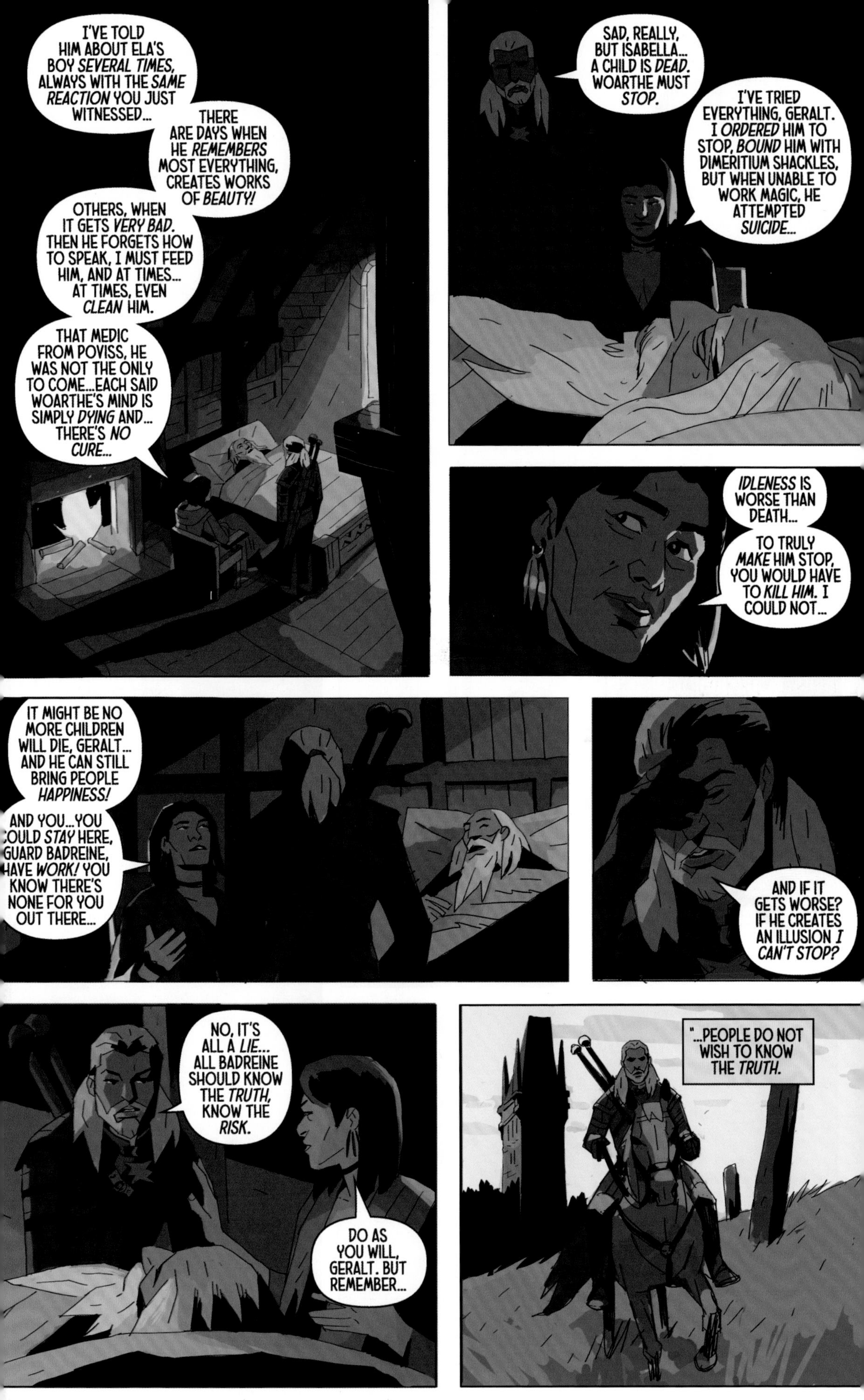
I'VE TOLD HIM ABOUT ELA'S BOY *SEVERAL TIMES*, ALWAYS WITH THE *SAME REACTION* YOU JUST WITNESSED...
THERE ARE DAYS WHEN HE *REMEMBERS* MOST EVERYTHING, CREATES WORKS OF *BEAUTY!*
OTHERS, WHEN IT GETS *VERY BAD*. THEN HE FORGETS HOW TO SPEAK, I MUST FEED HIM, AND AT TIMES... AT TIMES, EVEN *CLEAN* HIM.
THAT MEDIC FROM POVISS, HE WAS NOT THE ONLY TO COME...EACH SAID WOARTHE'S MIND IS SIMPLY *DYING* AND... THERE'S *NO CURE*...
SAD, REALLY, BUT ISABELLA... A CHILD IS *DEAD*. WOARTHE MUST *STOP*.
I'VE TRIED EVERYTHING, GERALT. I *ORDERED* HIM TO STOP, *BOUND* HIM WITH DIMERITIUM SHACKLES, BUT WHEN UNABLE TO WORK MAGIC, HE ATTEMPTED *SUICIDE*...
IDLENESS IS WORSE THAN DEATH...
TO TRULY *MAKE* HIM STOP, YOU WOULD HAVE TO *KILL HIM*. I COULD NOT...
IT MIGHT BE NO MORE CHILDREN WILL DIE, GERALT... AND HE CAN STILL BRING PEOPLE *HAPPINESS!*
AND YOU...YOU OULD *STAY* HERE, GUARD BADREINE, AVE *WORK!* YOU KNOW THERE'S NONE FOR YOU OUT THERE...
AND IF IT GETS WORSE? IF HE CREATES AN ILLUSION *I CAN'T STOP?*
NO, IT'S ALL A *LIE*... ALL BADREINE SHOULD KNOW THE *TRUTH*, KNOW THE *RISK*.
DO AS YOU WILL, GERALT. BUT REMEMBER...
"...PEOPLE DO NOT WISH TO KNOW THE *TRUTH*.

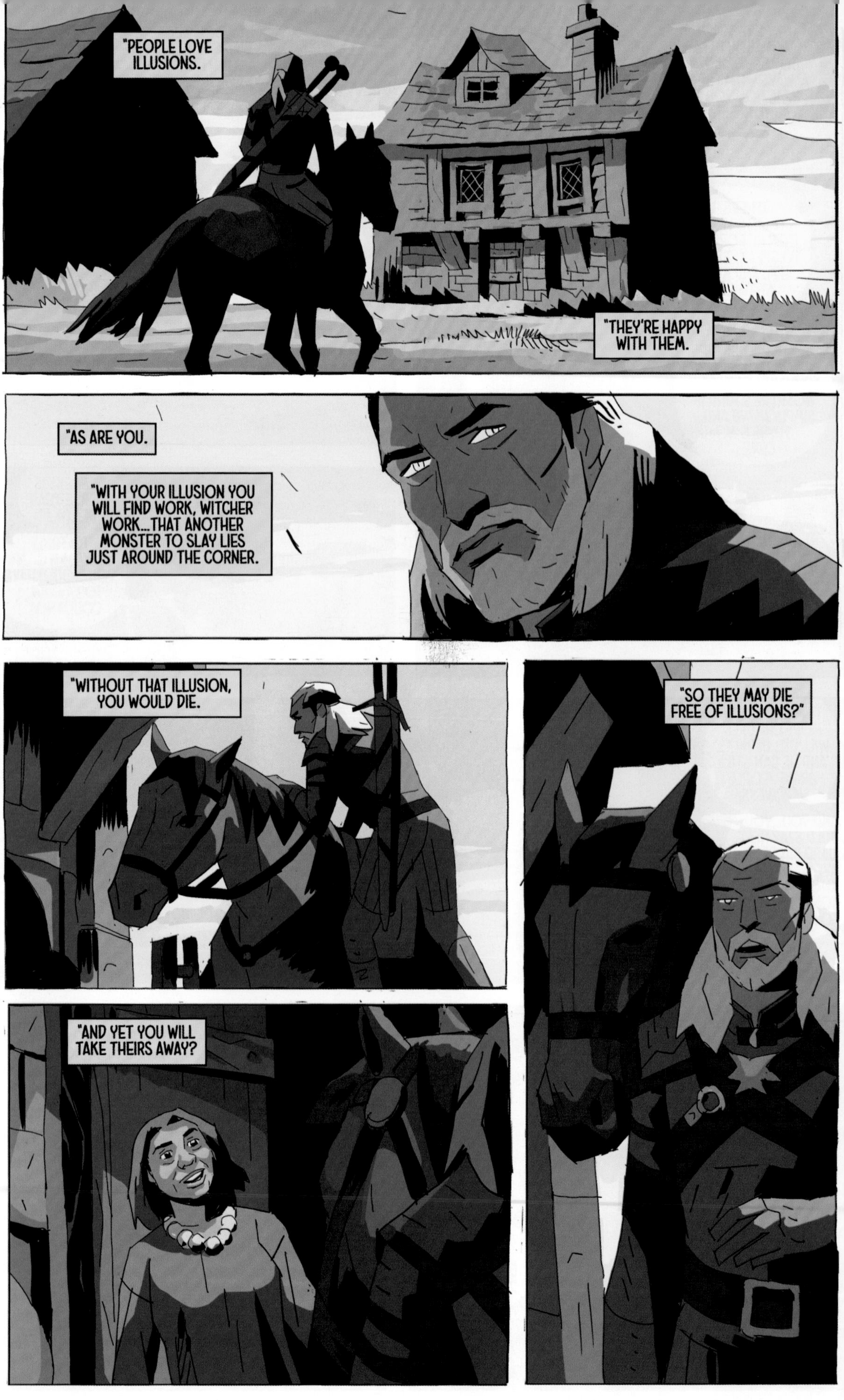
"PEOPLE LOVE ILLUSIONS.
"THEY'RE HAPPY WITH THEM.
"AS ARE YOU.
"WITH YOUR ILLUSION YOU WILL FIND WORK, WITCHER WORK...THAT ANOTHER MONSTER TO SLAY LIES JUST AROUND THE CORNER.
"WITHOUT THAT ILLUSION, YOU WOULD DIE.
"AND YET YOU WILL TAKE THEIRS AWAY?
"SO THEY MAY DIE FREE OF ILLUSIONS?"

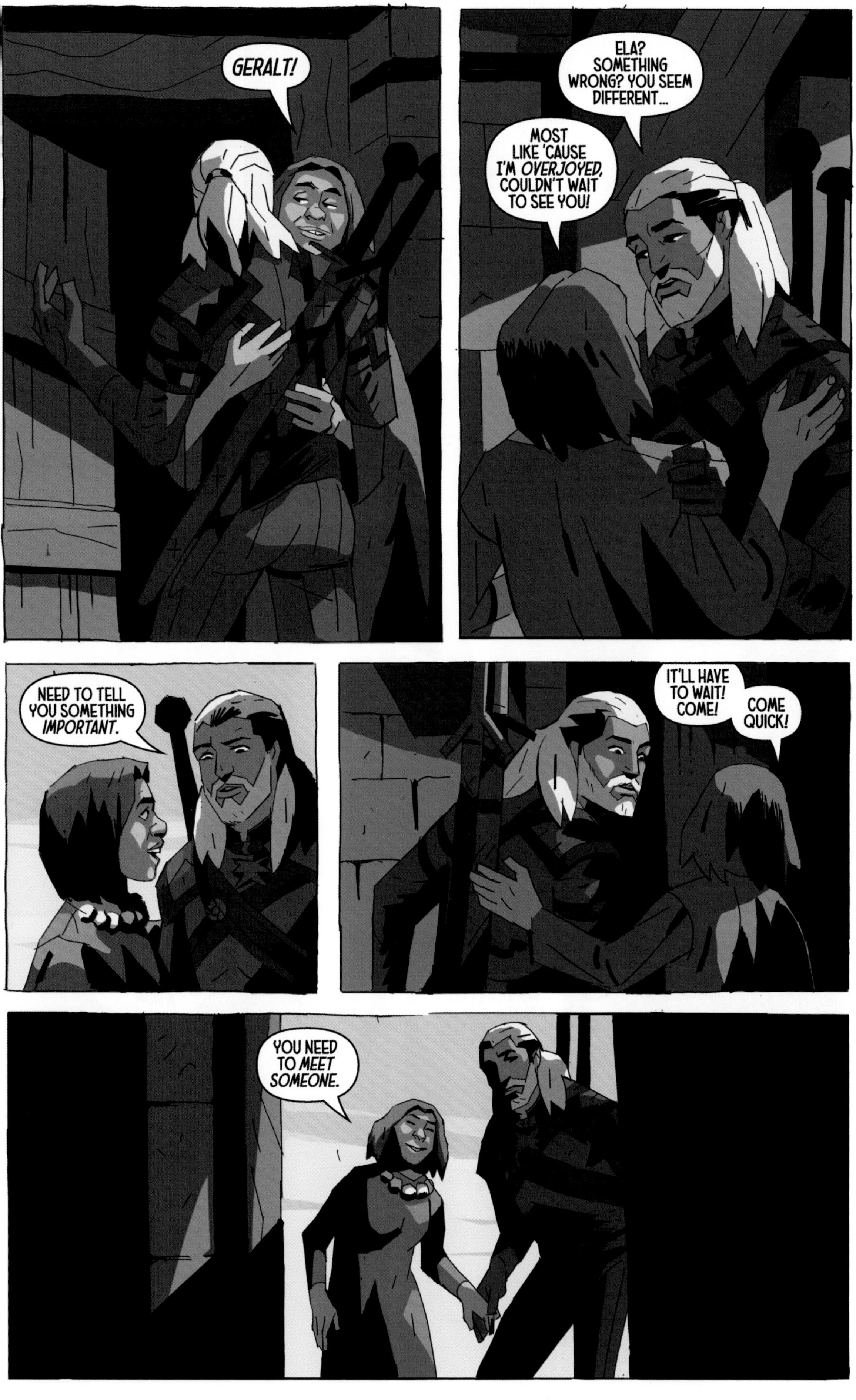
GERALT!
ELA? SOMETHING WRONG? YOU SEEM DIFFERENT...
MOST LIKE 'CAUSE I'M *OVERJOYED*, COULDN'T WAIT TO SEE YOU!
NEED TO TELL YOU SOMETHING *IMPORTANT*.
IT'LL HAVE TO WAIT! COME!
COME QUICK!
YOU NEED TO *MEET* SOMEONE.

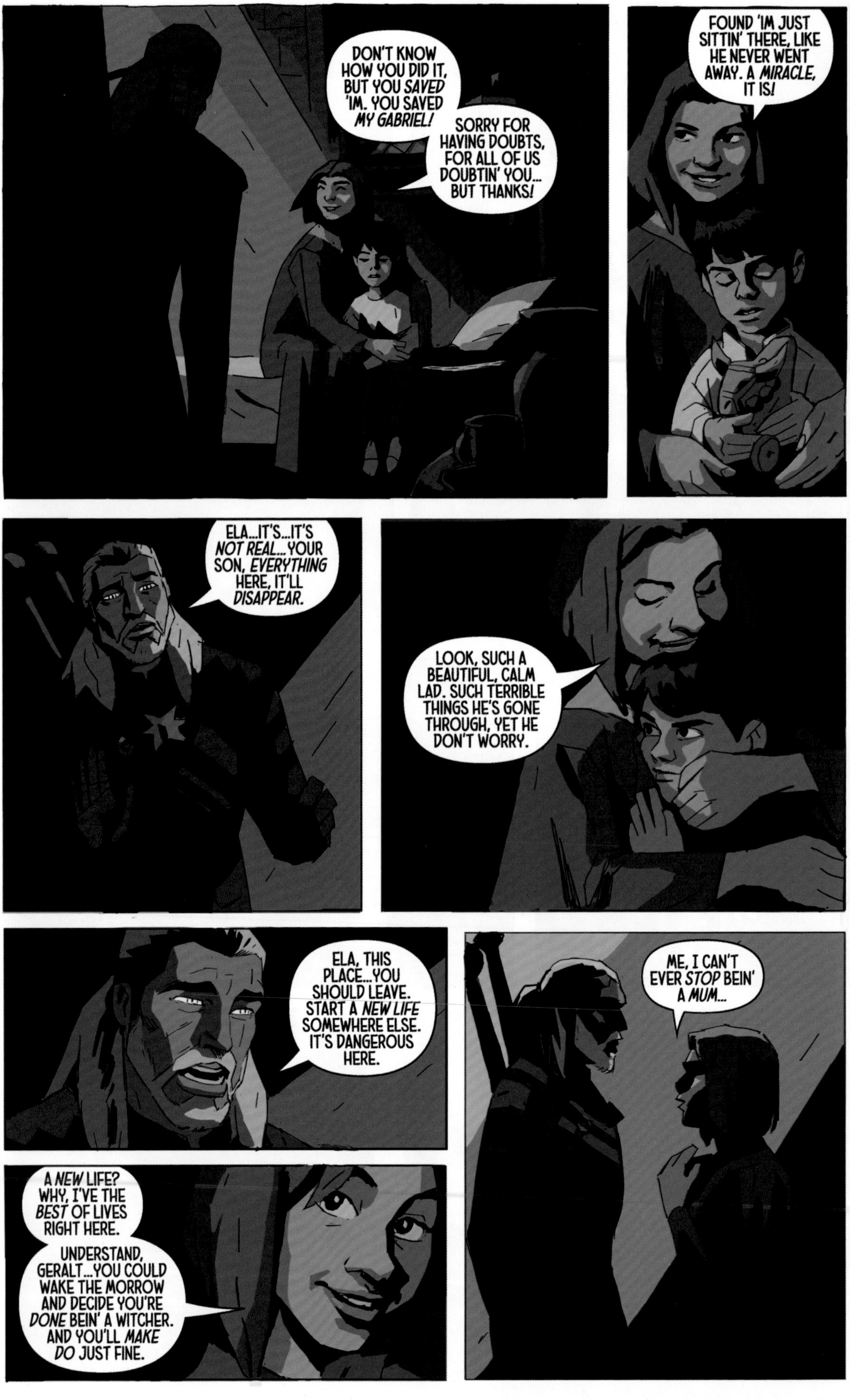
DON'T KNOW HOW YOU DID IT, BUT YOU *SAVED* 'IM. YOU SAVED *MY GABRIEL!*
SORRY FOR HAVING DOUBTS, FOR ALL OF US DOUBTIN' YOU... BUT THANKS!
FOUND 'IM JUST SITTIN' THERE, LIKE HE NEVER WENT AWAY. A *MIRACLE,* IT IS!
ELA...IT'S...IT'S *NOT REAL...* YOUR SON, *EVERYTHING* HERE, IT'LL *DISAPPEAR.*
LOOK, SUCH A BEAUTIFUL, CALM LAD. SUCH TERRIBLE THINGS HE'S GONE THROUGH, YET HE DON'T WORRY.
ELA, THIS PLACE...YOU SHOULD LEAVE. START A *NEW LIFE* SOMEWHERE ELSE. IT'S DANGEROUS HERE.
A *NEW* LIFE? WHY, I'VE THE *BEST* OF LIVES RIGHT HERE.
UNDERSTAND, GERALT...YOU COULD WAKE THE MORROW AND DECIDE YOU'RE *DONE* BEIN' A WITCHER. AND YOU'LL *MAKE DO* JUST FINE.
ME, I CAN'T EVER *STOP* BEIN' A *MUM*...

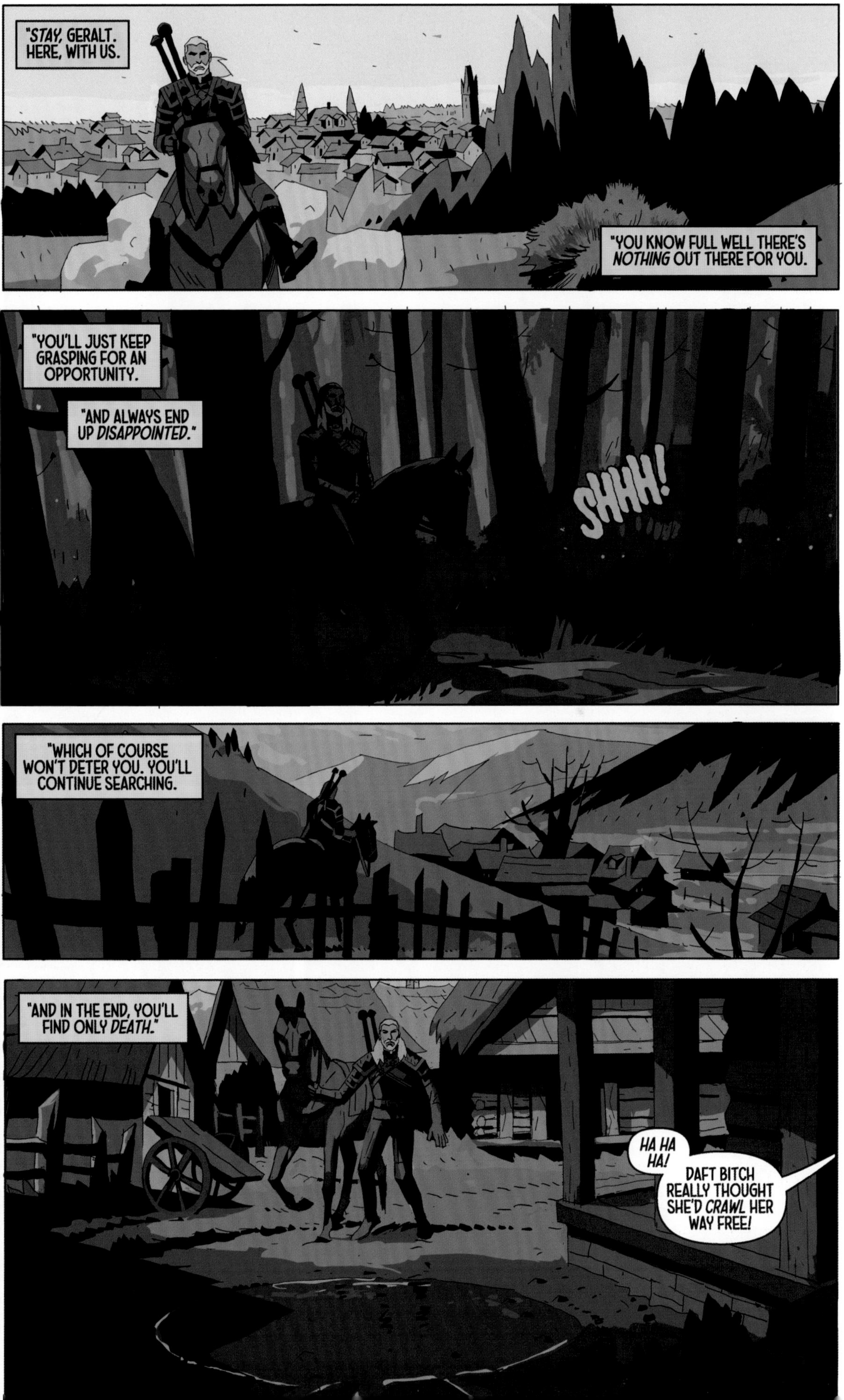
"STAY, GERALT. HERE, WITH US.
"YOU KNOW FULL WELL THERE'S NOTHING OUT THERE FOR YOU.
"YOU'LL JUST KEEP GRASPING FOR AN OPPORTUNITY.
"AND ALWAYS END UP DISAPPOINTED."
SHHH!
"WHICH OF COURSE WON'T DETER YOU. YOU'LL CONTINUE SEARCHING.
"AND IN THE END, YOU'LL FIND ONLY DEATH."
HA HA HA! DAFT BITCH REALLY THOUGHT SHE'D CRAWL HER WAY FREE!

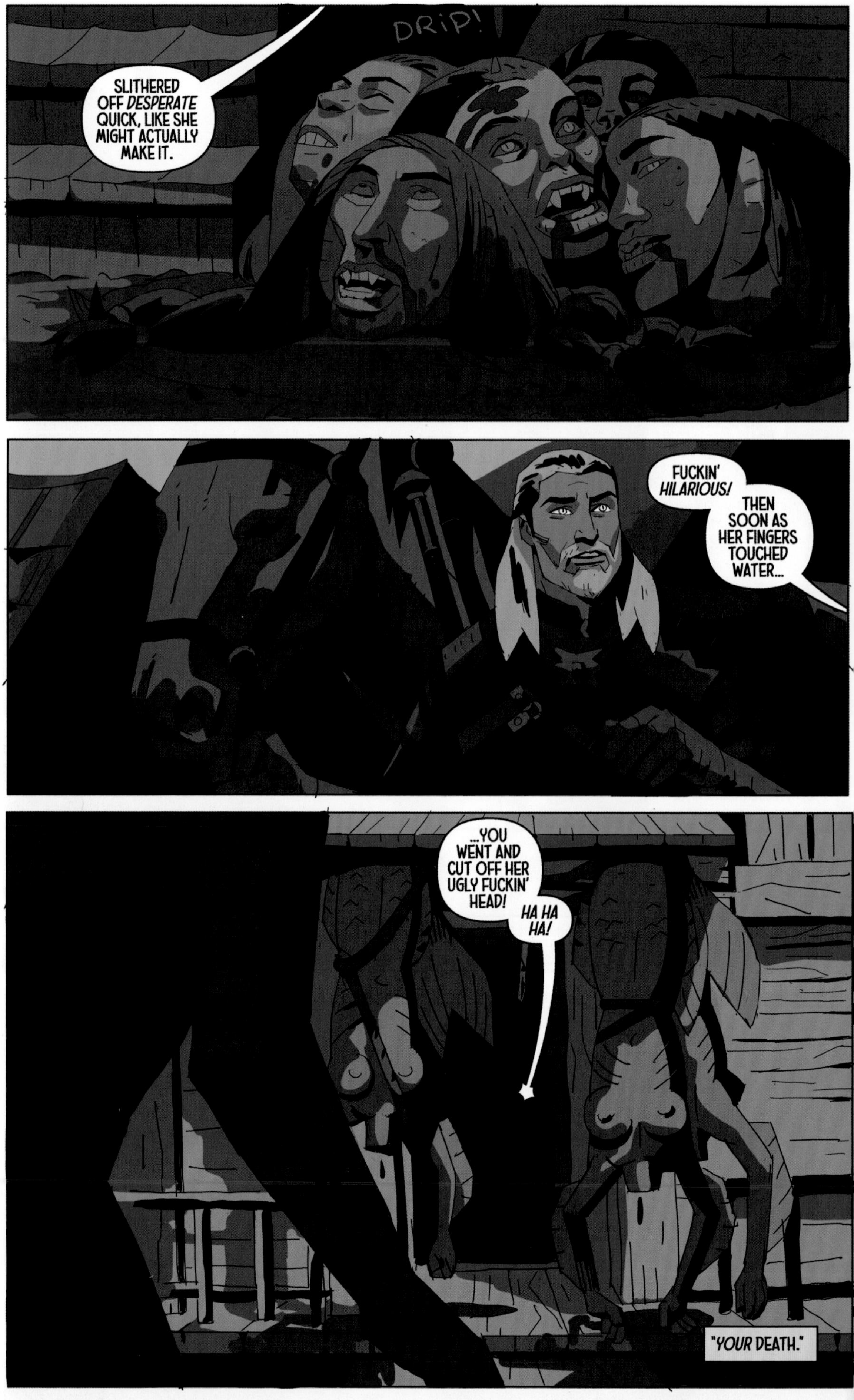
DRIP!
SLITHERED OFF *DESPERATE* QUICK, LIKE SHE MIGHT ACTUALLY MAKE IT.
FUCKIN' *HILARIOUS!*
THEN SOON AS HER FINGERS TOUCHED WATER...
...YOU WENT AND CUT OFF HER UGLY FUCKIN' HEAD!
HA HA HA!
"*YOUR* DEATH."

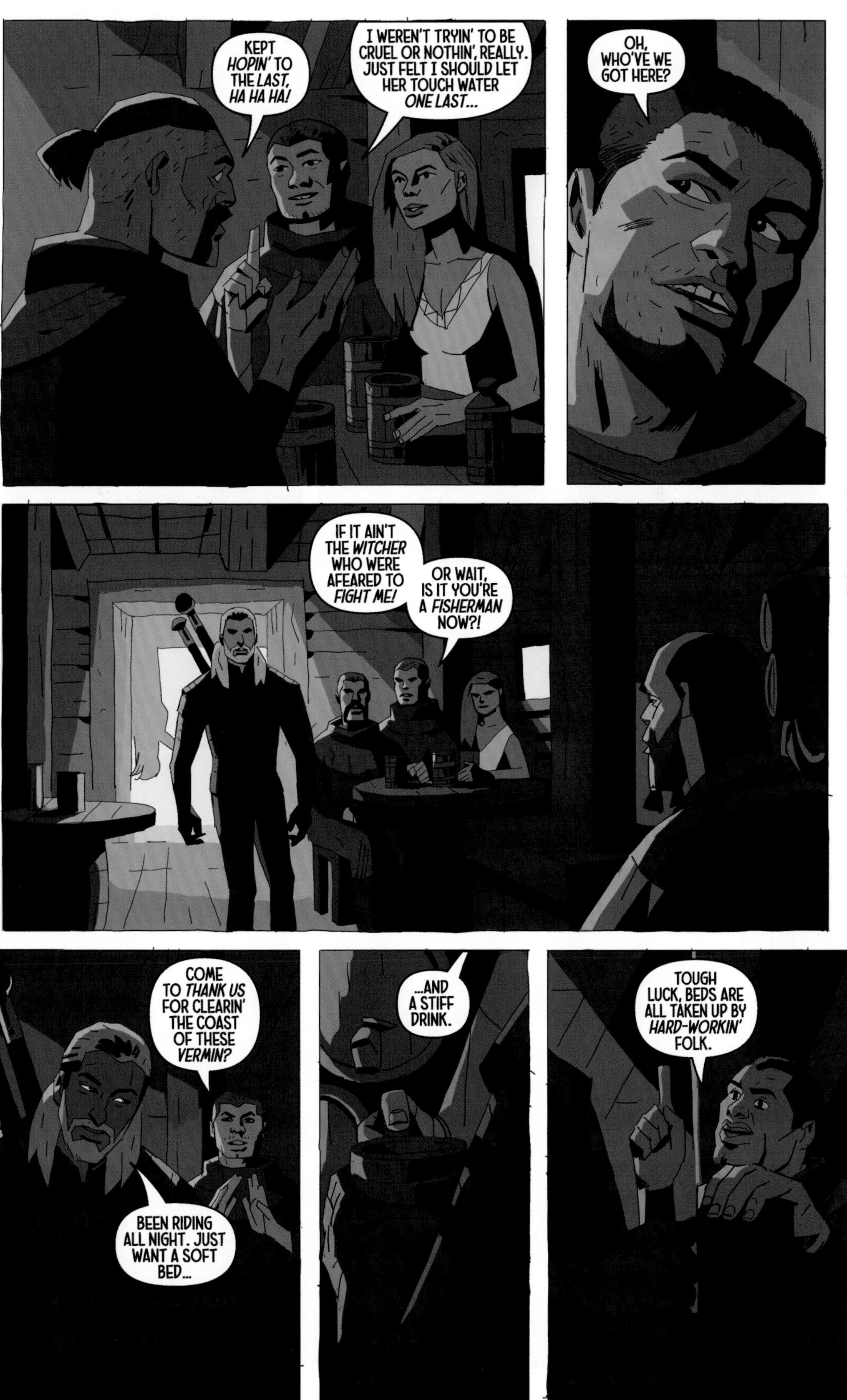
KEPT HOPIN' TO THE LAST, HA HA HA!
I WEREN'T TRYIN' TO BE CRUEL OR NOTHIN', REALLY. JUST FELT I SHOULD LET HER TOUCH WATER ONE LAST...
OH, WHO'VE WE GOT HERE?
IF IT AIN'T THE WITCHER WHO WERE AFEARED TO FIGHT ME!
OR WAIT, IS IT YOU'RE A FISHERMAN NOW?!
COME TO THANK US FOR CLEARIN' THE COAST OF THESE VERMIN?
BEEN RIDING ALL NIGHT. JUST WANT A SOFT BED...
...AND A STIFF DRINK.
TOUGH LUCK, BEDS ARE ALL TAKEN UP BY HARD-WORKIN' FOLK.

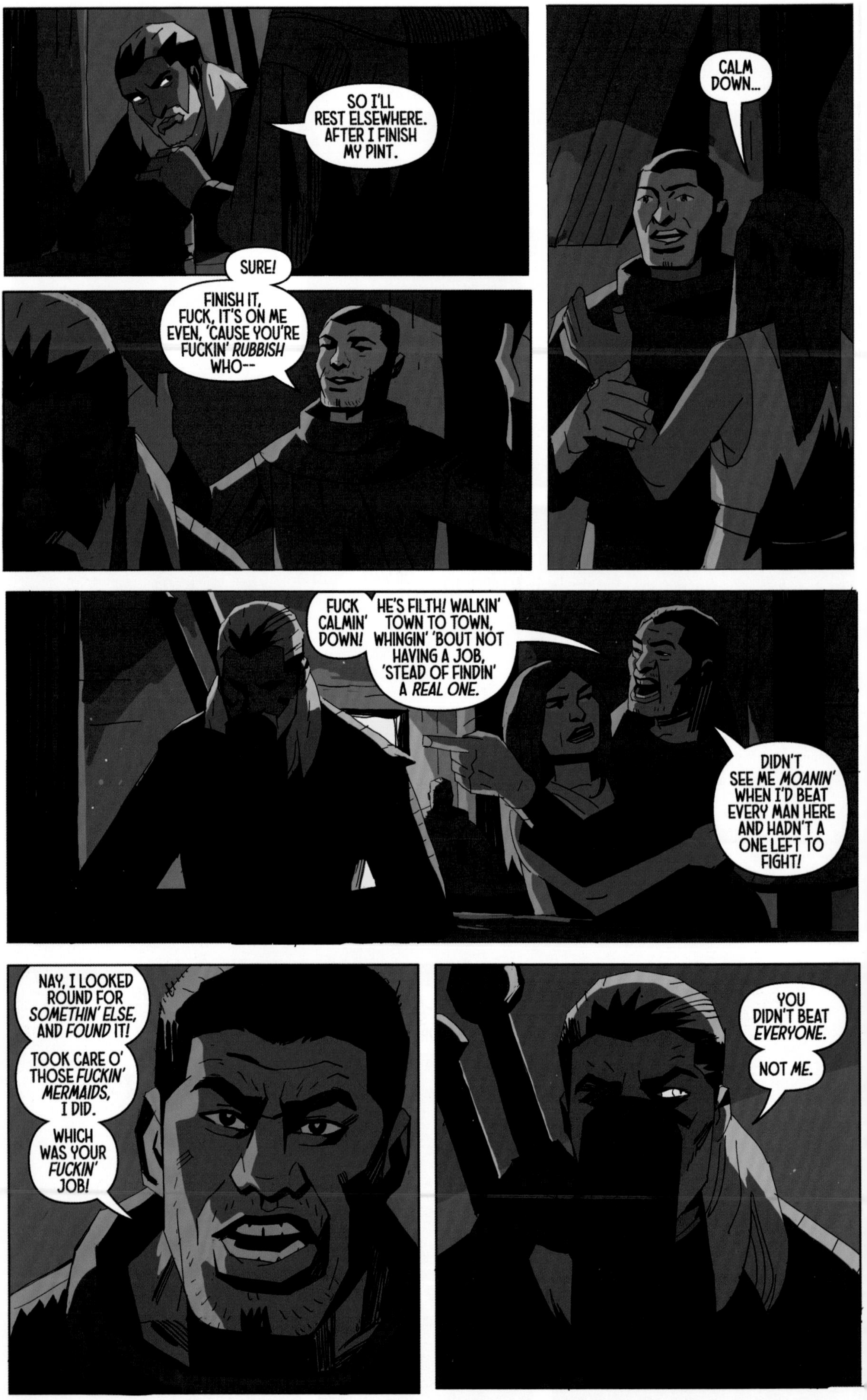
SO I'LL REST ELSEWHERE. AFTER I FINISH MY PINT.
CALM DOWN...
SURE!
FINISH IT, FUCK, IT'S ON ME EVEN, 'CAUSE YOU'RE FUCKIN' *RUBBISH* WHO--
FUCK CALMIN' DOWN!
HE'S FILTH! WALKIN' TOWN TO TOWN, WHINGIN' 'BOUT NOT HAVING A JOB, 'STEAD OF FINDIN' A *REAL ONE.*
DIDN'T SEE ME *MOANIN'* WHEN I'D BEAT EVERY MAN HERE AND HADN'T A ONE LEFT TO FIGHT!
NAY, I LOOKED ROUND FOR *SOMETHIN' ELSE,* AND *FOUND* IT!
TOOK CARE O' THOSE *FUCKIN' MERMAIDS,* I DID.
WHICH WAS YOUR *FUCKIN'* JOB!
YOU DIDN'T BEAT *EVERYONE.*
NOT *ME.*

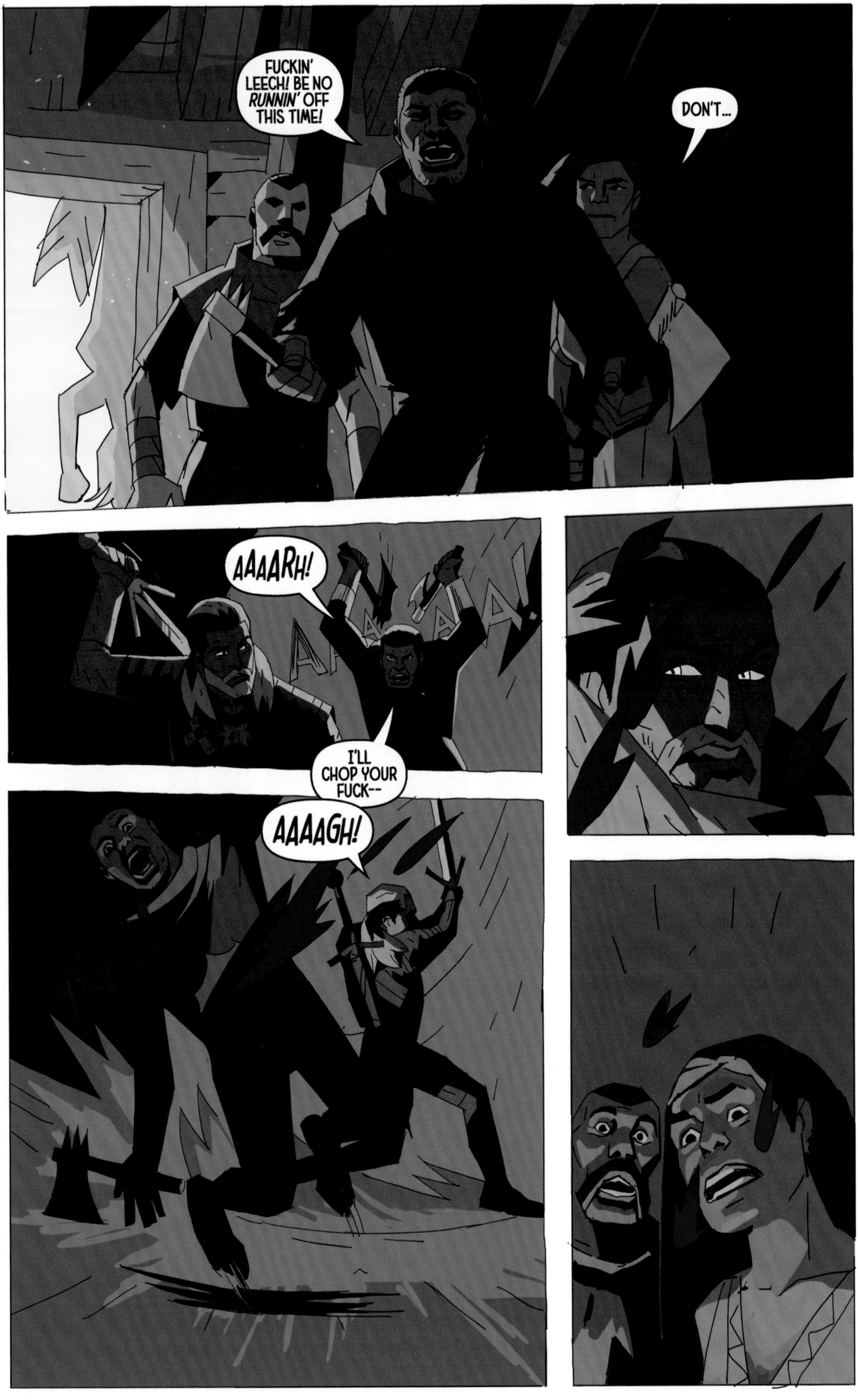
FUCKIN' LEECH! BE NO *RUNNIN'* OFF THIS TIME!
DON'T...
AAAARH!
I'LL CHOP YOUR FUCK--
AAAAGH!

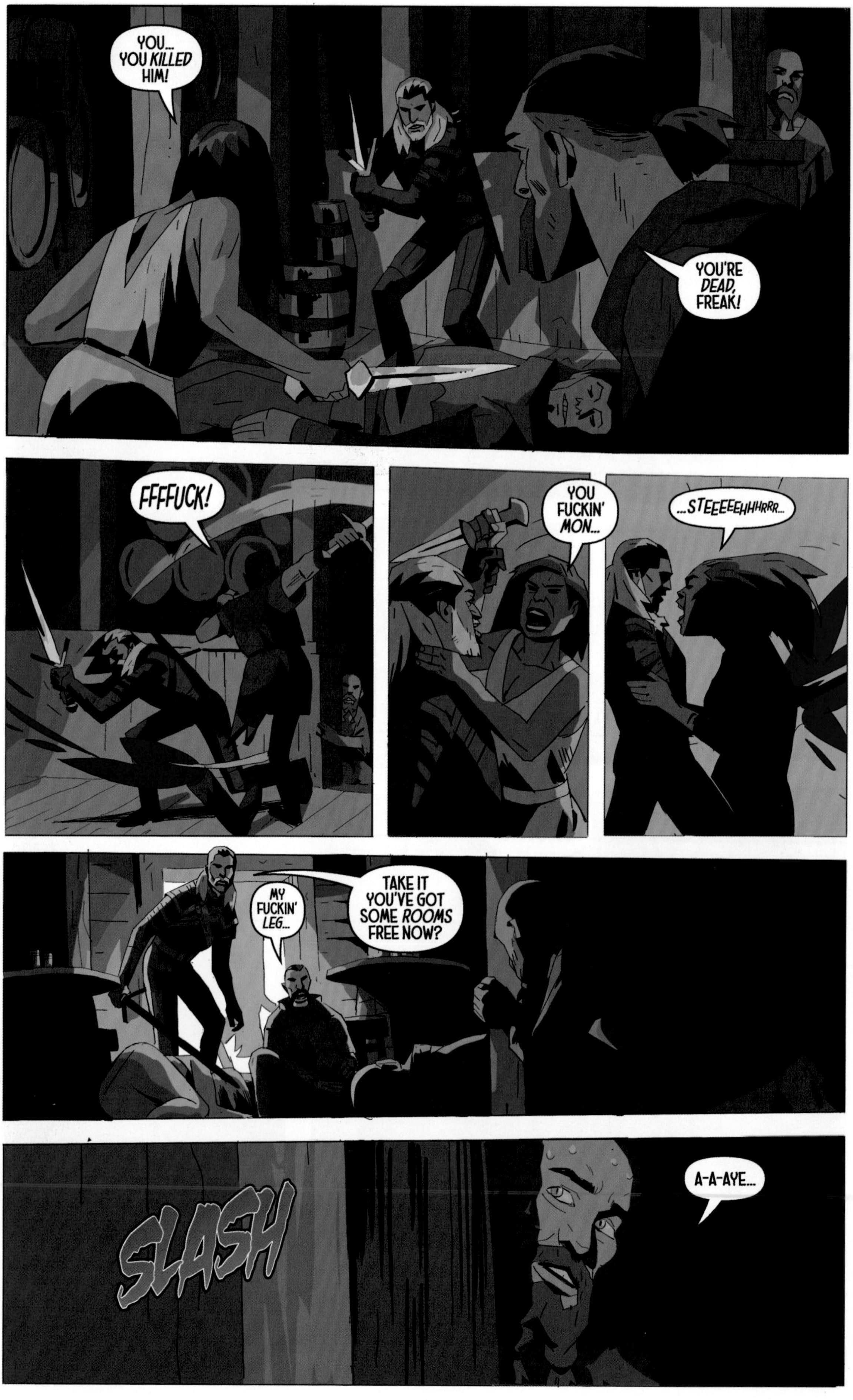
YOU... YOU KILLED HIM!
YOU'RE DEAD, FREAK!
FFFFUCK!
YOU FUCKIN' MON...
...STEEEEEHHHRRR...
MY FUCKIN' LEG...
TAKE IT YOU'VE GOT SOME ROOMS FREE NOW?
SLASH
A-A-AYE...

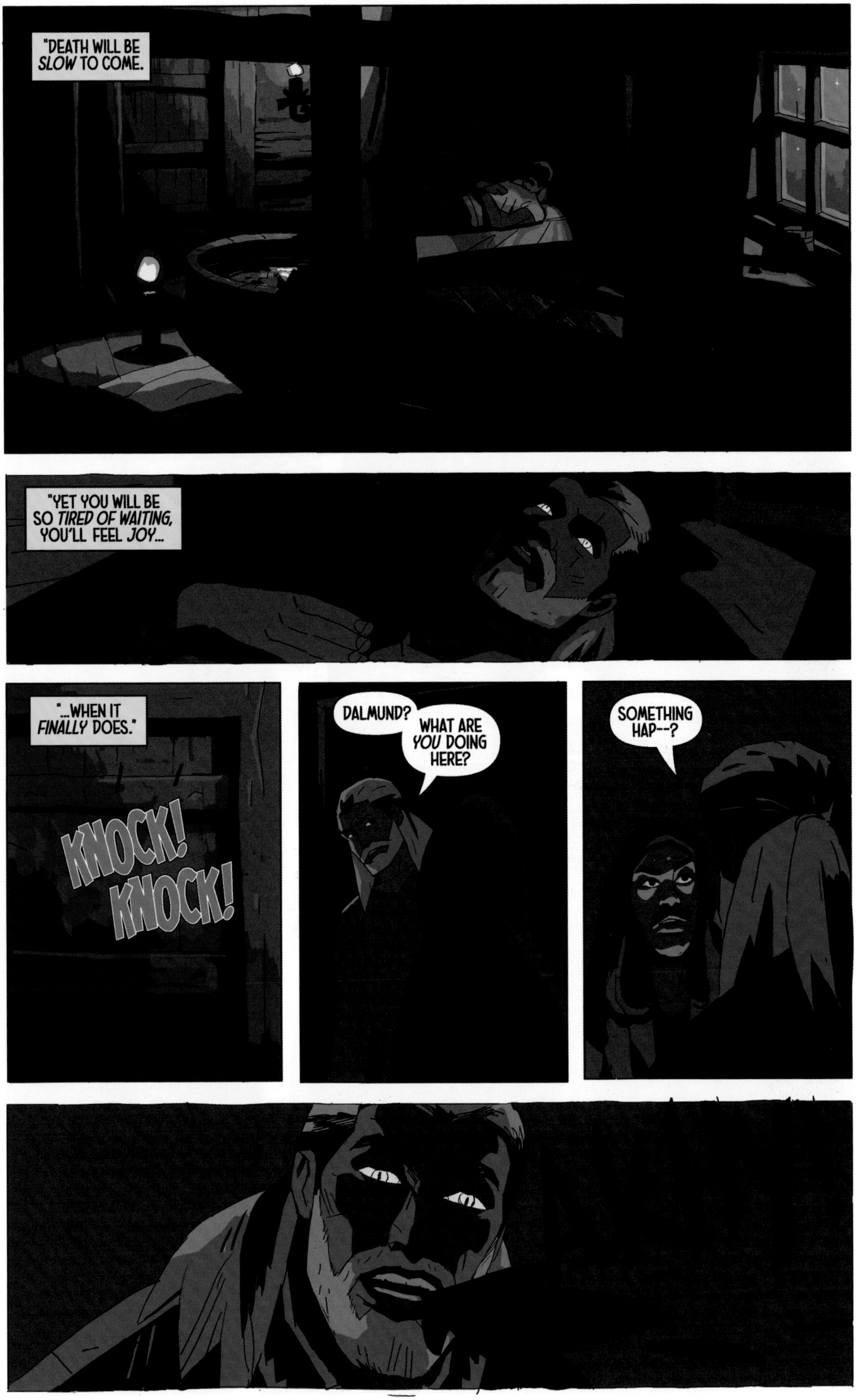
"DEATH WILL BE *SLOW* TO COME.
"YET YOU WILL BE SO *TIRED OF WAITING,* YOU'LL FEEL *JOY*...
"...WHEN IT *FINALLY* DOES."
KNOCK! KNOCK!
DALMUND?
WHAT ARE *YOU* DOING HERE?
SOMETHING HAP--?

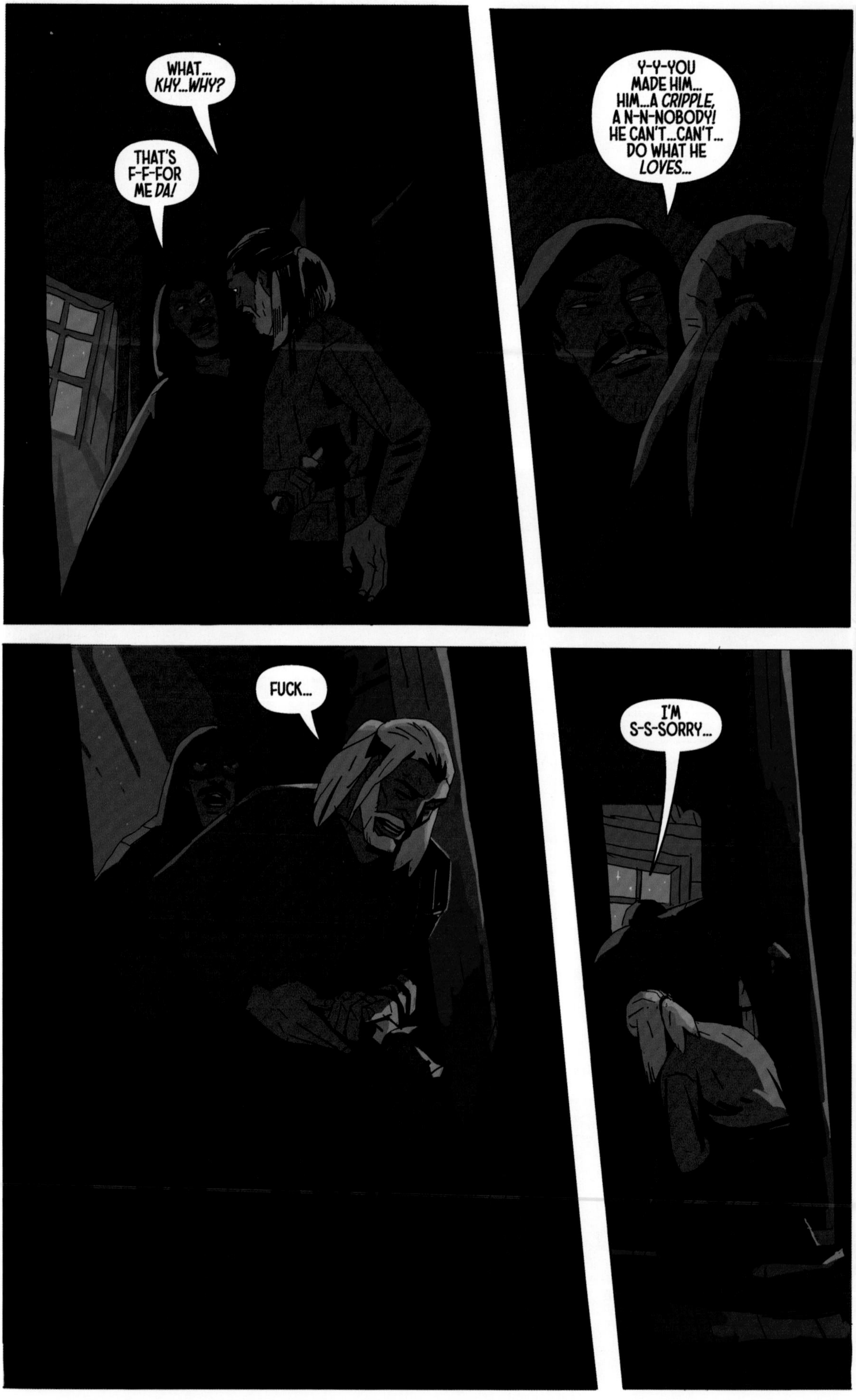
WHAT... KHY...WHY?
THAT'S F-F-FOR ME DA!
Y-Y-YOU MADE HIM... HIM...A CRIPPLE, A N-N-NOBODY! HE CAN'T...CAN'T... DO WHAT HE LOVES...
FUCK...
I'M S-S-SORRY...

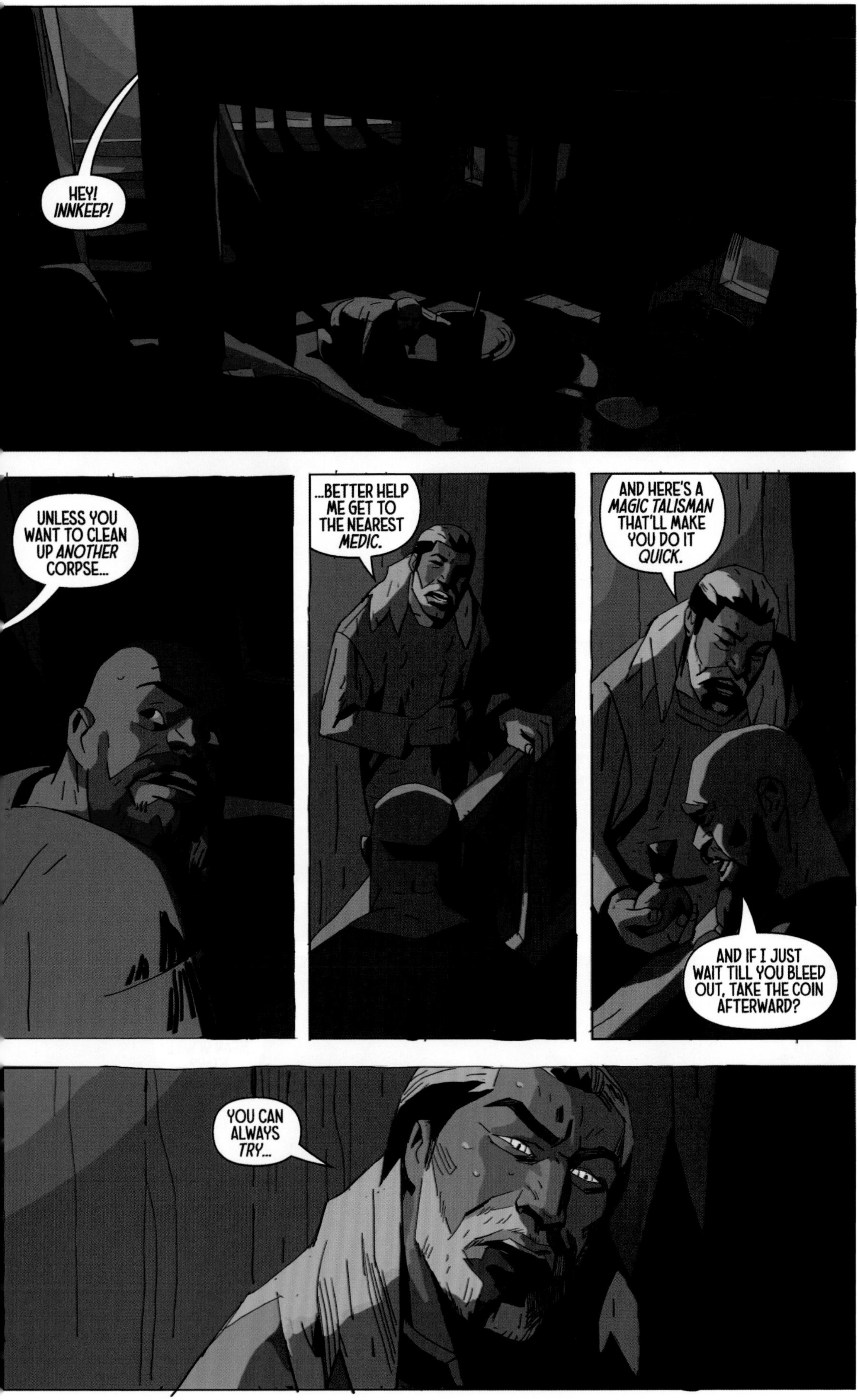
HEY! INNKEEP!
UNLESS YOU WANT TO CLEAN UP ANOTHER CORPSE...
...BETTER HELP ME GET TO THE NEAREST MEDIC.
AND HERE'S A MAGIC TALISMAN THAT'LL MAKE YOU DO IT QUICK.
AND IF I JUST WAIT TILL YOU BLEED OUT, TAKE THE COIN AFTERWARD?
YOU CAN ALWAYS TRY...

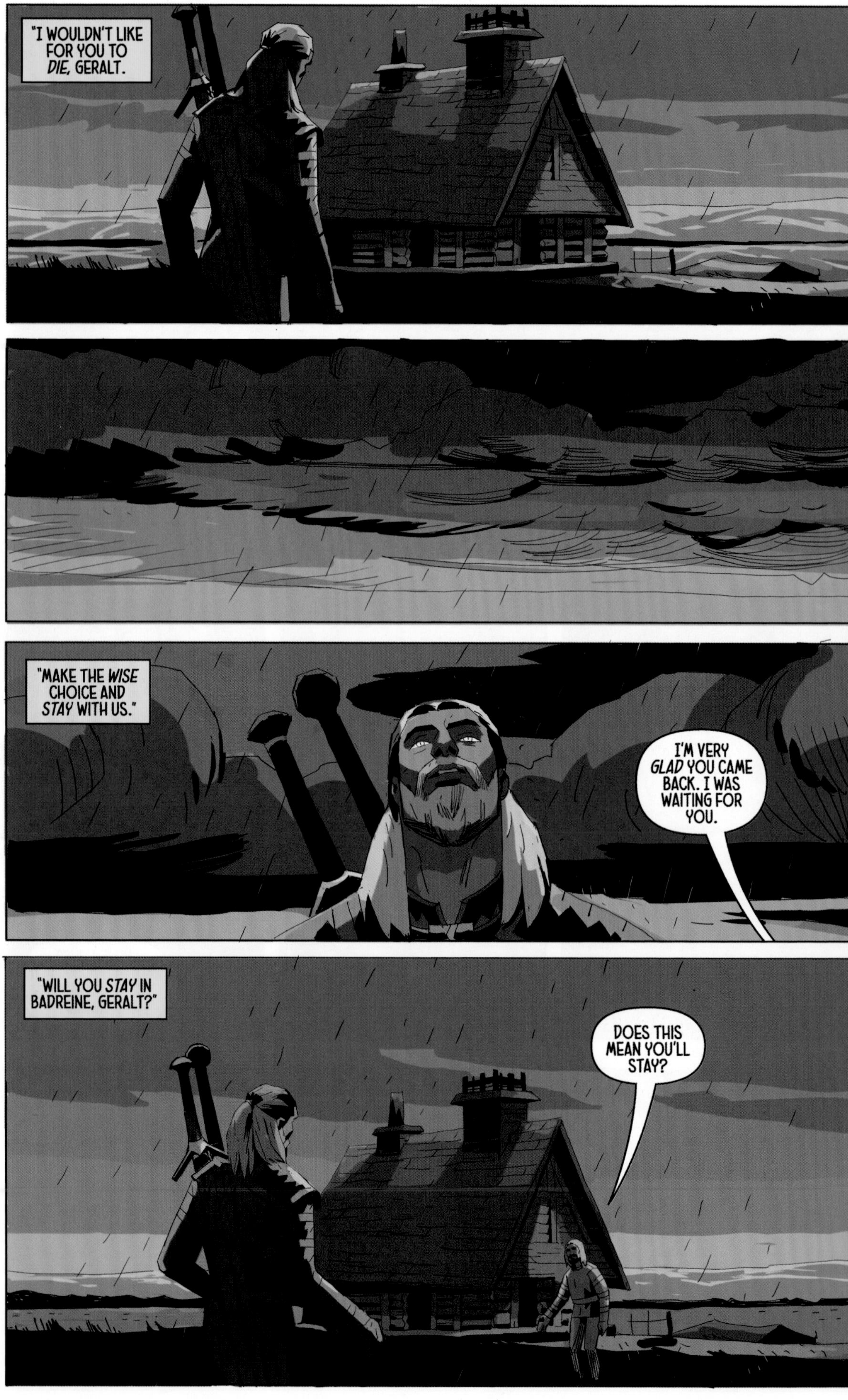
"I WOULDN'T LIKE FOR YOU TO *DIE,* GERALT.
"MAKE THE *WISE* CHOICE AND *STAY* WITH US."
I'M VERY *GLAD* YOU CAME BACK. I WAS WAITING FOR YOU.
"WILL YOU *STAY* IN BADREINE, GERALT?"
DOES THIS MEAN YOU'LL STAY?

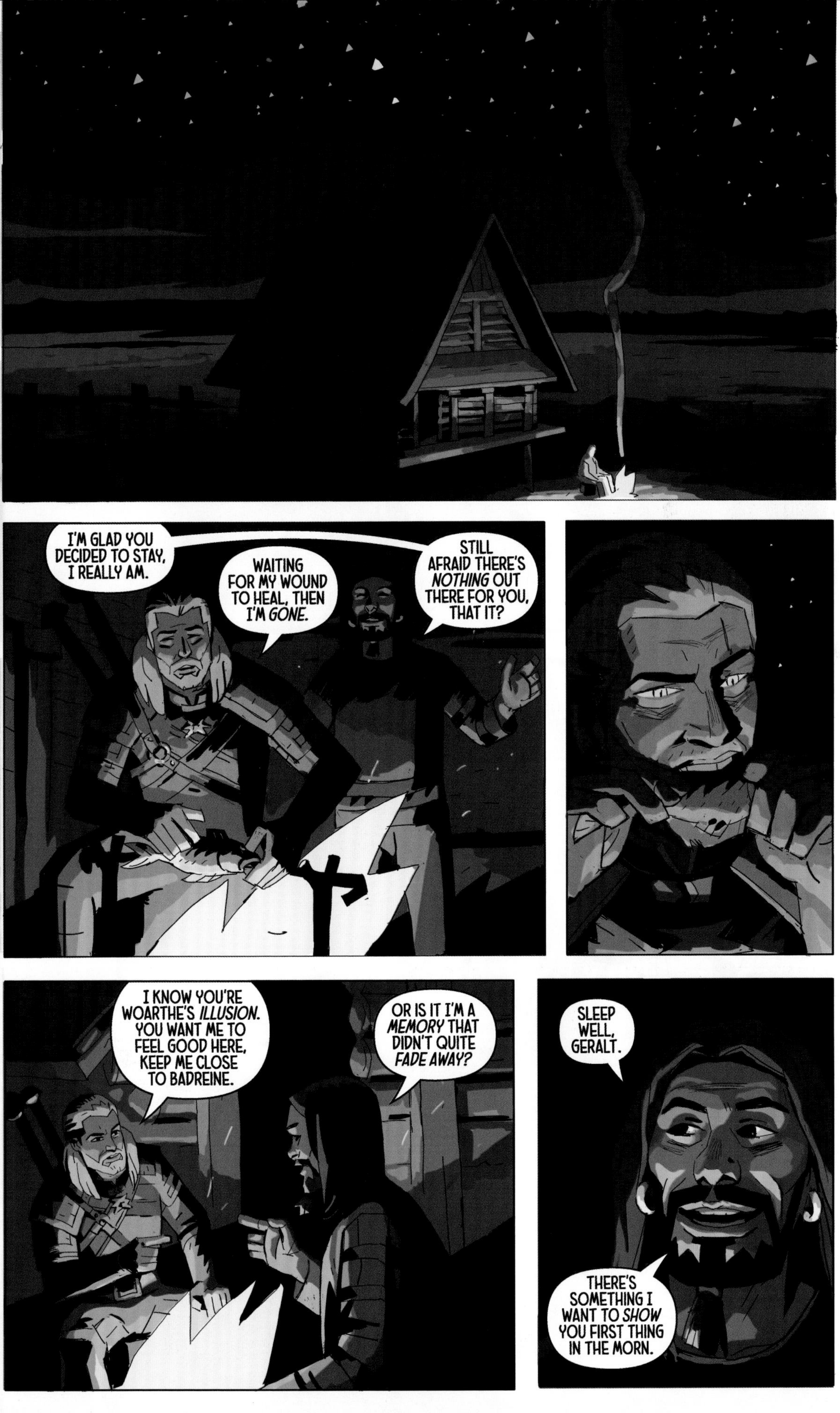
I'M GLAD YOU DECIDED TO STAY, I REALLY AM.
WAITING FOR MY WOUND TO HEAL, THEN I'M *GONE*.
STILL AFRAID THERE'S *NOTHING* OUT THERE FOR YOU, THAT IT?
I KNOW YOU'RE WOARTHE'S *ILLUSION*. YOU WANT ME TO FEEL GOOD HERE, KEEP ME CLOSE TO BADREINE.
OR IS IT I'M A *MEMORY* THAT DIDN'T QUITE *FADE AWAY?*
SLEEP WELL, GERALT.
THERE'S SOMETHING I WANT TO *SHOW* YOU FIRST THING IN THE MORN.

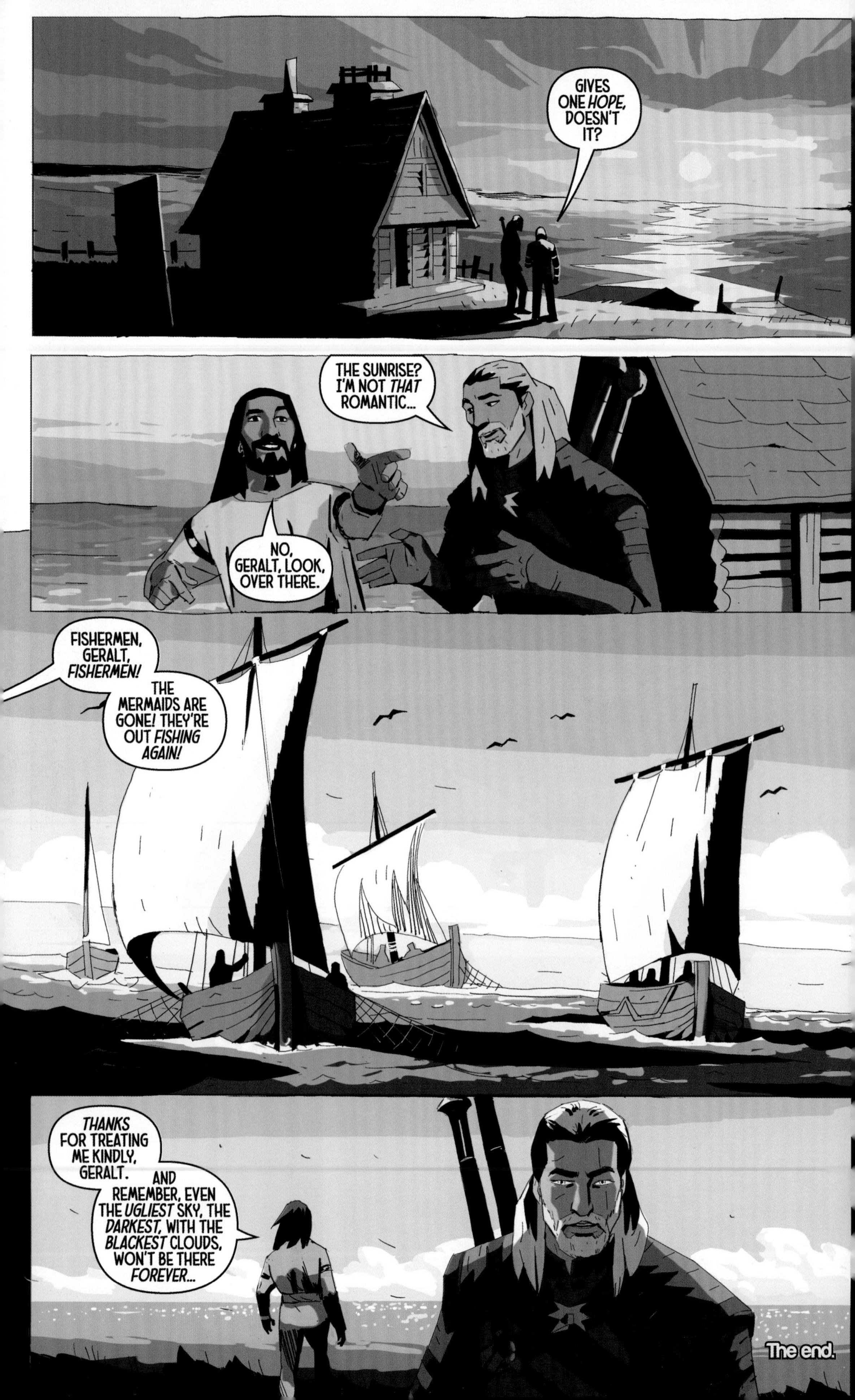
GIVES ONE *HOPE,* DOESN'T IT?
THE SUNRISE? I'M NOT *THAT* ROMANTIC...
NO, GERALT, LOOK, OVER THERE.
FISHERMEN, GERALT, *FISHERMEN!*
THE MERMAIDS ARE GONE! THEY'RE OUT *FISHING AGAIN!*
THANKS FOR TREATING ME KINDLY, GERALT.
AND REMEMBER, EVEN THE *UGLIEST* SKY, THE *DARKEST,* WITH THE *BLACKEST* CLOUDS, WON'T BE THERE *FOREVER...*
The end.

THE WITCHER: FADING MEMORIES #2 VARIANT COVER ART BY
JEREMY WILSON

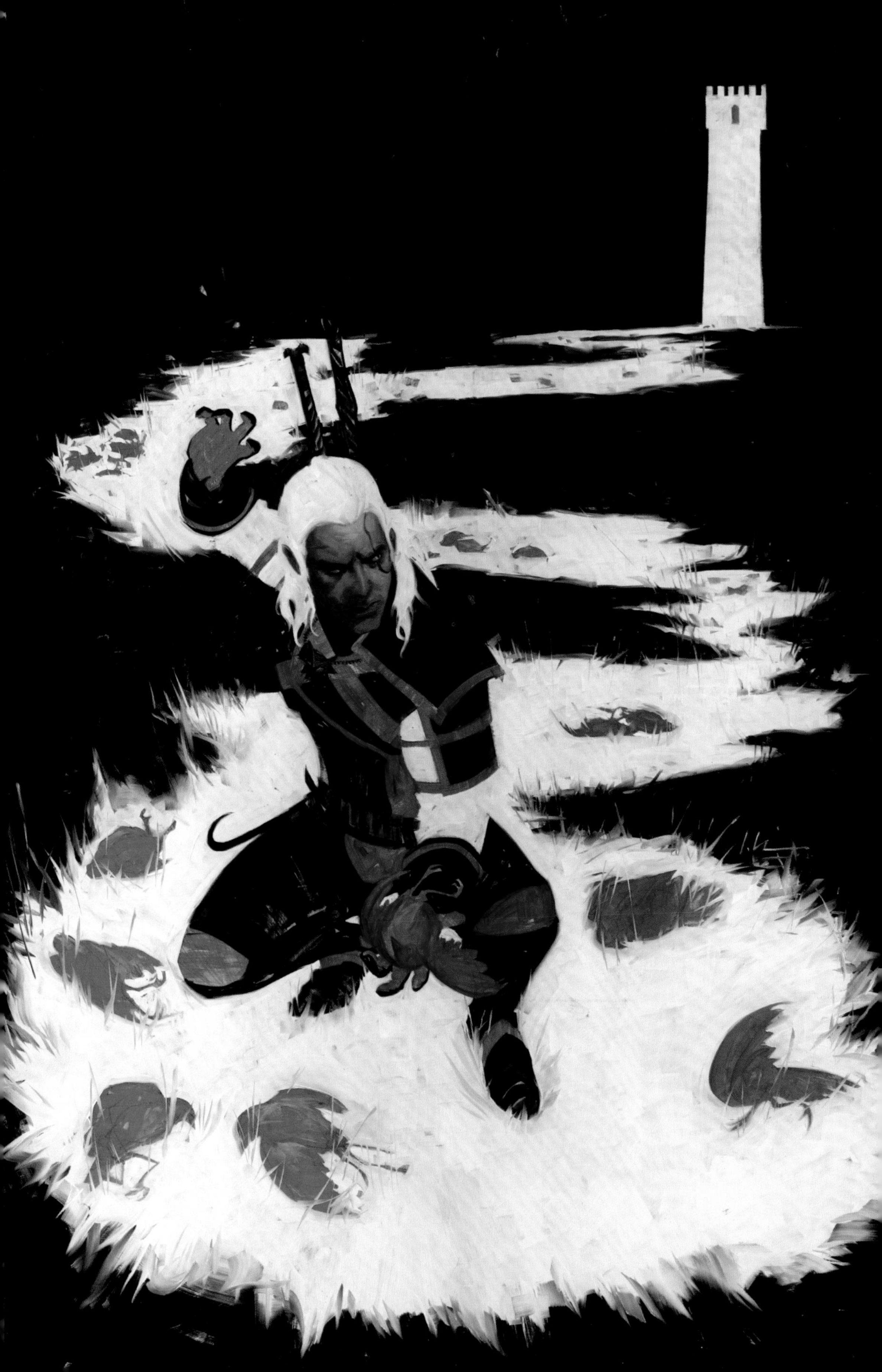

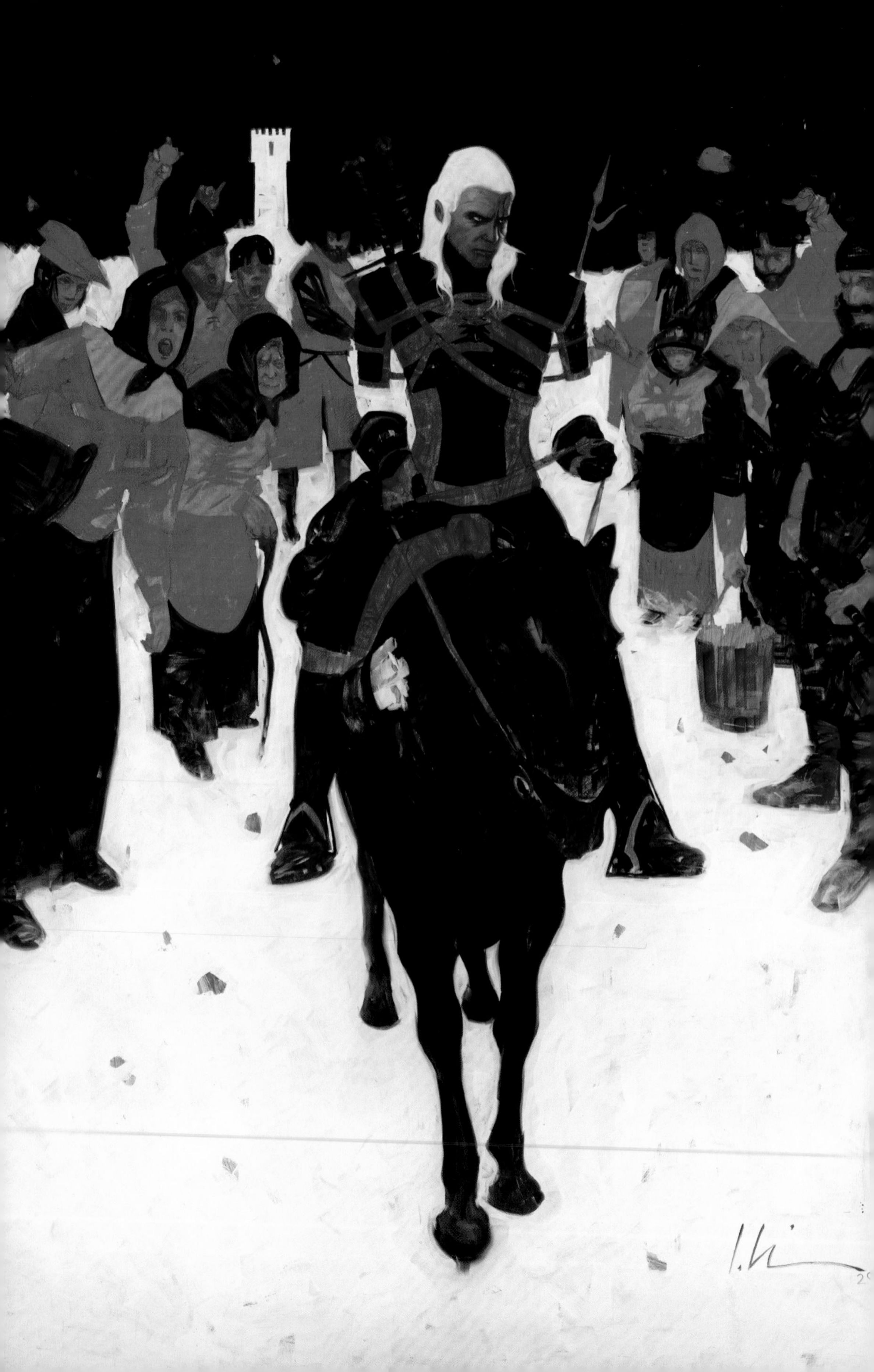

THE WITCHER: FADING MEMORIES #3 VARIANT COVER ART BY
JEREMY WILSON

THE WITCHER: FADING MEMORIES #4 VARIANT COVER ART BY
JEREMY WILSON

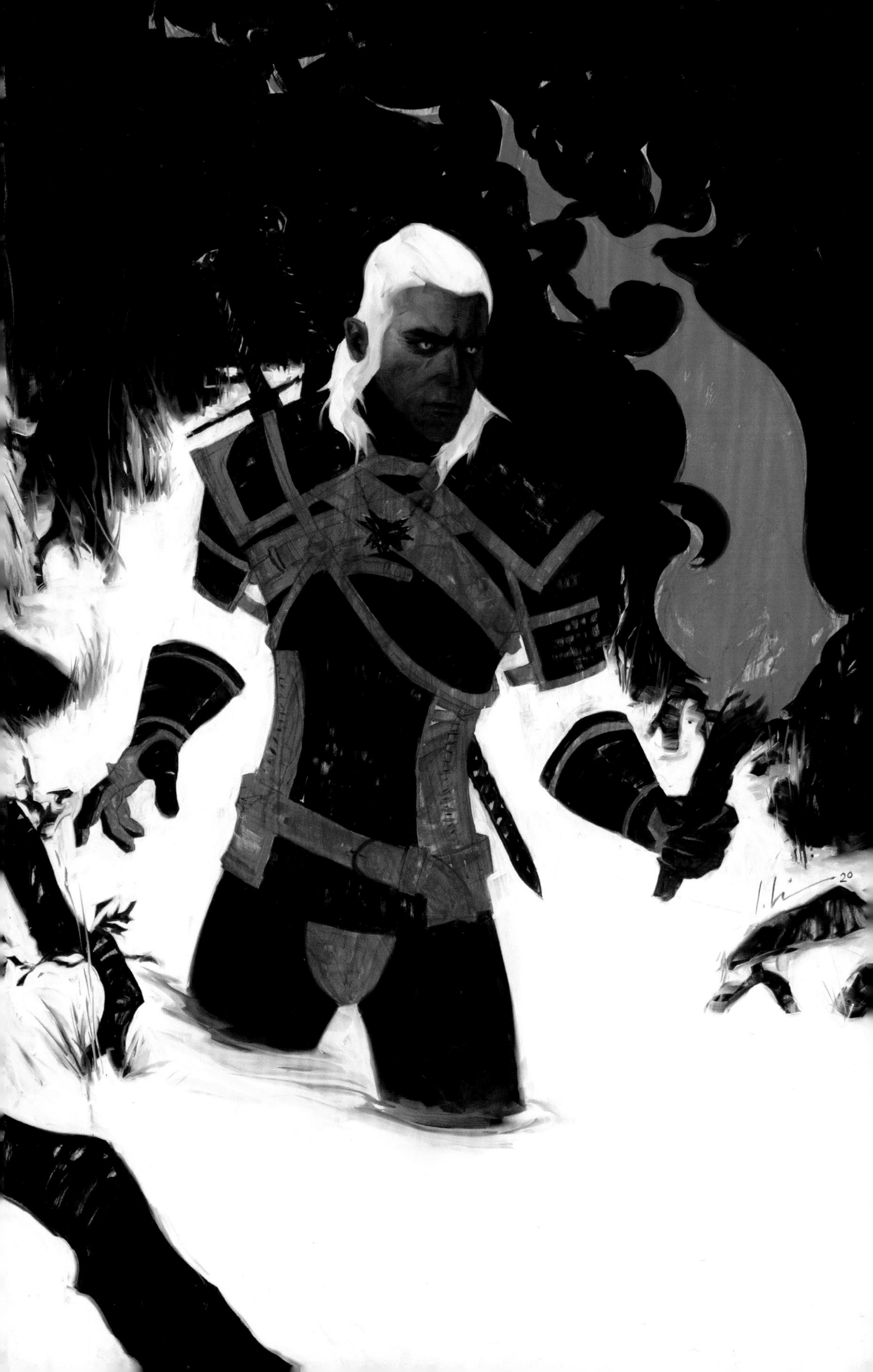

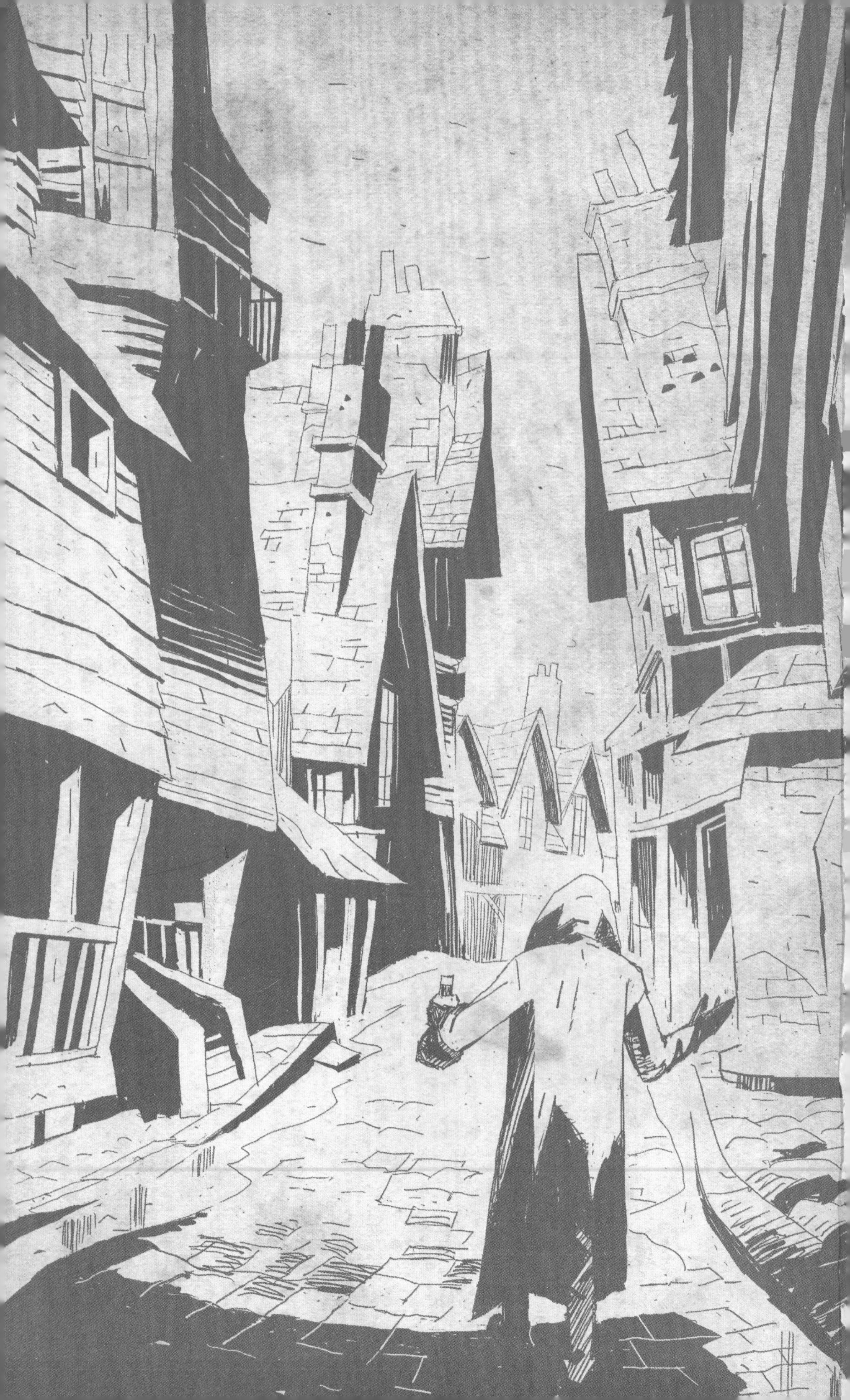